BOOK 1 OF THE SONGFORGE TRILOGY

JAMES BECKINGHAM

Publisher: Audiobooksradio
website: www.audiobooksradio.com.au

This edition published 2023

Cover design and illustration by Myke Mollard (bushcreatures.com.au)
Typesetting: WorkingType (www.workingtype.com.au)

This book is a work of fiction. Names, characters, places and incidents are either a product of the author's imagination or are used fictitiously. Any resemblance to actual people living or dead, events or locales is entirely coincidental.

ISBN: 978-0-6455996-6-4

For Cath, whose patience and encouragement has made all this possible. I couldn't have done it without you.

Prologue

Samurai General Ibaz watched impassively as the last of his troops moved into position in readiness for the assault of the walled keep. The war had been raging for close to a full decade and now it was one assault away from finally being over. The Drakes had pushed their enemy back step by step until this keep was all that remained.

But despite all that, there was still no guarantee of victory — not against this foe.

'Are the infantry in position?' Ibaz asked his aide, without taking his eyes from the battlefield.

'Yes, my lord. They await your command to begin the attack.'

'They have it,' Ibaz said. 'Tell them to begin their assault on the north and south walls, then send a messenger to make sure the Forgers and Sorcerers are ready to bombard the gatehouse.'

The aide saluted and sprinted away into the horde of troops but Ibaz had already forgotten him. He was calculating his next tactic as he saw the infantry lurch forward to attack.

It was a strangely graceful sight, watching the Drake army charge the walled city. Drakes had once been human, or so the legends said, until their Dragon gods had blessed them with a fragment of Draconic power and changed them forever. They were still mostly human shaped, but the similarities stopped there. A dragon's head now sat on their shoulders, two leathery wings sprouted from their back and a thick tail extended to the ground. Their bodies were covered by hard scales and they were stronger, faster and more resilient than any human could ever hope to be. They charged the city walls without hesitation, confidant that they were superior to their human enemy in every way.

'Tell the cavalry to be ready,' Ibaz said to another aide. 'As soon as those humans poke their heads up from behind the wall I want a cavalry charge to knock them right back down again!'

Five minutes later, Ibaz watched the cavalry shoot towards the battlements, fifty Drakes mounted on Keldarkan battle dragons, flying in an arrow formation as they assaulted the archers who had started to fire on the advancing infantry. The dragons hit the walls hard and fast, causing as much chaos as they could before the humans could form a proper resistance, then they leaped into the sky to wait for another opportunity.

Ibaz nodded grimly as the infantry crossed the last few metres to the city walls — the cavalry had kept the human archers distracted and unable to pepper his Samurai with arrows as they approached. Now, as the Drakes threw ladders and grapnels up against the battlements, the archers were of little use. It would be hand-to-hand combat as soon as the Drakes reached the top of the walls, and Ibaz would back a Drake against a human in melee every time.

'Come on, Taan,' Ibaz muttered. 'You're going to lose the walls unless you show yourself. Come and stop us.'

In the distance, the Drake infantry scaled the city walls while the dragon cavalry strafed the defenders. The walls had become a chaotic mess of fighting and dying as Drake Samurai expanded their foothold and pushed the humans back into their own city.

'Come on, come on,' Ibaz said. 'You've got to show yourself now or it will be too late.'

The human lines wavered as more and more Drakes clambered up the ladders and reinforced their comrades. A moment longer and the lines would have collapsed completely, but the humans still had some tricks of their own to play.

The stone of the walls melted and twisted, forming onto a giant hand that held the Drakes in its palm. Before the stunned Samurai could react, the hand closed into a fist and squeezed, then hurled the debris back at the attacking army. The single, bloody hand then writhed and split, breaking onto a multitude of smaller limbs which attacked any remaining Drakes, hurling them and their ladders from the wall to land in a broken heap on the ground. Ibaz watched impassively, mentally recording each death to add to the tally of crimes that his enemy would pay for.

'Is it him, sir?' a lieutenant asked. 'Is it Taan?'

'No, it's not him,' Ibaz replied. 'He's sent his pet Baradiarche out to play. Still, with them occupied it might be all we need. Signal the Sorcerers to attack — the Forgers are to wait five minutes, then hit those gates with everything they've got.'

It took a minute for the command to be passed down and his troops to mobilise, then Ibaz saw the Sorcerers turn in unison and unleash their magic. Wave after wave of fire crashed into the massive city gates, scorching the ground for fifty metres in every direction and sending smoke billowing into the sky. They didn't even scratch the gates, but then, they were never meant to. They were just a distraction, giving the newly discovered Forgers the time to work their magic.

Under the cover of smoke and fire, the sound of singing rose over the chaos of the battlefield. It was haunting and beautiful, and totally out of place amidst the carnage. But everyone could feel the power in that music and the humans on the battlements stared in disbelief as they realised the Drakes had found their own Forgers. They were so shocked they barely reacted when five fountains of metal burst from the ground in front of the gate and started shaping themselves into huge, cylindrical battering rams.

'It's time I joined my command,' Ibaz said as he saw the rams po nd against the gates, unimpeded by the defenders. 'I want to be there when the gates fall and I want Taan's head on my blade.'

Ibaz yanked on his dragon's reins, launching it into the air towards the mass of Drake Samurai lying in wait for the gates to fall. As he swept across the plains he heard the splinter of wood and the cries of human defiance as the gates sagged and prepared to shatter completely.

'Infantry, charge!' Ibaz shouted as the cavalry formed up behind him. The roar from the Drake army drowned out the shriek of tearing hinges and shattered locks. When the gates crumbled, they sprinted forward to claim the honour of being the first warrior inside the keep.

The humans had set up a hasty defence, setting their most heavily armoured warriors in a phalanx in the front courtyard. To their credit, they held for several minutes as the Drakes poured through the gatehouse and crashed against their spears, but they were fighting a losing battle. Ibaz spearheaded a dragon charge that shattered their formation, and with their cohesion lost they were easy pickings.

Ibaz left the fighting behind as he shot through the courtyard to the base of the huge tower that dominated the keep centre. On his barked command, his mount dropped to all fours and swung its powerful tail to smash the door to kindling. Ibaz had slipped to the ground and was running up the tower stairs in an instant, not even waiting for his guard to catch up. He knew Taan was the key to this battle, and if he wasn't removed quickly then everything could still be lost. Time was of the essence.

The further Ibaz charged into the tower, the more his fears grew. There were no guards and no servants; there was no one at all to stop them. Surely Taan's inner sanctum should be guarded more than this? It was only when Ibaz heard the beautiful sound of the ForgeSong echoing off the stones that he understood, and that dread pushed him faster up the stairs.

'No, no, no,' he shouted. 'Not this time!'

His breath was coming in ragged gasps as he finally reached the top of the tower. He ran up the last few stairs and dropped his shoulder to the door that barred his way. The lock gave way with a satisfying crack and Ibaz slid through the archway on his knees, holding his sword at shoulder level to ward off any attacks.

He found himself in an open room at the very top of the tower, surrounded by two dozen frightened humans who were huddled around the outer wall of the room. In the centre stood an old man in vivid rainbow robes, holding his hands to the sky as he sang at the top of his voice.

'Taan!'

Ibaz raised his sword in challenge but the old man ignored him. He arched his back as the last notes of his song filled the room with power, then he looked at Ibaz and smiled. The room filled with a kaleidoscope of colour and thunderous noise which hurled Ibaz back down the stairs. Then there was nothing.

'What in The Dragon's name happened in there?' one of Ibaz's guards asked as he rounded the corner.

'Taan,' Ibaz snarled.

He scrambled to his feet and ran through the door to face his hated enemy, but the tower room was no longer there. It had been blasted apart, leaving nothing but scorched stone floor and swirling ash. The howling wind swept away Ibaz's cry of rage and the last remnants of Taan's command room.

'Find him,' Ibaz said, turning to his guards. 'Scour the city and the surrounding countryside. He had at least twenty humans with him, so look for group tracks!'

But Ibaz knew it was futile. Taan had slipped the net and he would return, one day. He couldn't know, standing on the shattered tower, that it would be over four hundred years before the events this day had set in motion would come to fruition. Four hundred years of Drake rule and human slavery before the world would once again erupt into war.

CHAPTER 1

The huge figure strode down the street, oblivious to the rain that drenched his cloak and ran in torrents down his back. He moved with the strength of a born warrior and not even his heavy limp, nor the three bottles of scalett he'd drunk before he set out, could change that. The thugs of the city slums were smart enough to leave him alone and searched for easier prey, but occasionally even they would wonder why a Drake Samurai of the Royal Guard was walking these squalid streets.

The Warrior stopped at a crossroads and looked blearily at the street sign, eventually making out the words and turning down another unremarkable street. Three blocks later, the muddy road gave way to a plaza of cobblestones and the dingy hovels became opulent market stalls. The scene looked completely out of place with its surroundings — a desert style slave market in the middle of the worst slums in the city, where those rich enough or those with tastes outside social acceptance could buy humans in anonymity.

The Warrior stopped, drew back his hood and looked in disgust at the decadent scenery. His iron grey scales glinted in the rain, while droplets of water gathered at the tip of his snout and ran in rivulets past his protruding teeth. He waved a clawed hand at the nearest vendor, who ran from his dry stall into the soaking wet.

'What can this humble Drake do for you, Gracious Lord?' the Copper scaled Merchant asked.

'I am called Kelkh,' the Warrior snapped, 'and I am no Gracious Lord.'

'Of course, good Master Kelkh,' the Merchant said, bowing again. 'Please accept my apologies. Your demeanour was so noble I simply assumed you were from the Palace.'

Kelkh snorted at the obvious lie. He was what he was, a Samurai Warrior who had taken one too many injuries in battle. There was nothing noble about him.

'Curse you, Dragath for forcing me into this,' he thought, closing his eyes and swaying drunkenly. He opened them again and saw the merchant staring expectantly.

'I seek to purchase a ... a ...'

'A slave? But of course, good Master, I have received a new shipment of humans just this week. Come, I will show you.'

The merchant bowed and waved towards the nearest stall where twenty humans of all ages and gender huddled together. Kelkh wrinkled his snout angrily and for an instant he knew he couldn't go through with such a farce; then he remembered who had told him to do it and what the repercussions were of ignoring such on order.

With a snarl he stormed into the stall and grabbed a bottle of scalett from the merchant's dinner table. He gulped down the fiery liquid while the merchant barked orders at the humans and pushed them into a line, kneeling with their heads bowed.

'Here you are, good Master,' the merchant said. 'Do you have any special ... requests for your slave?'

'Requests?' Kelkh asked.

'Yes, good Master,' the merchant grinned lecherously. 'Any

special qualities your slave should possess.'

Kelkh's expression darkened as his spirit soaked brain caught on. 'No, they should not!'

'Very well, good Master. I will let you inspect my stock and choose for yourself.'

Kelkh took another long draught of scalett and started his inspection. The humans all looked the same; dark hair ranging from brown to black, with skin bronzed from too much time in the sun. All of them cringed under the watchful gaze of the merchant.

He was almost at the end of the row when one of them caught his eye. She was tall for a human, with the awkwardness of youth still in her limbs. She was around sixteen with skin the soft colour of cream and shimmering hair like molten gold tied in a club behind her head. She looked up when he stopped in front of her and Kelkh noticed that her eyes were sapphire blue.

With a cry of outrage, the merchant launched himself in front of Kelkh and brought a thick cane down on the girl's back. 'How dare you raise your eyes to a Warrior, slave! Good Master, I apologise most humbly for this insult. Her last master was old and failed to discipline her appropriately. I will have her whipped the moment you depart.'

'No, that's not necessary,' Kelkh said. 'How much is she?'

'Good Master, I must advise you against her,' the merchant gasped. 'She is not a fit slave for a Warrior such as yourself.'

'And why not?'

'Good Master, this human is cursed. She has been marked by The Dragon.' He pointed at her golden hair, making absolutely certain that his fingers never touched it.

'If she's cursed, then why is she for sale?' Kelkh asked.

'She is a specialty item,' the merchant grovelled. 'I have clients who are drawn to such things. They enjoy the thrill of danger that such a curse adds to their dalliance.'

Kelkh's face turned an ugly black and he rammed his snout against the merchant's. 'Who would *dare* act with such dishonour and still call themselves a Drake?'

'Good Master, I do not know such things. I never know my customer's names, because most prefer it that way.'

'Swear by The Dragon that you don't know who they are.'

'I swear it, I swear!'

Kelkh dropped the merchant in disgust and threw a pouch of gold into his lap. 'This girl is mine. That coin should cover your price and more — your customers will have to look elsewhere for their entertainment.'

The merchant nodded dumbly and Kelkh left him sitting on the wet stones while he hoisted the girl to her feet. 'You are coming with me, understand?' She nodded uncertainly but didn't reply. 'Good. Let's go.'

Kelkh stepped out into the rain and the girl followed obediently behind him, shivering in the cold. Kelkh took one look at her, then stepped back into the stall and grabbed the merchant's thick cloak. Ignoring the merchant's look of shock, he tossed the garment to the girl and turned to go home. Two blocks later, he decided that he was nowhere near drunk enough to deal with this evening.

Kelkh opened a bleary eye and was grateful that the blinds in his room were drawn shut. He sat up slowly and gripped his thumping head as the world started spinning. He kicked over a wooden bucket that he couldn't remember putting on the floor and with a supreme effort he managed to focus enough to consider if he needed it. Not yet, he decided.

When he finally felt well enough to get up and get dressed, he noticed that his normally messy room had been carefully cleaned and ordered. The smell of stale scalett that usually permeated it was almost gone, replaced with a pleasant fragrance of lemongrass. Kelkh sifted through his hazy memory and tried to figure out what the hell had happened last night.

He was jolted from his thoughts as the door opened and a young girl with shining golden hair walked inside. She bowed and knelt in the middle of the room with her head lowered.

'Good morning, Master.'

'Master?' Kelkh asked confused. 'Who are you, girl?'

'My name is Annah Tress, Master. You purchased me last night from Iriel the slave trader.'

Kelkh massaged his jaw as he tried to recall last night. Dragath had told him to get a slave, so he had gone out to do just that. But the feeling that keeping a slave was not honourable had rankled him until he found a bottle of scalett. After that ...

Blurred images slowly filtered back of a copper scaled merchant desperately warning him of a cursed slave. He remembered being angry at the merchant and buying the slave, then he remembered little else.

'Damn Dragath, anyway,' he muttered. 'What do I need a slave for?'

Kelkh looked at the girl, still kneeling on the floor, and he noticed she was trembling. She was frightened, he realised;

frightened that she had done something wrong. She didn't know him well enough to know if he would beat her for it. He cleared his throat awkwardly and tried to put her at ease.

'So tell me, girl, what can you do?'

'I can do whatever you require of me, Master,' she replied, touching her head to the floor.

'I presume it was you who cleaned my quarters?'

'I'm sorry if that was wrong, Master. My last master required me to keep his home clean at all times.'

Kelkh sighed and pinched the scales between his eyes. 'No, girl, you weren't wrong. If cleaning a house is what you're used to doing then by all means keep doing it. Do you know how to cook?'

'Yes, Master.'

'Good, then you can cook me breakfast. There's boar steaks and krat in the cool room, and bread in the pantry.'

Kelkh led Annah into the kitchen and sat at the table while she busied herself making breakfast. Before long, the smells of cooking boar reached his snout and his stomach growled in anticipation. A few minutes later, Annah put the boar steak on the table next to a plate of fried krat, a thick Drake blood sausage.

Kelkh plunged eagerly into his breakfast, wolfing it down with none of the decorum found in more noble houses. He stuffed his mouth full and was chewing happily when he realised that Annah was standing against the back wall.

'What are you doing back there, girl?' he demanded. 'Don't just stand there, go and make yourself some breakfast, then sit down and eat. There's human food in the pantry.'

Annah gaped in surprise before her training took over and sent her into action.

Kelkh finished his steak and was mopping the grease up with a thick slice of bread when Annah sat down. He shoved his plate aside and reached for the krat, then frowned when he saw Annah nervously picking at her food.

'Eat up, girl,' he said. 'You'll be no good to me if you're fainting from hunger.'

Annah was so nervous she crammed a whole rasher of bacon into her mouth and almost choked on it. Kelkh sighed and ran a hand over his eyes, muttering about the stupidity of humans. Annah finished her breakfast in record time and jumped to her feet to clear the table.

'Leave all that for now, girl,' Kelkh said. 'It's time I showed you what I do here. Then I can start training you for what you'll be doing.'

'I saw your armour, Master, and your sword,' Annah said. 'My last master taught me the basics of caring for his equipment and I could learn more if—'

'No,' Kelkh snapped. 'My armour and weapons are none of your concern. He climbed abruptly to his feet and winced as the movement made his leg twinge. 'Come, girl, let me show you.'

He led Annah to a large stone barn at the back of his home, kept clean of straw, paper and anything else that was potentially flammable. A large furnace stood at the back of the room looking cold and vacant, and a heavy anvil sat in the centre. It looked just like a blacksmith's forge should, but it felt unused. The only things that did seem lovingly worn were a set of exquisite metalworking tools that hung near the door.

Kelkh picked up a brick of steel from a supply bin and tossed it on top of the anvil with a dull clang.

'This is what I do now, girl,' he said heavily. 'I'm a Forger.'

'I understand, Master,' Annah replied. 'I've seen the blacksmiths work in the city and I know some of what's required. I must bring coal for the fires—'

Kelkh cut her off with a bitter snort. 'You don't know any more than I did, girl. I'm a Forger, not a blacksmith. Do you know the difference?'

Annah shook her head nervously.

'Then you'll learn,' he said. 'Sit over there.'

Annah knelt with her hands folded in her lap and waited, not certain if she should be afraid or not.

Kelkh ignored her, lost in his own imagination. He picked up the steel brick and held it at eye level, watching as the early morning sunlight flickered across its shiny surface. Heaving a great sigh, he placed the brick back on the anvil and started to sing. It was obviously the last thing Annah had expected, judging by her expression, but the soft baritone of his voice and the power of the music quickly seeped into her bones and put her at ease.

Kelkh didn't see her expression change; he was lost to the music as he sang the song of creation. The words flowed through him unbidden and unknown, filling the room with sweet harmonies that made his spirit soar. He reached out for the steel brick with his hands and his song, holding it firmly in both as he gave it shape.

The metal moved beneath his thick fingers like bread dough, melding itself to the whim of song and hand. The metal glowed faintly as he worked it, a soft silvery light that grew brighter with every second. A dagger quickly took shape; a slender blade with a thick crosspiece and plain hilt, all from the same block of metal with no seams or joins. It was a thing of beauty, flawless and perfect.

The tone of Kelkh's song changed, the smooth, steady notes giving way to a softer, faster gait. He reached for his metalworking tools and used them with a delicate touch that was at odds with his bulky physique and fearsome manner. He carved elaborate scrollwork up and down the length of the blade until it was a masterpiece all of its own, depicting a scene that was holy to all citizens in the Empire; the Ascension, when the true Dragons gifted Kelkh's people with a fraction of their power and gave birth to the Drake nation. The Dragons looked so real that even Kelkh imagined they might leap up and fly out of the metal. With an unconscious grin, he spun the knife around to work on the hilt.

With a blade so detailed, Kelkh felt that elaborate decoration on the hilt would detract from the overall effect. The song seemed to agree with him and it remained in harmony with his hands as they smoothed the metal to a polished shine. He crafted it in the shape of a dragon's tooth, broad and flared at the top, curving to a delicate point at the pommel.

He turned the dagger over and over in his hands as he inspected his work, looking with eyes and music for any flaw in its creation and finding none. Satisfied that the Forging was complete, he let his voice trail off and brought his song to an end. The look of joy and absolute peace fled from his face as reality once again took hold and he saw his creation truly for the first time.

'So now you know what a Forger does,' he said, looking at Annah who still knelt in the same spot, enraptured by the beauty of his song. 'You see the difference.'

'Yes, Master,' she whispered.

'Good.'

He stretched his sore arms and flexed his wings to ease out the cramp. The sun had passed its zenith and was approaching the mountaintops — four or five hours had passed by unnoticed while he Forged.

'Go and make us some lunch, girl,' he sighed. 'I'm starved.'

Annah bowed awkwardly from the floor, then jumped to her feet and hurried away. Kelkh watched her go then looked at the beautiful dagger in his hand, glowing brightly like a sliver of moonlight. He walked to the far corner of the room and opened an iron chest with his toe, then dropped the dagger unceremoniously into it and kicked it shut. Shaking his head in disgust, he followed the growls of his stomach towards the kitchen.

CHAPTER 2

Aerik stretched his aching back as he hefted a full sack of ro-khill over his shoulder. The Drakes loved the stuff, using it to make their foul brew, scalett; but it was a tricky thing to grow. It needed huge amounts of water to reach maturity, which meant that Aerik and dozens of other human slaves spent twelve hours each day wading in thigh deep water as they tended and harvested the plants.

It wasn't bad work as far as slavery went — you were allowed a degree of freedom while you worked because the Drakes on guard weren't keen on dirtying their armour by wading into the muddy water. Every now and then they would line up the slaves and whip some of them for minor infractions, just to remind them of their station, but Aerik knew other slaves suffered much worse.

He waded through the mire until he reached a set of steps up to a wooden walkway running around the outer edge of the ro-khill paddy. He climbed out of the water under the bored gaze of two emerald scaled Drakes and hurried along the slick walkway to the weighing station. The Drakes had no difficulty walking on the slippery wood with their thick, clawed feet, but it amused them to watch their human slaves slide about. If you lost too much ro-khill from your sack when you fell, they would give you a beating for your mistake as well.

Aerik sighed and shifted the sack to his other shoulder. It was his life and he was used to it. Besides, it wasn't all bad. At least he had something to look forward to.

He stepped into line behind the other slaves, waiting for his turn in front of the sapphire scaled clerk who ran the weighing station. The Drakes lived in a rigid caste system, where the colour of their scales indicated which Great Dragon they were descended from and what clan they belonged to. Sapphire Drakes were born and trained into academics, and their clan produced all the scribes and low level administrators for the Empire.

When it was his turn, Aerik stepped forward and placed his sack on the scales. The sapphire Drake stared at the weight, flicking his tongue in and out of his mouth as he recorded the result in a thick ledger.

'Very good,' he said patronizingly. 'You've exceeded your quota by three kilograms. You may leave for the day.'

'Thank you, Master,' Aerik said, kneeling and bowing his head until the Drake waved him away. With another bow of obedience, he turned and hurried from the ro-khill paddies.

Aerik knew the way by heart as he sped through the squalid streets of Tingra, the slave ghetto on the outskirts of the Imperial City. He slipped between the tired pedestrian traffic returning home from a hard day's work, weaving through the crowd as he ran towards home. There were a few calls of greeting and a few shouts of annoyance as he hurried along, but none of them slowed him down.

He almost slipped in the deep mud as he came around the last corner, but mercifully managed to keep his feet. His brother,

Monta, was already waiting outside their sparse home and the last thing Aerik needed was to fall flat on his face in a puddle of mud and give his brother more ammunition.

'You're late,' Monta said. 'Where have you been?'

'Sorry,' he replied. 'It was a slow day in the field. The storms knocked the bushes about, so pickings were slim.'

Monta's look of annoyance changed quickly to one of concern. 'The Drakes weren't angry, were they?'

'No more than usual,' Aerik shrugged. 'They know it isn't our fault. They gave out a few extra lashes but we kept our heads down just in case. They didn't take anyone today.'

'Thank god for that,' Monta sighed. 'Now come on, we're late. Tisa's going to be beside herself if we take too much longer.'

Monta grabbed his brother by the elbow and propelled him back out into the steadily darkening streets. Twilight gave way to complete darkness as they reached their destination, a former horse stable that had been converted into a slave hostel when it had grown too decrepit. It had been lovingly repaired and maintained by the slaves who called it home, and from time to time it had been used as a meeting hall of sorts. When a daring slave succeeded in brewing a palatable drink called scrum from apple scraps and off cuts, the nature of this humble meeting hall rapidly changed.

The new bar, dubbed 'The Stable', quickly grew an underground reputation amongst the slaves as a place to relax, have fun, meet people and drink merrily. It was an escape from the horrors of their everyday world and a luxury that they had never known. The Drakes knew, there was no doubt about that, but they turned a blind eye. The bar kept the slaves happy, and a happy worker was a busy worker; plus they were less likely to lash out in a fit of pent up anger. They raided The Stable from time to time, just to keep up appearances, but they left the scrum alone and those who were arrested were usually let off with a light flogging. In all, the slaves thought the rewards more than worth the risks.

Monta and Aerik came to The Stable almost every night, swapping Aerik's considerable barding skills for food, drink and companionship. The slaves had no money and owned few possessions, so people paid their way at The Stable with services. The roof and walls were kept in good repair by people paying their tab, the garden was beautifully tended and the pebble beds behind the building were constantly changed to display different symbols and patterns. Monta's love, Tisa, worked three nights a week as a waitress and Monta himself earned his keep as a cook.

When the doors opened to admit them, they almost ran inside, drinking in the sights and smells of their home away from home. Monta scanned the room until he found Tisa, sitting at a small table against the far wall. She wasn't working that night and Monta left his brother's side straight away to enjoy as much time with her as he could. Aerik laughed at how quickly he was abandoned and slapped Monta on the back of the head as he ran by.

Aerik didn't mind, though. He had enough friends in The Stable that he was never lacking for company. He headed towards the bar to see who was working and was immediately swamped by a crowd of young children. They clambered over him, squealing and begging him to tell them a story. He laughed at their antics and quickly agreed, ushering them into a corner of the building where he could spin his tale and keep the children out of everyone's way. One of his friends brought him a mug of scrum to keep his voice flowing, then he was left to his captive audience.

The children were enraptured as Aerik told them a tale of great deeds and romance, abounding with heroes and monsters. They sat in awed silence, listening as he took their imagination to far away places that they would never see. He was good at what he did and it made him feel worthwhile to put a spark in the children's lives. He knew all too well that most of them would have two or three years left before they were put to work in the mines and the ro-khill paddies.

He hurriedly swept that thought aside and put all his skill into his finale, drawing gasps of shock and squeals of delight from the spellbound audience. The children cheered him as he stood up and gave them a foppish bow, and the parents who came to collect their sons and daughters gave him a smile of thanks. He waved at them all as they were led away, then hurried to the bar for another mug of scrum.

With a full mug in hand, he saw a table of his friends across the room and made straight for it. He picked up a free chair as he weaved through the crowd and set it down next to his friend, Japheth, who worked in the mines.

'Good to see you, Aerik,' Japheth grinned. 'How were the kids?'

'Happy and entertained as usual,' he replied.

'They do love a good story,' Japheth laughed. 'My daughter will be re-enacting that tale for me tomorrow. Every bit of it, more than once.'

'You'll cope, I'm sure.'

'Aye, that I will,' Japheth nodded. 'So are there any plans for you to have any yourself?'

'What, kids?' Aerik asked, surprised. 'Not likely. I need to find the right woman first.'

'What about that lass, Mara, who you were seeing last week?'

Aerik shrugged sheepishly.

'Damn it, boy,' Japheth groaned. 'Some day soon, one of these girls is going to clock you good, and you'll deserve it, too.'

'It's not my fault I've got high standards.'

'There's no one that's ever had any higher,' Japheth replied. 'Why can't you be like Monta, find a nice girl and start a family?'

'Monta's not about to start a family,' Aerik laughed.

'Don't tell me he hasn't told you,' Japheth said. Aerik just stared at him in confusion. 'You mean he doesn't know?'

Aerik's expression lit up as understanding dawned on him. 'How long?'

'Long enough to have the morning sickness,' Japheth said. 'That's the downside of wedding a midwife — you have to put up with sick mothers-to-be in your living room. The good side is I find out things before anyone else does.'

'Will she tell him tonight?'

'I don't know. I thought she would have told him already! But it's all the more reason you should start behaving like a responsible uncle-to-be and settle down.'

'Oh, enough,' Aerik snapped. 'Where's Timbal?'

'Dead,' Japheth replied, his expression darkening. 'One of the Drakes overheard him calling them 'lizards' behind their back. They ran him through on the spot.'

Aerik sighed and banged his fist against the table. 'Idiot! Damned fool. I warned him not to say that within earshot of a Drake.'

'We all did,' Japheth replied. 'I think deep down, he wanted them to hear him. He'd had enough of this life and now he's free of it. Be free, brother.'

Japheth raised his mug and Aerik raised his own in response.

'Be free,' Aerik toasted, giving the slave's last honour and taking a long drink. They both lapsed into silence, listening to their friends talk around them, moving on with their lives despite their loss. Death was too frequent a visitor to the slaves for anyone to dwell on it.

Japheth and Aerik were soon enmeshed in a new mix of gossip and tale spinning, and both the hours and the scrum flew by unnoticed. It was only when a familiar voice shouted a whoop of joy that Aerik looked up.

'Looks like Tisa finally let your brother know,' Japheth said.

Aerik didn't disagree, as he watched Monta pick up his girlfriend and spin her in his arms. 'There'll be a wedding on the horizon then,' he grinned.

Japheth's reply was lost as Monta called for his brother to sing in celebration of the moment and the crowd quickly caught on; Aerik's skill was well known and loved around The Stable.

Aerik hopped to his feet and ran through the crowd until he reached his brother and enveloped him in a crushing hug. He hugged Tisa as well, then rushed to the bar where one of the waitresses handed him his lute. The crowd parted to make way for him as he skipped to the stage, and then closed ranks when he passed, jostling for the best position.

Aerik's deft fingers plucked at the worn strings, and he sang a soft ballad that almost brought the half drunk crowd to tears. He grinned when he saw Tisa grab Monta and drag him to the centre of the room, where other young couples had already gathered to dance cheek to cheek. Monta, ordinarily the most bashful of dancers, laughed joyously as he hugged Tisa to him and swung her gently around the room.

When the song finished, there was a moment of silence as the crowd composed themselves, then they erupted into a roar of applause that soon became a call for something else. Judging the crowd the way only the best of bards can, Aerik burst into a raucous tune, quick and lively that sent every person in The Stable grabbing a partner and running for the cleared dance area. There was another song after that and another until all hours of the morning, and the happy dancers all made sure that Aerik was never without at least one mug of scrum. It was almost midnight when the carousing wound down and the slaves grabbed their families to go home and rest before another long day's work.

Aerik walked unsteadily home from The Stable, humming happily to himself. It had been a fantastic night and he was in the best mood he'd been in for a long time. When he tripped and fell, he didn't even utter his usual curse — well, not loudly anyway — he just rolled onto his back and stared at the stars, oblivious to what the mud was doing to his clothes. He would probably earn a lashing for his appearance, but as he watched the stars sparkle like diamonds on black velvet, he decided he didn't care.

Tomorrow he would work in the ro-khill fields, and the day after, and after, and after until he either died from disease or random chance, or until he lost the will to go on and did something stupid. It was his lot in life and he had known it since he was twelve, but for tonight at least, it didn't bother him. His brother would soon be married and a father, and he would have a little niece or nephew to watch grow up. He was happier than he'd ever been, and nothing was going to take that away from him.

And who knew, perhaps there was something to Japheth's idea of settling down after all.

CHAPTER 3

Annah hurried to the door when she heard a heavy knocking from outside. Kelkh was in his forge and she dared not disturb his work, so she opened the door to give her apologies to the visitor. She saw a strange Drake with golden scales waiting on the cottage veranda, looking around the newly tended garden beds with interest. She immediately stepped back and fell to her knees.

'Can I help you, honourable Lord?' she asked.

There was a long pause, which Annah hoped was due to the Drake adjusting to the unexpected presence of a human slave. The Drakes could be very finicky where their honour was concerned, and something as simple as being greeted by a slave and not their master could be taken as a great slight. Drakes had been known to slay the slave in response to such a thing, sparking a feud between Noble Houses when the slave owner claimed compensation.

'Well well,' the Drake said, as his golden clawed hand reached out and took a lock of her hair. 'Why would Kelkh have gone and bought a slave?'

Annah saw her hair glitter golden in the sunlight, almost the same colour as the scales on the Drake's hand, and she started to tremble. The Drake rubbed her hair thoughtfully between thumb and forefinger, then let it fall in front of her face.

'What is your name, young one?'

'Annah Tress, servant of Kelkh Ironbound, honourable Lord,' she replied.

'Well, Annah Tress, my name is Ishkal, or Ishkal the Gold if you wish to be formal. I'm an old friend of your Master's and I would be indebted if you would fetch him for me. Don't worry about disturbing him; he won't be angry when you tell him I'm here.'

'Of course, Lord Ishkal,' Annah said, bowing until her forehead touched the mat. 'Please enter and I will let the Master know you're here.'

Ishkal walked past her and headed towards the living room without any prompting, moving with a familiarity that gave credence to his friendship to Kelkh. Annah left him to find his own way and rushed to the forge to fetch her master.

Music flooded into the hallway as soon as she opened the door, bringing tears to her eyes from the sheer captivating beauty of it. For a moment Annah was torn between doing her duty and listening to the sweet music, but that moment didn't last long; to fail in her duty was to invite the often fatal wrath of a Drake Master. She hurried over to Kelkh and knelt in front of him as his song waned and came to a halt.

'What do you want, girl?' he asked. Annah couldn't tell if he was annoyed or not.

'Pardon my interruption, Master, but there is someone here to see you. He claims to be a friend of yours, called Ishkal the Gold.'

Kelkh's face broke into a toothy grin and he let loose a loud laugh. He stepped past Annah, patting her on the shoulder on his way through. 'Come on, girl,' he said happily. 'It's time you met one of the finest Drakes in the Empire.'

Annah hurried after Kelkh, who was walking to the living room as quickly as his crippled leg would allow. He waved at Annah to wait in the doorway, then limped across the room to his friend.

Standing in the gloom of the corridor, Annah had her first chance to properly study Ishkal the Gold. He was shorter than Kelkh and not as broad, but he had an aura of calm and tranquillity. Where Kelkh had a ponytail of thick hair that looked like a bunch of iron ropes, Ishkal's head was clean shaven with the soft scales reflecting brightly in the afternoon sunlight. He was clothed in soft brown robes that hugged him closely and he was crisscrossed from foot to neck in finger thick metal bands. He looked like a brown fish caught in a tight metal net and he was the strangest Drake Annah had ever seen.

'Ishkal, what are you doing here?' Kelkh bellowed.

Ishkal gave a dignified smile that matched Kelkh's happy grin and gave his friend a back thumping warrior's hug. 'It's been far too long since I've seen you, old friend. It was time I took a sabbatical from the Abbey anyway, so I thought I would visit and reminisce about old times.'

'You're always welcome here, my friend,' Kelkh replied. 'And you'll find the service far better than the last time you stayed!'

Knowing what was expected, Annah was already moving forward when Kelkh turned and beckoned her.

'Ah yes, young Annah Tress,' Ishkal nodded. 'I was going to ask you about her. Not something I had expected at all.'

'No, nor I in truth,' Kelkh sighed. 'Annah, go and fetch us some lunch, then you can feed Mange. You'll find a sack of ro-khill by the back door and you'll find Mange in his pen. It's a big open air enclosure, you can't miss it. Just feed him ro-khill until he's full and come back again.'

'Yes, Master.'

'Annah Tress,' Ishkal called, stopping her as she turned to leave. 'Have you ever seen a Keldarkan Rock Dragon?'

'No, Lord Ishkal.'

'Then show no fear. Have courage and it will respect you.'

'Thank you, Lord Ishkal.' She bowed and left for the kitchen to make a meal that her Master would be proud to serve to his best friend.

After she'd brought lunch to Kelkh and Ishkal, Annah found the sack of ro-khill outside the back door, heaved it over her shoulder and made her way to the large rock enclosure at the back of the property. As she drew closer, she heard the hard scrabbling of a large creature moving around. She cautiously approached the pen and peered inside.

Half of the enclosure was covered in, giving shelter during the worst of weather, but that part of the pen was currently not in use. Lying full length on the ground, basking in the late winter sun, was a creature of rock and magic. Mange, the Keldarkan Rock Dragon, was the size of a draft horse, with a tail that stretched out as far again. Each wing was at least as long as his body and both were currently stretched at full length to gain the most from the unseasonable warmth.

As Annah approached, the Dragon's head came up slowly. It

twisted its sinuous neck, expecting to see Kelkh approaching. When it focused on Annah instead, it moved with amazing speed, flipping onto its legs and opening its gaping maw in challenge. Annah fought down the urge to run away and gulped as she stared down the stone gullet.

'Show courage,' she whispered. 'Show courage and it will respect you.'

With agonizing slowness, she reached into the sack and pulled out a lump of ro-khill. Looking like a cross between a black avocado and a sponge, this ro-khill had somehow been laced with metal; Annah could clearly see the silver lines crisscrossing it. She didn't know if that was meant to make the food more appealing to the Rock Dragon and she honestly didn't care as she held out the dull lump and waited.

Time passed unnoticed as she kept her arm straight and prayed that the Dragon would lower its claws and close its tooth filled mouth. When she was certain that her arm would break under the strain, the Dragon finally dropped onto all fours and trotted cautiously over to sniff her hand. With a surprisingly gentle touch the Dragon took the ro-khill in its mouth, took a step back and tossed it upwards. Its head snapped forward, catching the black lump in mid air and crunching it loudly before swallowing it down. A rough stone tongue flicked out and licked around the sharp teeth, catching any crumbs that escaped its notice.

Digging into the sack again, Annah quickly produced another lump of ro-khill and held it out. The Dragon's head snaked back out to grab the food, and again it was tossed into the air and snapped up. By the third lump, Annah started to overcome her fear of the creature and she felt confident enough to look at it more closely.

The Rock Dragon lived up to its name, looking every part like a dragon statue roughly chiselled out of granite. When it moved, Annah almost expected it to crack at the joints, but that wasn't the case. The magic that flowed through every Dragon was still the lifeblood of this, the least of Dragons. The joints flowed and moved as though they were liquid, adding a hint of grace to the otherwise ungainly creature.

Without thinking, Annah reached out her hand and stroked the Dragon between the horns on its rough head. The Dragon closed its eyes and scratched the floor happily, leaning its head into Annah like a giant cat. She laughed at the unexpected antics from such a fearsome creature, dropping the ro-khill sack and lifting her other hand to tickle under its chin. The Dragon's head pushed into her, almost knocking her over when it nuzzled against her chest. She smiled in relief that her fears were apparently unfounded and retrieved the sack from the ground, reaching in and grabbing another lump of ro-khill.

Ishkal sat back in his chair and pushed the remains of his lunch away. 'So, Kelkh, tell me about this girl, Annah Tress.'

'It's all Dragath's fault,' Kelkh sighed. 'When I left the Marauders he told me that most blacksmiths have slaves to assist them and he gave me the address of a Slave Market.'

'But you're not a blacksmith,' Ishkal pointed out.

'Do you think that matters to Dragath?'

'No, I suppose not. And one doesn't ignore a suggestion from a Prince of the Realm.'

'No, one doesn't.' Kelkh sighed and ran his hands over his snout. 'I don't know what I'm going to do with her. She's been here for a week and I've already run out of things for her to do. Keeping the house clean and cooking meals only fills up a few hours.'

'Yes, I noticed everything was unusually tidy,' Ishkal chuckled. 'I never understood how someone of your military background kept such a messy house — your command tent was always immaculate.'

Kelkh grunted but otherwise ignored the comment. 'She's so timid,' he said. 'When she sat at the breakfast table, she was so scared she almost couldn't hold her fork!'

'That would be because she's never sat at a table with a Drake before,' Ishkal replied. 'Slaves aren't deemed worthy of dining with their masters; they just have to grab whatever they can when they have a spare moment.'

Kelkh frowned then shook his head irritably. 'Well I've already got her used to eating breakfast with me and I'm not going to change that on her now. I guess she's just stuck with it.'

'Good,' Ishkal grinned. 'It will make breakfasts far more interesting while I'm here.'

'And how long are you here for?'

'The usual. Two weeks of the wide world before I return to the Abbey.'

'I'm glad that you're here, my friend. You can help me think of what to do with this girl.'

As if on cue, Annah entered the room and knelt on the carpet. 'Mange has been fed, Master.'

'Did you have any trouble?' Ishkal asked.

'No, Lord Ishkal,' she replied. 'He was very gentle once he grew accustomed to me. I thank you for your advice. It was most useful.'

'I'm surprised he took to you so well,' Kelkh said. 'Mange doesn't usually like strangers. I expected you to have a few bruises on you when you came back.'

Not knowing quite what to say to that, Annah just kept quiet and bowed.

'Now, young Annah, your Master and I were just discussing what to do with you,' Ishkal said. 'Do you have any suggestions?'

'I can do whatever you require, Master,' she replied.

'I've no doubt,' Ishkal said. 'But I asked if *you* had any suggestions.'

'Lord, I ...'

Ishkal saw the confusion on her face and the fear that she might say the wrong thing and enrage him. He cut her short with a wave of his hand. 'What are you naturally good at, Annah? A skill that you never had to try to develop.'

'I have some skill at drawing, Lord Ishkal,' she replied.

'Drawing,' Ishkal said thoughtfully, leaning back in his chair and steepling his fingers over his chest. 'Kelkh, what work do you have outstanding at the moment.'

'Enough to sink a ship,' Kelkh snorted. 'I have an order for three katana from Duke Crawall for himself and his two bodyguards, a dress pike for Darian, the younger son of Count Falker, and a cavalry sabre for the Count himself. Plus there's that damned great sword for Duke Inral.'

'Nothing else?' Ishkal asked. 'Nothing less ... martial?'

Kelkh shrugged irritably. 'Dame Lorous keeps asking me to make something for her granddaughter's coming of age and she's becoming annoyingly persistent.'

'You haven't accepted?' Ishkal asked.

'I can make weapons with my eyes closed,' Kelkh said. 'But some useless ornament, I just don't see the point. And if I can't visualise it in my mind, I can't visualise it with my song.'

'So you can't Forge what you can't imagine?' Ishkal asked. Kelkh nodded and Ishkal grabbed a pencil and some parchment, which he pushed towards Annah. 'You can draw, Annah Tress, so visualise something that will be fit for a Dame's granddaughter.'

Annah's eyes widened as she gripped the pencil, until Kelkh patted her awkwardly on the shoulder. She took a deep breath and put pencil to parchment, sketching the first thing that came to her mind. At one stage she grabbed a lump of bread from the table and used it to rub away a mistake, but other than that she kept her head down to her task. Minutes passed by while Kelkh and Ishkal watched, until finally Annah bowed and held the parchment out in both hands to her Master.

Kelkh rubbed his jaw with one hand, holding the parchment in the other as he looked at her design. Ishkal coughed delicately and Kelkh put the parchment on the table for them both to see. Drawn roughly on the page was a metal and glass vase, fashioned in the shape of a dragon. The four metal legs made the stand, with the body making the base. The glass vase sat on the dragon's back, held in place on four sides by the long neck, two upswept wings and a thick tail.

'Well?' Ishkal asked. 'What do you think?'

'It can be done,' Kelkh said, eyeing the parchment critically. 'I can get the glass from the blower in the morning, but I think the dragon needs a little work. The head should be arched more.'

Ishkal tore off another piece of bread and rubbed away the dragon's head. Grabbing the pencil, he placed it in Annah's hand, took her wrist and led her gently to the table. 'Arch the head a little more for me, please, Annah.'

Annah nodded and carefully drew the head again, this time arching it at the neck and opening the mouth in a miniature roar.

'Yes, that's much better,' Kelkh said. 'I like the roar, too. But I think the wings should be longer and the tail a fraction thicker.'

Annah scrabbled on the parchment again, leaving charcoal blackened clumps of bread littered around the floor as she rubbed the parchment clean.

'Good. But no Dragon's scales are ever so perfect,' Kelkh said. 'I think we should take one out here and here, and add a damaged one here.'

Ishkal sat back and smiled serenely to himself. He always enjoyed it when he made people happy, and he had just solved what Kelkh could do with all of Annah's spare time. If this one vase was anything to go by, Kelkh would soon be swamped with orders for goblets, platters and all manner of other things.

'He might even learn to enjoy himself,' Ishkal said under his breath. With a contented sigh, he closed his eyes and left Annah and Kelkh to their work.

CHAPTER 4

A roar went up in The Stable as Monta, Tisa and Aerik stepped inside. Every patron seemed truly happy to see them and Errol, the bartender for the evening, even left his post to give them each a hug. It had been many months since they had been there, not since the birth of Tisa's baby, Rebecca. With Tisa recovering from the birthing and Monta and Aerik looking after all the house chores as well as their own slave work, none of them had time to spare.

This was Tisa's first night away from the house and Aerik had gone out of his way to make it a memorable one. He had reserved a table for two right in front of the stage and reworked the duty roster so that her favourite cook was working. He led Monta and Tisa through the cheering crowd to their table, then left them to enjoy each other's company and sought out Japheth. He found him without too much trouble, on a table that ran the length of the back wall.

'Aerik, it's about damned time you showed up here again,' Japheth said, standing up and giving the bard a backslapping hug. 'I haven't seen you since the wedding! My wife made me promise to tell you how much she enjoyed your singing at the reception. She said that Monta and Tisa looked thrilled when you got up and played.'

'It was my tribute to them,' Aerik shrugged. 'I can play songs, tell stories and be a slave. I wanted to do something they'd always remember and slaving didn't seem appropriate.'

Japheth laughed and took a long drink of scrum. 'Well there wasn't a dry eye in the house, I can tell you that much. But that still doesn't explain why you haven't been to The Stable in so long.'

'I've been busy,' Aerik replied. 'With Tisa moving into the house and then the baby, Monta and I haven't had time for anything.'

'Bah, I think you just like playing uncle,' Japheth said. 'My wife said that the night the baby was born, you were almost as nervous as Monta!'

'It's a nervous time,' Aerik shrugged.

'And I hear talk that you rush home at night to play babysitter so Monta and Tisa get some time to themselves.' Aerik shrugged again. '*And* I hear you sing the bubs to sleep most nights with that beautiful voice of yours.'

'Enough, enough,' Aerik sighed. 'She is my niece, you know.'

'True, but I still think you're smitten.'

Japheth ducked under the table as Aerik swiped at him, coming up laughing and clutching his empty mug. As a peace offering, he ordered another round from a passing waitress.

'So what have they named her?'

'Rebecca,' Aerik replied.

'Rebecca? That's a free man's name,' Japheth frowned.

'I know,' Aerik replied. 'Tisa named her after her own mother. Apparently she was free for her entire childhood before she was captured by the lizards. I think Tisa dreams that her daughter will be free some day, too.'

'Not in this lifetime,' Japheth scoffed. 'We're slaves and slaves we'll stay. Anything else is a dangerous pipe dream.'

'That's a bleak outlook.'

'No — just a realistic one.'

Aerik shrugged and returned to his drink, too happy to be back at The Stable to argue with Japheth about his thoughts on life. He drained the last of his glass and caught the eye of one of this evening's barmaids, one he knew well and was trying to know better. She flashed him a smile and deftly slipped through the crowd to refill his mug, and Japheth's as well when he asked.

Aerik watched her disappear into the crowd while Japheth sighed and shook his head in despair. 'You're hopeless,' he growled. 'The way you've been acting around Rebecca, I thought you might want to settle down and have one of your own.'

'And who says I don't?' Aerik asked.

Japheth just snorted and shook his head again. 'Don't get me started.'

Aerik grinned and left the topic alone. He looked around the room while Japheth disappeared out the side door to water the garden and was surprised by the number of unfamiliar faces. At least one in three was unknown to him and he said as much to Japheth when he returned.

'What do you expect?' Japheth grunted. 'You've been away for months. New guys come, old guys pass on.'

'I suppose,' Aerik said. 'There just seems like a lot of new guys around.'

Catching Aerik's eye, one of the new faces in the room broke away from his group of friends and walked over. He was tall, with tan skin and brown hair, and he had the kind of stocky build that came with working in the slave mines. He smiled amiably as he approached the table.

'Good evening,' he said. 'My name's Ebon and I'm new around here.'

'Nice to meet you, Ebon,' Aerik said, shaking the man's hand. 'I'm Aerik and the surly one over there is Japheth. What can we do for you?'

'I was just looking for some information,' Ebon said. 'I've seen this brew being served at the bar and I've got no idea what it is or how you pay for it. I've tried to get the barmaid's attention, but she always seems to skip past me and head for this table.'

Japheth snorted into his scrum and Aerik had the good grace to blush. 'I'm sorry about that, Ebon. The drink's called scrum and we brew it from apple core pulp and apple skin that we all keep aside. We pay for it in favours, which is why this building is in such good repair and the gardens are so beautiful. If you speak to Tabalt, the manager, he'll set you up with an account.'

'Quite an enterprise he's made here,' Ebon said. 'Thank you for the information.'

'You're welcome,' Aerik replied. 'But even if you set up an account tonight, it might be a while before you can charge a drink to it. Let me buy you one, seeing as you're new to our slums.'

Ebon looked taken aback by the unexpected offer, then his face broke into a wide grin. 'Thank you, I'd appreciate that.'

Aerik waved at the barmaid, who quickly stepped over with an extra mug and topped up both the others for the promise of a dance later on. Japheth rolled his eyes and Ebon chuckled into his scrum, but Aerik just smiled and watched her walk away to refill her serving jug.

There was an outbreak of coughing and spluttering from the far side of the table as Ebon took his first sip, and Japheth casually stretched out his arm and gave the man a hard slap on the back. Ebon coughed again, then picked up his mug and took another long drink.

'By the gods, that is *good!*' he wheezed, banging his hand on the table.

'You'd better believe it,' Japheth smiled.

'Cheers,' Aerik added.

Ebon laughed and the trio fell into an easy banter about the more mundane things in the area. Japheth and Aerik took turns in explaining the dos and don'ts of the ghetto, letting Ebon know in no uncertain terms what would get him killed. When the doors creaked open, none of them thought anything of it, assuming that another group of slaves had finished late from their work in the fields. But when the hall fell into a hush that radiated like a wave from the entry, they knew that something more sinister had arrived. Five Drake Samurai stood in the doorway, hands on their sword hilts and armour glinting in the torchlight.

'Damn, it's a Drake patrol,' Japheth said.

'We've got to get out of here,' Ebon whispered urgently.

'Take it easy, Ebon,' Aerik said calmly, patting his shoulder. 'The Drakes come here to shake up the bar and show that they're still in command. They don't want us to forget it. They'll hand out a few lashes for show and leave.'

Ebon looked like he might disagree but eventually nodded and rose to his feet with the others, watching the Drakes warily. The Drakes split up and strode through the room, sneering at the humans as they backed away to create a path. One Drake walked to the centre of the room and looked around disdainfully.

'This is an illegal gathering,' he said, his voice almost echoing in the silence. 'It is a violation of our laws and every one of you is accountable. You humans must be taught your place.' He paced up and down the crowd until he stopped in front of Ebon's friends. 'You, you will come with me.'

Ebon hissed between his teeth and started forward but Aerik grabbed his arm and held him back.

'Don't go,' Aerik whispered. 'I know he's your friend, but you'll get him killed if you try to stop the Drakes from taking him. They'll whip him and toss him in the cells tonight, then turn him loose tomorrow. It's happened before; don't worry about him.'

'It's not him I'm worried for,' Ebon said grimly.

Aerik shrugged but kept his hand firmly gripped on Ebon's arm. Ebon's friend still hadn't moved and the Drake was getting angry.

'Didn't you hear me, slave?' he asked. 'You come, now!'

The man hesitated again and the Drake's patience wore out. He barged through the crowd and reached out to grab the man by the scruff of the neck. The Drake was so disdainful of the slaves that he didn't even look at the man's companions as he pushed them out of the way. That was why he never saw the danger, but from across the room with a clear line of site, Aerik did.

One of the slaves grabbed the Samurai's arm and lifted, while another slid a knife from her sleeve and stabbed upwards into the unprotected armpit. The Drake gaped as the knife slid home, but made no other sound as he slid to the floor. The girl withdrew the knife as he fell, wrapping it in a cloth and wiping her hands, then she passed the bundle to one of her companions. The group dispersed into the crowd, who had seen nothing and simply assumed that the Drake had slipped over — and as the Drakes were touchy about honour, no one wanted to admit that they had seen the Samurai fall. By the time people realised what had happened, the knife had changed hands five times and been dropped in a slop bucket. The perpetrators had all but disappeared.

Aerik stood dumbfounded, desperate to disbelieve what he had seen. He knew that this was the sort of trouble he didn't want, a thing he never should have seen. It grew worse when one of the Samurai's companions saw him on the floor, lying in a steadily growing halo of blood. The roar of outrage was simply frightening and those at the front of the crowd paled and fell to their knees.

'Who?' the Drake screamed. 'Who did this? One of you must have seen! Tell me!'

The crowd was silent; either no one had seen or no one wished to be the target of the Drake's wrath by stepping forward. The Drake hissed in fury and plunged his sword into the chest of the closest slave. He tore the weapon free with ease, ignoring the body as it slumped to the floor.

'Who?' he screamed again.

The slaves said nothing, all staring in horror at the bloody sword in the Drake's hand. The Samurai whipped around, staring at every one of the slaves that surrounded him, commanding them to speak. He reached back his arm for another strike but a second Samurai stepped into the middle of the room and grabbed his comrade's elbow. The newcomer whispered something to his comrade, who nodded and lowered his bloody sword. The newcomer then faced the crowd, scanning the faces for some that met his needs.

'A Drake Samurai has been killed,' the newcomer said. 'Some of you committed this deed and some of you saw it. I don't care which of you step forward, but someone *will* step forward. You, you and you,' he pointed, picking his chosen faces out of the crowd. 'Come here, now.'

Three slaves stepped forward and Aerik sweated profusely as he strained to see who they were. Two of them were new, barely a week in the fields to judge by the state of their skin and hands. The third was Tisa. Aerik felt sick, as though a giant fist had grabbed his insides and squeezed. The air in his body didn't seem to be enough as he thought about his brother's love and the baby they'd brought into the world. He almost fell until Japheth reached out and took hold of his shoulder to keep him steady.

The Samurai paced up and down, circling the three as they stood trembling in the middle of the room, alone and defenceless. The Samurai with the bloody sword had backed up against a support column where he could see almost the whole crowd.

'These three,' the pacing Samurai said ominously. 'These three shall be an example to you all. They die, now.'

The Drake with the bloody sword stepped forward and plunged his blade into the first slave's back. He didn't even have time to realise his death sentence before the blade had finished its cruel work. The second slave saw what was coming and tried to run. He took one step before the Drake's backswing caught him in the neck.

The crowd watched horror-struck as the Drake advanced on Tisa, yet none of them dared do anything. Aerik fought past his fear and grabbed an empty bottle of scrum from the table, but before he could do anything, a strong hand gripped his wrist and another clamped around his mouth.

'Don't do it,' Ebon said. 'We'll just be burying four people instead of three.'

Aerik struggled in vain against the iron grip, but another was already leaping to Tisa's defence. An anguished cry rose from the crowd and Monta rushed forward, desperate to save his wife. With no idea how to fight, driven instead by fear and love, Monta charged the Samurai with his bare hands. The Samurai pivoted on his back heel, spinning into a crouch to duck Monta's wild blow and whipping his bloody blade around as he turned.

Monta took two heavy steps as his momentum took him past the Samurai, then he looked down at the bloody stripe along his torso left by the wicked blade. He wobbled on his feet like a puppet, then as though the strings had been cut, he fell to the floor in a broken heap.

Aerik sagged into Ebon's arms as he watched first Monta, then Tisa lose their lives to a Drake blade. His happy world crumbled down around him so quickly that he lost all thought of where he was and what was happening. When the room erupted in a bang and smoke billowed into every corner, he didn't even react. It was only Ebon's strong grip that pulled him out of the building under cover of the smoke screen.

In an alley at the back of The Stable, reality finally set in and Aerik dropped to his knees to be sick. Figures moved around him, but he didn't care. Monta, his beloved brother, was dead. And Tisa, too, who had never harmed anyone in her life. He'd loved them both fiercely as the only family that he had and now they were gone. A single thought hit him, pushing through his haze of grief; he wasn't alone, not entirely.

'Rebecca,' he whispered. 'I have to keep her safe.'

A maniacal energy flooded his limbs as he thought of little Rebecca, the last remaining member of his family. He charged out of the alley so quickly that the slaves who dragged him from The Stable had no chance to stop him. He never heard their cries of warning, he just ran. The dark streets that he'd known every day of his life now looked frightening, as though they harboured a Drake in every shadow; but with the power of sheer terror driving him on, he ran.

The lights of his home were still burning when he came around the last corner, and Aerik hoped it was a good sign. He burst through the door and found Tisa's sister, Lysa, looking up at him in surprise, baby Rebecca cradled in her arms. Aerik sobbed in relief and wrapped them both in his arms.

'Aerik, what is it?' Lysa asked. 'What's wrong?'

He looked down at her, her face so like her sister's, and the tears sprang to his eyes. 'They're dead, Lysa. The Drakes killed them.'

Lysa gaped at him as her mind frantically fought to understand, then she bowed her head and her tears joined his. 'Be free, sister,' she muttered. 'Be free, brother.'

The simple words of the slave's last honour jolted Aerik out of his shock and reminded him who he was. They knew, all of them, that their lives would come to an untimely end some way or another, and they had already laid plans for Rebecca's future. It didn't remove the hurt, but his mind was no longer locked to inaction.

'Be free,' he whispered. 'You will be missed and never forgotten.'

The solemn moment was ended as the door shuddered from a heavy blow, then splintered as it was torn from its hinges. Aerik turned and pushed Lysa and Rebecca behind him, but his heart dropped as he saw a Drake Samurai in the doorway, bloody sword drawn.

'Running somewhere?' the Drake hissed, stepping past the shattered wood splinters. 'You thought no one saw your escape from the bar, eh, slave? Well now you will pay for the death of a Samurai, you and your mate!'

Aerik pushed Lysa and Rebecca to the floor and dove to the left as the Samurai stabbed forward. He felt a tug at his side, followed by a wave of pain as he hit the ground. He touched a hand to his ribs and flinched when it came away red with blood. The Samurai flicked its tongue in and out of its mouth and looked from Lysa to Aerik, trying to decide which was the greater threat. When the Drake's eyes locked on Aerik and narrowed, he knew his time was up.

The Samurai stepped forward and was preparing to strike, when a hand reached around his body and yanked the short Tanto dagger from his belt. The Samurai acted purely on trained instinct, dropping to one knee and scything his blade around horizontally to slice his new foe in half. It should have worked and would have worked were he anywhere but a slave's quarters — the wood and wicker walls were built close together to make the most use of space in the slave city and they were far too cramped to swing a Katana. There was a sound of splintering wood and an annoyed grunt as the Samurai realised his sword was stuck, then the dagger struck home. Driven with expert precision, it slipped between the chest plate and the helm, finding the Drake's unprotected neck.

The Samurai staggered back, staring glassy eyed and amazed at his attacker, then fell to the floor. Suddenly the hall was clear and Aerik looked into the grim face of Ebon, still holding a bloody dagger in his hand.

'Come with me, Aerik. Hurry!'

Chapter 5

Annah rose early to complete her morning chores. She cleaned the living area, removed the dishes that Kelkh and Ishkal had dined off the night before, washed them and stacked them neatly away. She straightened the throw rugs on the furniture and gathered the rubbish to be discarded, heaving the sack of refuse over her shoulder and carrying it outside.

By now used to Kelkh's habit of sleeping in, Annah quietly closed the door and headed for the rubbish pile at the very back of the property, as far away as possible from the house itself. She hadn't even left the porch when she noticed Ishkal on the lawn in front of her.

Dressed in his usual robes crossed with metal bands, Ishkal swung his arms and legs in a continuous fluid motion that looked like a slow motion dance. One arm reached out, palm flat and open, then the other swung upwards with a clenched fist. Turning his head so that he looked the other way, he then kicked out his back leg until it was higher than his shoulder. There he stayed, eyes closed and balanced on one leg as the chilly mountain air washed over him. Annah watched until she was certain he wouldn't move again, and then he swung once more into slow motion and continued his exercises.

Annah suddenly realised that she was staring and hoped desperately that Ishkal wouldn't take offence if he realised. Resettling the sack on her shoulders, she headed for the rubbish pile.

'Leaving so soon, Annah Tress?' Ishkal asked.

Annah jumped and dropped her sack, which hit the porch with a loud thump. She turned back to Ishkal and fell to her knees, nose touching the ground. 'I am sorry, Lord Ishkal. I didn't mean to disturb you.'

'You didn't disturb me, child,' he said, smoothly continuing his exercises. 'And you shouldn't apologise either. You did nothing wrong and showed a laudable curiosity. It was I who frightened you, so I should be the one who apologises.'

'My Lord, no,' Annah said, shocked at the thought of a Drake apologising to her. What would her Master think?

Ishkal laughed at her reaction but didn't push the point. 'So you're interested in my Kata, are you?'

'My Lord, I've never seen it before, that's all,' she stammered. 'I meant no offence.'

'And none was taken,' Ishkal smiled. 'But you haven't answered my question — you're interested in my Kata, yes?'

'I ... I am, Lord Ishkal,' she said. 'I've never seen anything so beautiful.'

'And you're interested in learning it, am I correct?' he asked.

Annah paled and pushed her face towards the ground. 'My Lord, I would never presume—'

'Annah, I want you to tell me the truth,' Ishkal sighed. 'If you have no interest in learning, then say so. But if you *are* interested in learning, then I want you to tell me.'

Annah shook like a leaf, caught between her desire to learn

the beautiful dance of Ishkal's Kata and her fear of angering her master with her presumption — a terminal mistake in most houses.

'Annah, do you want me to teach you?' he asked.

She raised her head and looked at Ishkal, his gold scales glinting in the morning light. 'Yes,' she whispered, fear almost choking her.

'Then I shall,' he grinned. 'I'll let Kelkh know and we can start tomorrow.'

'But you won't be allowed to,' she blurted. 'It's forbidden. I'm a slave and I learn only what I must to do the tasks assigned to me.'

Ishkal laughed and spun in a complex circle, then hopped lightly over to Annah and knelt beside her. 'The laws of the Dragon Empire were created by the Ruby Drakes. They were the most powerful clan after the Golds, but we chose to follow a life of meditation and enlightenment rather than rulership. The Ruby clan acknowledge us as the more powerful descendants of The Dragon, so they don't presume to give us orders. We, as a clan, respect their position as the leaders of the Empire and we don't undermine their authority by flagrantly disobeying their laws.' He leaned back on his heels and grinned. 'But we can disobey them if we chose to.'

'Why would you disobey them just to teach me?' she asked.

She knew she might be pushing the boundaries of his patience, but she had to know. Ishkal reached out and took a lock of her hair in his hand, turning it this way and that so that it caught the morning light and shimmered the same gold as his own glittering scales.

'Because you interest me,' he said simply.

Annah spent the rest of the day in the Forging room with Kelkh, basking in the warm glow of his song and assisting him with the final touches of the dragon vase they had sketched the night before. For all his irritable ways, Kelkh proved a patient craftsman and the forging took far longer than she expected. It was evening by the time they were finished and despite her pride at seeing the vase she had designed, she hurried from the room to make dinner.

While she cooked, she kept one ear open as only a slave can do, listening for Ishkal to make his request. He didn't wait long and Annah was amazed when Kelkh just shrugged and agreed with no argument. Ishkal knew his friend better though, and he knew the old warrior was happy that Annah would have something to keep herself occupied.

And like that, it was done. Ishkal told Annah to meet him the next morning in the front yard and left for bed. Kelkh sat at the table, drinking a glass of scalett as he turned the newly forged vase over and over in his hands, lost in thought.

The next morning Annah woke early and completed her chores, determined to give Kelkh no reason to be angry with Ishkal for keeping her busy. She rushed outside at the appointed time and found Ishkal sitting cross legged on the ground waiting for her.

'Greetings, Annah Tress,' he smiled. 'Your first lesson today will be a simple introduction to the meditation of the Gold Drakes. If you can master this, then I will teach you more. If not, then I will have to find something else to keep your time occupied. Perhaps a vegetable garden.'

Annah smiled shyly at the joke, then stepped onto the grass next to him and lost herself to his teaching. To begin the lesson he showed her the steps of a simple Kata, teaching her how to move her arms and legs in symphony and keep her balance focused. It felt strange at first, and the hardest part was trying not to fall over when she reached her arms out to one side and lifted one leg off the ground. She stumbled the first few times, but she eventually succeeded.

The steps weren't difficult to remember — punch forward, turn and crouch, punch to the side and hold; stand and kick to the other side, balance, then return to standing position and repeat. It was all done in slow motion, which was very useful while Annah was trying to memorise and perfect the movements, but quickly grew painful as her muscles strained with the unaccustomed effort of holding her body in unusual positions.

At the end of every revolution, Ishkal held the leg balance for a fraction longer than the time before, and even though Annah's body screamed out from exhaustion, she was determined to hold the position for as long as required. Her leg cramped on one revolution and she thought it would buckle from underneath her, but she gritted her teeth and pushed on. That was when she heard the singing.

It filled her with a pleasant sensation, rolling around her and through her as it floated on the air. She recognised it immediately, having heard it for several hours in Kelkh's forge — it was the song of creation magic. But at the same time it wasn't, not really, not quite. It didn't have the same soul-soaring feeling of joy and awe-inspiring sense of power that Kelkh's song had. It was similar, but on a far smaller scale.

Where Kelkh's song was fluid, changing continually with his mood and accommodating what he was trying to create, this song seemed static, rehearsed until it was perfect but never different.

Annah looked at Ishkal and watched him sing, eyes closed as he moved with effortless grace through his exercises, and she wondered what it all meant.

When they finished their lesson and Annah was stretching out her muscles as she was instructed, she decided to ask. It was a huge leap for her after a lifetime of obeying without thought, but she believed Ishkal would not chastise her for her presumption.

'Lord Ishkal, I have a question, if I may ask it?'

'Of course, Annah. What do you wish to know?'

'I just wondered, Lord, if you were a Forger?'

Ishkal looked at her and scratched his chin thoughtfully. 'What makes you ask that, young Annah?'

'I heard you singing while we practiced and it sounded similar to Master Kelkh's forging song.'

'Yes it does, doesn't it?' Ishkal said. 'Well, Annah, there's a reason for that and it has to do with these.' He pointed to the metal bands that crisscrossed his body. 'Do you know what these are?'

'No, my Lord.'

'These bands are made out of steel forged by the magic of the SongForge,' he said. 'Our friend Kelkh made them for me many, many years ago, before he became a Forger. They're a magic that we Gold Drakes have spent hundreds of years learning to control.'

Ishkal closed his eyes and started to sing softly. Annah kept her eyes locked on his face, waiting to see what he was doing. She jumped in fright when she felt something tap her on her knee.

Looking down, she saw one of the metal bands stretch into the likeness of a finger and tap her gently again. Ishkal's voice grew stronger now that he had her full attention and several more bands leapt to his command, stretching away from his body and weaving themselves into a wiry hand that waved jauntily at her.

Ishkal let his voice trail away and the metal unravelled back into thick bands that settled against his clothes. He opened his eyes and smiled at Annah's wonderstruck face.

'The SongForge is a magic that is beyond our comprehension,' he said. 'We of the Golden clan have trained for generations to learn how to use it, but we can only do so much. We can't create magical metal from ordinary metal the way Kelkh can and we're nowhere near as powerful. No one knows why some Drakes have such immense power of the Song; it seems sometimes that The Dragon picks us at random for the honour. But we of the Gold can use the magic metal in a way no others can and bend it to our will.'

Annah looked in awe at the monk, staring at the humble metal bands with a new respect. Ishkal saw in her expression that she wanted to ask more questions, to know all she could know, but her fear kept her silent. With time, he knew she would find the courage to ask.

Suddenly her head snapped up and she looked over her shoulder at the house like a startled dog. Ishkal heard noises from inside and knew that Kelkh had finally surfaced. Annah shot to her feet and ran inside to make the breakfast. Ishkal watched her go and sighed — it was a start, at least.

CHAPTER 6

Aerik sat in the sparse cell, trying to sort things through in his mind. He had tried to sleep, but eventually decided it just wasn't going to come. Lysa lay stretched out next to him, her breathing soft and regular, and he felt glad for that at least. Rebecca slept as well, cradled in his arms, blissfully unaware of the tragedy that had claimed her mother and father, and changed the course of her uncle's life forever. He stroked the soft wisps of hair on her head and prayed that her life would be a good one, despite her loss.

There was a knock on the door, a light tapping as though the person wasn't sure whether he was awake or not. Sighing, Aerik took Lysa's head off his lap and rested it on the ground, using his rolled up vest as a cushion. He put Rebecca down on the blanket that they had set up for her, then opened the door and stepped outside. Ebon waited patiently in the corridor while he shut the door.

'I thought you might be having trouble sleeping,' Ebon said.

'Some,' Aerik shrugged. 'But I guess that's to be expected. Yesterday I was a happy man, with a family, good friends and a place in the world. Now ...'

'I understand,' Ebon said. 'I lost my family too. I lost my parents to the mines when I was young, my sister to the lecherous grasp of a Drake Noble and my brother to a Samurai who had nothing better to do. He said my brother didn't kneel quickly enough, so he ran him through.'

Aerik swallowed painfully, thinking of Monta as he crumbled to the ground and Tisa as she watched her husband fall.

'I want to offer you something,' Ebon said. 'I want to give you a new place in the world, a new purpose.'

'As what?' Aerik snorted. 'The Drakes want me dead; I know that already. What could I possibly do?'

'You could fight.'

Ebon watched closely as Aerik struggled with the idea. He didn't need it explained to him; he understood perfectly. Ebon was asking him to help start a revolt, to strike back at the Drakes who had taken everything from him. Ebon was offering him a lifetime of fear and danger, but also a chance for the one thing he hungered for at that moment. Ebon offered a chance for revenge.

'What are the rules?' he asked.

'They're simple. You can join, but Lysa can't — not in the actual missions anyway.'

'You don't accept women?' Aerik asked, surprised at the segregation.

'Oh, we accept women,' Ebon grinned. 'We'd halve our forces if we turned them away and we'd lose some of our best warriors as well. No, Lysa has to stay behind because if you die, and that is a very real possibility, Rebecca will need someone of her own blood to look after her.'

'I die here or I die in the fields,' Aerik shrugged. 'I know where I'd rather die. I think Lysa will be relieved to watch over Rebecca. What else?'

'No brother of this revolution will harm another,' Ebon said. 'We're all each other has and we're not about to let some petty argument tear apart everything we've worked for. Our existence is balanced on a knife edge as it is, and dissention will be the end of us. Betrayal needs retribution, blood for blood.'

Aerik nodded and scratched the stubble of his beard irritably. 'What else?'

'Nothing,' Ebon replied. 'Just give me your word that you'll join us and fight, and honour our ways.'

'You have my word,' Aerik said, holding out his hand to Ebon. Ebon reached out and grasped his forearm just below the elbow, clasping in the way of free men.

'Be free, brother,' he whispered.

'Be free,' Aerik echoed. 'When do I start?'

'Now,' Ebon grinned. 'We're not the Drakes; we don't have the time, money or equipment to train you into a Samurai. The skills you learn, you'll learn in your own time or on missions.'

'So when's my first mission?'

'Tomorrow night,' Ebon said. 'It's your initiation, and it will help put your past where it belongs.'

Aerik started to ask what Ebon meant, but was cut off before he could speak. 'Get some sleep, brother. You'll need it before tomorrow.'

By the next evening Aerik was full of nervous energy, waiting for the mission to start. He was used to the constant work of the rokhill paddies and having nothing to do was wearing at him. He told Lysa about his choice and it was one of the hardest things he'd ever done in his life. She kept up a brave face but Aerik saw the unshed tears in her eyes. He saw her silent agony at the thought of losing the last family she had and her only friend.

He gave her no assurances, as he had none to give and he would never lie to her. He just hugged her and told her that it was what he had to do; for Monta and Tisa, and for little Rebecca, too. She understood, he knew. She may not have agreed and she certainly feared but she understood. He drew strength from that and it gave him the courage to kiss Rebecca on the forehead and walk from the room.

Ebon waited for him in the corridor, carrying a single torch to light the way. He didn't say anything, respecting Aerik's need for silence and his own thoughts, but he was a comforting presence nonetheless. They walked silently through the shabby corridors of their hideout, carefully stepping over rotted floorboards and splintered debris. Ebon stopped at a door, no different to the others that dotted the hallway, and rapped twice. He waited six seconds then rapped three times and Aerik heard the sound of bolts sliding back. The door swung open with an aged creak and Ebon waved Aerik inside.

The room was darker than the corridor but better maintained. It was split into numerous alcoves, with shelves that held folded black clothing. Ebon led Aerik to an alcove and put the torch into a bracket on the wall.

'You had a locker at the ro-khill paddies where you kept your tools, right?' Ebon asked. Aerik nodded. 'This is the same thing.'

He reached up and took a bundle of black clothes from the shelf, which he tossed to Aerik. They were made of coarse slave cloth and dyed to blend into the shadows.

'These are yours now,' Ebon said. 'Wear them only when you're on a mission. If you're caught wearing them you'll be killed and you'll reveal us to the Drakes. They're a superstitious lot and we rely on them thinking of us as spirits and shadows not flesh and blood. If you shatter that illusion, they won't be so afraid of us and that will weaken us badly.'

Aerik stripped off his mud stained work garb and pulled on the flowing black pants, tunic and soft leather boots. Ebon showed him how to adjust the hood and face mask so no skin showed through, then he stood back to admire his handiwork.

'And that's how we appear to the Drakes,' Ebon smiled. 'As shadows, monsters from their own mythology striking them at will and disappearing without a trace.'

He took a Tanto dagger from the shelf and tied it to Aerik's belt. It was stolen from a Samurai and painted matte black from blade to pommel to make it harder to see.

'You're ready,' Ebon said. 'But listen to my warning — don't ever face a Drake Samurai in open combat. They'll kill you in an instant without even thinking about it. They've been trained far beyond what you or I can ever imagine and their skill is almost supernatural. It's bred to them, in their heart and in their bones. Attack them from the shadows if you have to, or run into a house where their swords are too big to use, but never face them in the open. That's suicide.'

'Don't worry, I'm not that stupid,' Aerik replied.

'There're a lot who are,' Ebon said. 'Or they're so angry at the Drakes that they forget all reason. Just be careful.'

'I will,' Aerik promised.

'Good. Then let's go.'

Ebon led Aerik and four other revolutionaries out of the building into the dark, quiet streets of Tingra. There was no one around, it was late and no slave would dare risk arriving tired to work — that would result in a lashing at best and a sword blade at worst. Despite the lack of people, Ebon and his comrades kept to the shadows, moving swiftly down the street as they blended their black clothes to the black corners. Even Aerik had to look twice for his comrades, and he knew they were meant to be there. He shook his head in amazement and did his best to copy them.

They made their way carefully through the town and after a while Aerik overcame his fear and took note of where they were. It was his neighbourhood, five blocks from his old home and ten minutes walk from The Stable . Aerik picked up his pace until he caught up to Ebon and tapped him on the shoulder. Ebon's hooded head whipped back to look at him and Aerik moved his hands to imitate a talking mouth the way he had been shown. Ebon looked around the street and up at the dark building faces to make sure there was no danger nearby, then nodded curtly.

'What are we doing here?' Aerik asked. 'This is my neighbourhood.'

'Our target is staying in your old slave ghetto,' Ebon replied.

'Where are we going?' Aerik asked.

Ebon looked at him long and hard, trying to decide whether he should tell the young man or keep the information until they reached their destination. Finally he shrugged and decided it didn't matter. 'We're heading for the Drake barracks on Diamond Street.'

'You're planning to follow Emerald Way to Oak Street, then follow that all the way up to Diamond?' Aerik guessed.

'That was the plan, yes,' Ebon said impatiently.

'Not a good idea,' Aerik replied. 'It's far too open and the Drakes sometimes set up hidden checkpoints along the road. The locals avoid it if we can, especially when we're coming home from The Stable. I know a better way.'

Ebon stared at him, judging his motive and determination, then finally nodded. He cupped his hands to his mouth and blew three soft owl hoots into the still night air. Within moments, four shadows emerged around Ebon, waiting expectantly.

'Aerik says our planned route goes through marked land,' he said. 'The Drakes set random checkpoints for the locals up and down those roads, so it goes without saying that we need to avoid them. Aerik knows a better way, so he's in the lead from now on.'

Ebon repeated the talking motion with one hand, then brought his other hand down in a swift chopping motion to indicate that the parley was done and silence had resumed. He pointed to Aerik and made a walking motion with two fingers. Aerik nodded and started off down one of the dismal side alleys.

He led them down the back streets and rubbish filled alleys, guiding them through the dark half of the slave sector from memories ingrained in him since he was five. At every corner he fought the urge to look over his shoulder, knowing that he probably wouldn't see the five black figures behind him and he'd just be slowing them down if he tried. After what seemed like both an eternity and the shortest of moments, Aerik finally stopped and raised his open palm into the air to signal a halt.

Ebon appeared at his shoulder and made the hand gesture for talk, deferring to Aerik's greater knowledge of the area to decide if it was safe. Aerik scanned every shadow, searching all the old haunts that he used as a child to spy on the Drakes. They were all empty and he nodded to Ebon.

'The guards change every hour, rotating one Samurai off patrol into the guardhouse and one from the guardhouse out onto patrol,' Ebon said. 'Our target is in command of these barracks for the night-time shift, so he'll be there the whole time. We'll wait fifteen minutes after the next shift change before we attack, just to make sure the Drake on patrol is too far away to know what's happening. I don't want to fight any more Samurai than we have to.'

Ebon's companions nodded and made themselves inconspicuous in the dark alleyway, crouching into a ball in a corner or lying full length on the ground in the shadows. If anyone walked by, even if they were looking for trouble, they would only see shadows and garbage.

It turned out they'd just missed a patrol change. Almost an hour before a Drake came walking down the street, hunched into his cloak to ward off the chilly night air. He walked up to the heavy door of the guardhouse, then knocked a complicated rhythm and muttered a password to gain entry. As the door swung open, Ebon looked at one of his comrades who nodded, then he motioned them all to hold tight for ten minutes.

Time crawled as one Samurai walked inside the guardhouse and another gathered his cloak around him and left. Aerik watched the Drake disappear into the torch lit streets and tried to calm his nerves. Ebon and the others barely moved a muscle, taking the situation with the stoic acceptance of experience. Aerik rubbed his stiff muscles to work out the cramp and beat back the cold, and prayed for time to hurry up.

When ten minutes had passed, Ebon rose to his feet and dropped a black cloth on the ground. From somewhere in his robes he took out a small wooden carving of a Dire Wolf and dropped it on the cloth. The others followed, dropping something they'd made with their own hands onto the cloth before they left the alley. It was their gift to the gods, to be taken to a hidden temple and burned when the mission was complete. It was a last act of defiance from people who had once been slaves, and as slaves had been forbidden to worship any deity other than The Dragon of the Drakes.

Ebon moved out of the alleyway and stood in the shadows of the street proper, motioning Aerik to follow. His comrades took the cue and padded silently across the street to the guardhouse. One crept to the side of the building and started to climb the rough brick walls. Using a glove fitted with bent nails to serve as climbing claws, the man dragged himself quietly to the top of the building. When he reached the roof, another girl stepped onto a comrade's offered back and hopped lightly on top of the door frame, where she perched like a gargoyle guarding the entrance from intruders. The two remaining revolutionaries took positions on either side of the door, knives out and ready to strike.

Ebon watched them all, making sure they were in the right positions and that their movements were unnoticed by the guards inside. Once they were all in place, he cupped his hands and gave a single owl hoot.

One of the revolutionaries by the door stood and rapped his hand against the wood, copying the knock he heard the Samurai give earlier. He knew he couldn't give the password; he hadn't heard it clearly enough, and even if he had, he didn't have a voice low or gravely enough to imitate a Drake. Instead, the man threw all his weight against the door, slamming into it to imitate the sound of a body that had been attacked and pushed from behind. When the peephole slid open to see what was happening, the slave jumped to his feet with his knife drawn and plunged the blade downward into the empty ground.

To the Drake behind the portal, it appeared that a Samurai had returned from patrol and given the correct knock code, then been attacked and knocked to the ground. He saw the attacker drive a knife home and his outrage at the death of a Samurai overrode his better sense. He called out to his companion, drew back the bolts on the door and charged outside to kill the attacker and defend his fallen comrade. When he yanked the door open and saw the ground empty, he knew that he had been tricked — but it was too late.

The girl above the doorway swung her knife down with all the power in her shoulders, stabbing the Samurai in his draconic head. The Samurai dropped to the ground without so much as a scream, and the girl knew it was time to leave. She sprung upwards and reached her arms to the sky, while her comrade on the roof leaned down and caught her by the wrists, then dragged her to safety.

The second Samurai roared in anger as he saw his friend fall and charged out of the building, dropping to a roll as he came through the door to avoid the same stabbing fate. The hoot of an owl echoed through the night sky as the Drake rolled out, and acting on their signal, the revolutionaries on either side of the door lashed out with their daggers. One of them hit the Samurai's armour, doing nothing but scratch the lacquered paint, while the other caught the Drake on the arm. The Drake's heavy emerald scales turned away most of the blow, but when he came to his feet he still had an angry red line from his shoulder to his elbow.

Now that the Samurai was on his feet with his sword drawn,

the two human revolutionaries were worried. Neither one had any illusions about their chances of fighting a Samurai one on one, or even two on one, but they still held their ground. This scenario had been catered for.

The Samurai advanced, drawing a Tanto dagger in his off hand so he could defend against both attackers if they fought him together. He never knew Ebon was there, never even guessed at his presence until a heavy body hit him square in the back, knocking him off balance. Two steps was all it took before he regained his footing, then he looked up stupidly at the black figures in front of him, blinked and fell flat on his face. The black hilt of Ebon's dagger was barely visible in the dark light, sticking up from the back of the Drake's neck.

It all happened so quickly that Aerik was stunned when Ebon beckoned him from the shadows. He approached the dark man as he waved his comrades into the guardhouse and yanked his dagger from the dead Samurai's neck.

'What now?' Aerik whispered.

'Now we find the Guardhouse commander and do what needs to be done.'

'Does he know we're here?'

Ebon looked at the two dead Samurai that his comrades were dragging inside, then looked back at Aerik. 'He knows, and he knows we're coming for him. He's waiting for us.'

With that comforting thought, Ebon led Aerik into the guardhouse and locked the door behind them. Inside the guardhouse, the two other revolutionaries were busy stripping the bodies of the Samurai, taking their knives, swords and any other useful items they came across. Ebon gave the room a cursory inspection, but his gaze was focused mainly on the single door set in the back wall.

Ebon's two companions quickly finished their task and joined him in the centre of the room, one of them carrying a pike that they'd taken from a weapon rack. Ebon nodded and they took up their positions on either side of the door, just as they had outside the entryway. Ebon stepped between them and pushed the door open. Inside, a single Drake Samurai knelt on the floor in front of an emerald statue of a Dragon.

'Great Dragon, save me from these spirits that seek to claim me for the hells,' he prayed. 'Smite their demonic powers from them and grant my sword the power to return them to the grave.'

Ebon turned his back on the Drake and walked across the room, still visible through the doorway but too far away for a desperate strike that would gut him where he stood.

'Mighty Samurai, look at what you huddle in fear of,' he shouted, drawing back his hood and pulling down his mask. The Drake hissed in fury as he saw Ebon's face and he jumped to his feet faster than any human could hope to move. He drew his sword and charged; his distain at the human and his outrage that a slave would usurp their status pushed him to recklessness.

'Now!'

At Ebon's command, one of the two kneeling men shoved the pike out across the door at ankle level. The other man grabbed the wooden shaft and they braced the weapon between their legs and the wall. The Samurai crashed into the makeshift trip-wire and pitched face first onto the floorboards. Ebon's companions rushed forward and grabbed the dazed Drake's arms, pushing his hands up behind his back towards his neck where the slightest movement would cause him pain. They dragged the Samurai to his knees and Ebon waved Aerik over.

'Do you recognise this Drake, Aerik?' Aerik shook his head. 'The Drake who killed Monta and Tisa is dead, I killed him to save you that night. But this, this is the Drake who ordered it done.'

Aerik's memory flashed as he remembered the Samurai in The Stable, the newcomer who chose three faces from the crowd and marked Tisa for death.

'You remember?' Ebon asked.

'I remember,' Aerik nodded.

'Then put Monta and Tisa to rest.'

Aerik pulled his black dagger from its sheath and stepped forward. The rage bubbled inside him, building like steam until he was sure it would explode. He saw the Drake picking Tisa out of the crowd, and he saw Monta die. This Drake had killed before and would kill again; to kill him now would save the lives of so many humans in the future. Aerik hated him beyond words ... but he still couldn't plunge the dagger home.

'I can't,' he said, tears filling his eyes as he thought of his dead brother.

'You can,' Ebon replied. 'The first is always the hardest.'

'I can't,' he repeated.

He lowered the dagger and wiped the tears from his eyes with his other hand while Ebon sighed in sympathy.

Taking advantage of the distraction, the Drake wrenched one arm free and backhanded one of his captors. The man flew to the ground and the Drake yanked a Tanto from his belt. He swung the blade towards his other attacker, who released the Drake's other arm to grab the dagger aimed at his belly. He stopped the blade before it struck, but now the Samurai was free and the man knew he would be dead in seconds.

Aerik moved without thinking, plunging the dagger deep into the Drake's neck above the armour line. The Drake punched out at Aerik, but there was no strength in the blow. He slumped to the ground, his mouth open in a silent scream and his face showing disbelief at his fate. Aerik stood rooted to the spot, his gaze locked on the bloody dagger in his hand.

'It's done,' Ebon said, nodding to each of his men as they rose and indicated that they were unharmed.

'I almost ruined everything,' Aerik replied, shaking his head. 'I just couldn't kill a helpless person. I couldn't do it!'

'I'd be worried if it came easily to you,' Ebon said. 'The first is always the hardest, but in time you'll understand that every one of them you kill saves the lives of countless slaves that they might kill on a whim.'

Aerik nodded but still harboured doubts about his own abilities. Ebon left him to his thoughts and unbolted the locks to the roof access. Throwing back the first hatch, he climbed up the rickety ladder into the roof space and unbolted the second hatch. Seconds later he was outside and seconds after that his companions joined him. They slipped quietly down into the alley, collected their offerings to the gods and disappeared into the night.

Chapter 7

Annah stood on top of a narrow wooden post balanced on one leg. Her body was stretched out to one side and her other leg stretched out to the other, forming a lopsided T. In her outstretched hands she held a heavy lead ball the size of her fist, weighing down her limbs and making her tremble under the strain of keeping straight. She'd seen Ishkal do it before, seen him do it with a lead ball the size of her head, but she never appreciated how hard it was until she had to do it herself.

Since her first day learning Kata, Annah had worked tirelessly with Ishkal morning and night to learn everything he had to teach. In the mornings she performed the Kata again and again until she could do it with her eyes closed — in fact she often did just that in her more recent sessions. In the time remaining, she followed all manner of other exercises that Ishkal could devise, like this one, that were designed to increase her strength and coordination.

In the three weeks she'd been training, Ishkal had made her carry buckets of water up the hill from the river, hold stones above her head or on her raised foot, and perfect her balance using the lead balls. So far she couldn't see much difference in her abilities, but Ishkal seemed pleased. He also gave her a number of stretches to do every night before she went to bed, which would keep her body supple and help her to move with the fluidity that some of the more intricate Kata required. She made certain she practiced it all diligently.

When she wasn't with Ishkal in the mornings or doing her own training at night, Annah was helping Kelkh in the forge and keeping his house in order. Since his outstanding success with the dragon vase, Kelkh's skills as a metalworker had been sorely in demand. He'd become the darling of the noble circuit and requests for induction gifts and birthday presents flooded him daily. Annah was kept busy sketching ideas for all manner of objects while Kelkh watched over her shoulder, adding suggestions from what he knew of the particular client.

It was only when Kelkh took time out to work on his backlog of weapon orders that Annah ever had a chance to catch her breath and put the house truly in order. Kelkh didn't need her assistance with weapons forging — he knew how to do that all by himself. But for some reason, forging weapons always put him in a melancholy mood and Annah learned very quickly to stay out of his way when he was like that. It wasn't that he was abusive in any way, but Annah felt a bond growing between her and the old Drake and she didn't like to see him unhappy.

In the last week, the number of requests flooding into Kelkh's workshop had trebled. The Festival of the Dragon was on the coming weekend and every Drake noble with the money to spare wanted a suitable gift from Kelkh to present to their families. Kelkh was so busy he almost cancelled Annah's lessons with Ishkal to get all the work done, but Ishkal had come up with a counter offer that proved to be acceptable.

'Switch!'

Annah gasped in relief as she brought her leg down to the post and raised the other one, then swapped the lead ball from one arm to the other. For the last few minutes she'd been afraid that she couldn't keep it aloft, but the thought of disappointing Ishkal or Kelkh, gave her the strength to go on.

Ishkal walked in a continuous circle around her, looking up and giving her a light tap with his finger whenever some part of her body dropped out of alignment. Kelkh sat to the side, leaning against a rock with a sheaf of papers in his hands that he rifled through impatiently.

'So which one was for the Countess Varggo?' he asked, flipping through the parchments for the third time.

'The silver candelabra, master,' Annah replied, barely keeping the strain out of her voice. 'Three pronged with a Dragon in the centre and a Samurai on either side.'

'Ah, yes, that was it,' Kelkh mumbled. He shuffled through the papers until he found what he was looking for and held it up with a cry of triumph. 'Yes, here it is. It will be a beautiful piece, Annah. You should be very proud.'

'Thank you, master,' she said. She felt the urge to curtsey, as was proper for a slave receiving praise from her master, despite the fact that she was balanced precariously on one leg on a pole four foot off the ground. But as soon as her knee started to bend, she felt Ishkal's hand swat her calf.

'Keep straight, Annah,' he admonished.

Kelkh didn't even notice; he was too engrossed in the sketch in his hands. 'Yes, a very fine piece. The magic will light the fires on command and keep them burning forever without ever needing a candle.'

'Then perhaps you should call it something other than a '*candel*abra',' Ishkal smiled.

Kelkh's brow furrowed as he caught up with Ishkal's joke, then he frowned and muttered to himself. 'I'll need Annah on time today. We've got a lot to get through before this evening.'

'She hasn't been late yet, old friend,' Ishkal grinned. 'Today will be no different. Switch.'

Annah brought her foot back down to the post, hopping lightly to swap them over, and brought her body back upright. She stretched her other foot out forward and reached her hands out in front of her. One hand held the lead ball underneath, while the other held it from above like a giant dragon's mouth. She ignored the strain that the weight caused and fell into the meditative mindset that Ishkal had taught her. She found that when she calmed her spirit, she could almost hear the illusive notes of the Song of Creation that Ishkal had sung to her, and that brought on a sense of peace like nothing else could.

A bell rang in the distance and Annah's eyes snapped open in an instant. 'There's someone at the door, master.'

'So there is,' Ishkal sighed. 'Off you go, child. Your kimono is by the back door.'

Annah dropped lightly down from the post and bowed to both Ishkal and Kelkh, then took off down the hill towards the house. Her thin, rough spun kimono hung by the back door — it was embroidered with the symbol of Kelkh's house and was a sign that she was his property. Both Ishkal and Kelkh thought the idea was ludicrous and told her not to bother wearing it unless she was answering the door; some Drakes did not take kindly to any slave breaching protocol, and Kelkh and Ishkal thought too much of

Annah to see her killed over something so petty.

As they watched her race towards the house, they both felt a sense of protectiveness that they had never experienced before. Kelkh broke the silence first, clearing his throat awkwardly and tearing his eyes away from the back door where she had disappeared.

'So, how long until she's a monk?'

'Years perhaps,' Ishkal shrugged. 'Perhaps never. I doubt the Emperor would be happy to have a human monk in the Order of the Gold Dragon.'

'Then why train her?'

'Because she asked. And, I think, because I wanted to show that a human slave was as much a person as a Drake.'

'Others would disagree with you,' Kelkh snorted. 'There's a whole Empire of them I could show you.'

'Do you disagree with me?'

Kelkh cleared his throat again and stuck his snout back into the sheaf of papers in his hands. But Ishkal saw his friend's eyes stray towards the house, looking for Annah's return, and he smiled. Kelkh was an old soldier and stuck in his ways. He probably didn't even realise the depth of his fondness for Annah, and Ishkal thought it best to let him come to that understanding himself.

'She learns quickly,' Ishkal said, breaking the silence. 'Quicker than most, in fact. She's very talented.'

'She tells me you're teaching her to sing the Forgesong,' Kelkh grunted.

'Yes, I am. The basics anyway.'

'You know she can never use it,' Kelkh said. 'Humans can't

use the Forgesong, they never could. You're setting her up for disappointment.'

'I don't think so,' Ishkal replied. 'I think it's more important for her to learn it as part of her meditation, not for any aspect of magic.'

'She might think differently, especially when she works with me in the forge,' Kelkh said. 'Just be careful.'

He lapsed into silence as Annah ran back up the hill with a letter in her hand. She knelt in front of Kelkh and held the letter out to him. He sighed and took it from her hands, snapping the seal and irritably reading the neat script.

'What is it?' Ishkal asked.

'It's an invitation to a dinner party,' Kelkh said with disgust. 'From Duke Inral. Tonight of all nights!'

'Are you going to go?' Ishkal asked.

'I'm in no position to refuse an invitation from a Duke of the Emperor's court,' Kelkh sighed. 'I have to go and I have to take Annah with me.'

Annah looked uncertainly from Ishkal to Kelkh, trying to mask her fear as best she could. While she stayed with Kelkh at his home, she was safe, protected. But out in the streets of Drake City, she was just another slave — worse than most, because she was marked as cursed by The Dragon. Clasping her shaking hands in front of her, she bowed her head in response to Kelkh's decision.

'Come on, Annah,' the old Drake sighed. 'You and I will have to get started early this morning. We've got a lot of Forging to do before we leave for the party.'

Kelkh and Annah flew through the city on the back of Kelkh's faithful Rock Dragon, Mange. Annah marvelled at how the rock wings were able to keep the creature afloat, despite the obvious weight of its bulk. But before long, her amazement found a new outlet as they entered the area surrounding the Emperor's palace where the rich nobility made their homes.

Huge buildings stretched into the sky, some with battlements and courtyards of their very own. Kelkh directed Mange to one of the larger courtyards in a house that was almost a castle itself. With the ease of experience, Kelkh brought Mange in to land and slipped off the dragon's back. He helped Annah get down and then gave his clothes a quick brush before he went inside.

Kelkh was dressed in a sky blue tunic trimmed in silver with matching pants. He wore a dress breastplate over the top and a sword at his belt, but had left the remainder of his warrior's attire at home. Annah wondered why he chose not to dress fully as a warrior when it was clearly his right, but she didn't dare to ask.

She was dressed in a slave outfit of slacks and kimono, made out of soft cotton in the same sky blue as Kelkh's outfit. He had ordered it specially that morning and had paid handsomely to have it made so quickly. Almost as an afterthought, he'd ordered a thick cloak made, to ward off the winter chill, which was multiplied threefold when riding unprotected on the back of a dragon through the cold night sky.

'Take Mange around the side,' Kelkh said, straightening his thick cloak over the top of his ensemble and handing over Mange's reigns. 'You'll find a stable hand to the left of the courtyard who will tell you what to do from there.'

'Yes, master,' Annah replied, curtsying awkwardly with one

hand resting on Mange's neck.

'Don't worry, girl,' he smiled. 'I have no wish to be here any longer than necessary. I'll come for you as soon as it's polite.'

Annah curtsied again and took hold of Mange's reigns in both hands, then led the Dragon towards the stables. The courtyard was well lit and she had no trouble finding the stable hand, a tall, lanky youth with tanned skin and dark hair. He took the reigns from her hands, making absolutely sure he didn't touch her. He muttered the directions to the slave lodge and hurried away with Mange in tow before Annah could thank him.

Alone in the courtyard, Annah shivered and gathered her new cloak around her to ward off the cold. The night was clear, which was both a blessing and a curse, for while there was no rain, there were also no clouds to stop the spirits of warmth from fleeing into the sky. The moon shone brightly, giving her all the light she needed to find the slave lodge once she left the torch-lit main courtyard. She only tripped once on a cracked pavestone near the slave mess hall, and thought ruefully that such a thing would never be allowed where a Drake could see it.

She pushed herself to her feet and limped over to the fence where a horse blanket had been hung to dry, then used it to wipe the mud off her hands as best she could — the last thing she wanted was to leave streaks of dirt on her new clothes. When she was finished, she made her way to the simple stone hall of the slave's quarters and knocked timidly on the door, shivering in the cold as the Drake Slave Master decided how long he would make her wait. Finally she heard the sound of bolts being thrown back and a mean, copper scaled face poked out from inside.

'Yes?' the Drake hissed.

'Forgive me for disturbing you, my Lord,' Annah said, keeping her eyes on the ground and curtsying formally. 'My name is Annah Tress, servant of Kelkh Ironbound who is a guest of Duke Inral's party this evening.'

The Drake's eyes narrowed and he looked her up and down as she stood shivering in the cold. With an almost lazy gesture, he reached out and swung a backhand blow across her jaw. Annah was sent sprawling, but she knew better than to wallow in the pain — that would just invite more blows. She scrambled to her knees and knelt in front of the Drake.

'I'm sorry, Lord, if I caused you offence,' she said, trying hard to control the trembling in her voice. 'That wasn't my intention.'

'You caused no offence other than your miserable existence, human,' the Drake sneered. 'That was just a warning. I won't tolerate any lip, any mischief or any slave who'll disturb me. If you even think about anything like that, then remember that blow and ask yourself if you'd enjoy another ten just like it! Now get inside, you've already made me colder than I care to be!'

Annah scrambled inside, tripping and falling flat on her face as the Drake stuck a clawed foot between her legs. He chuckled heartily as she dragged herself up, bowing and apologizing for getting in his way.

'The bunks are out the back,' he snarled. 'I don't want to see or hear you until a runner comes from the party to collect you. If I do ...'

He raised his hand threateningly and Annah bowed to show she understood. He grunted and took a seat beside the fire, where a table and chair had been set up. A book and half a bottle of scalett sat on the table, leaving Annah with no illusions about what the

Drake would do with his time. She headed for the corridor at the back of the room and fled to the relative safety of the slave barracks.

The corridor ran back a few meters, then opened into a large room crammed full of bunks. A small area had been cleared at the front of the room where far too many humans were gathered in front of a miserable looking fireplace. They all looked up when she entered and their looks of interest quickly changed to horror and disgust. A burly man with salt and pepper hair stepped forward reluctantly and looked her up and down.

'My name is Annah Tress—'

'I don't care what your name is,' the man said sharply. 'Nor does anyone else here if they know what's good for 'em.'

'You is cursed!' another voice piped up from the safety of the back of the crowd. 'Look at her hair — it's gold, just like the scales of them monk Drakes!'

Annah opened her mouth to protest, but the grey haired leader cut her off with a look. 'Don't say a damned word, girlie,' he growled. 'We're good, honest folk. We work hard and keep our noses out of trouble, and the Drakes treat us good because o' that. Three whole months and not one execution! We don't need no cursed girl spoilin' all our luck, you hear me?'

Annah opened her mouth to reply but once again the leader beat her to it. 'Don't talk! We won't be put under any o' your spells, understand?'

There was an angry murmur of agreement from the crowd. Annah wisely kept her mouth shut and nodded, which seemed to calm the man.

'Well and good,' he said. 'There's a bunk in the back corner that you can use, so long as you keep clear of us. If anythin' strange happens around here, we'll come lookin' for you, don't doubt, so you'd best keep out o' trouble.'

Annah nodded again and hurried to the bunk the man had indicated as quickly as she dared. She could feel their eyes on her and it was all she could do to keep herself from tears. She heard the low murmur of gossip behind her as she reached the bunk, which was just a dirty straw pallet laid on the floor in the corner. She dropped onto the filthy bundle, hugged her knees into her chest, and tried her best to ignore the muttered comments and dark looks thrown her way.

Annah had never had much contact with other slaves. She was captured at the age of four and remembered almost nothing of what life was like as a free woman. For two years she was trained by a Drake overseer to learn what it was to be a slave; to serve without question and obey the Drakes in all things. The humans who joined her in the indoctrination were too young and too frightened to care what colour her hair was.

When her training was complete, she was bought by a former Imperial Army Infantryman who spent his remaining days reliving the glories of his youth. She had polished his armour and weapons until they gleamed, cooked meals and cleaned the house while the old Drake drilled imaginary soldiers in the courtyard. She was his only slave and he had mostly ignored her. She hadn't been very upset when he passed away, but she had been worried about what her future would hold.

Because of her isolated upbringing, she'd always believed in the solidarity of her fellow human slaves. They had all been caught and forced into servitude against their will, and she imagined a tight knit fraternity forged from that bond of hardship. But sitting miserably in her corner, Annah realised how naïve she was; she was an outcast because something as simple as the colour of her hair had branded her apart. The other humans had no interest in her, other than worrying that she might ruin their comfortable posting just by being alive.

She looked up as she heard the scuffle of boots on the floor. One of the slaves had broken from the group and was standing in front of her, looking down darkly. He rubbed his hands unconsciously against the cold and finally shoved them into the pockets of his sparse tunic. Remembering the reaction she received the last time she tried to speak, Annah kept her mouth shut and waited for the man to make his intentions known.

'I lost a pair of gloves,' he said finally. 'Seeing's as how it's your fault, you should give me something to make up for it. That cloak o' yours will do nicely.'

'My fault?' Annah asked. 'How could it be my fault? I've been over here the whole time — I never came anywhere near you!'

'You brought your bad luck in here the moment you stepped through the door,' he growled. 'I had a winning streak o' five games before you got here and now I lost my winnings *and* my gloves.'

'It's not my fault,' Annah repeated. She looked over the man's shoulder to the other slaves still playing whatever gambling game they were involved in. She could tell they were all listening in with one ear, but she could expect no help from that quarter.

'Give me your cloak,' the man growled. 'I won't ask again.'

'But it's too cold,' she said, rising slowly to her feet and clutching her cloak with both hands. 'You've at least got the fire, but back here I've only got what I'm wearing...'

The man snarled, tired with the conversation, and swung an

open hand slap at her head. Acting completely on reflex, Annah raised her hand to block the strike and tilted her body away from the man. He grunted in surprise and swung his other hand to catch her off guard, but again she had her hand up to block him. Growling angrily, he threw a flurry of clumsy blows and Annah found herself falling into her daily Kata routine. The same fluid movements, the same hand and arm positions, but instead of Ishkal watching and repeating her actions, a sweaty slave grew more and more frustrated.

The man paused to catch his breath when it became clear that his attacks were getting nowhere. Annah stood trembling in the corner, still aghast that her own body seemed to have acted without her conscious control and terrified that she might suddenly forget her new found skills.

The man finally realised that trying to punch Annah was getting him nowhere and he gave up on subtlety. With a roar, he threw himself forward, intent on tackling her to the ground. She deftly twisted sideways, bending her body as Ishkal had trained her and slipped from the man's grasp. Surprised at her sudden move, the man couldn't stop himself as he slammed face first into the wall. There was a groan of sympathy from the slaves at the front of the room and the man stumbled backwards with a glassy look in his eyes.

Annah stepped back out of the man's reach, still worried that he might attack her again. But the man had no intention of continuing — Annah had beaten everything he'd thrown at her, and all he had to show for it was a bruised face and a bloody nose. Throwing her a dark look, he staggered back to the others.

Annah spent an hour standing in the corner, praying that

someone would come to tell her Kelkh was ready to leave. The other slaves occasionally muttered amongst themselves and threw her dark looks, but mostly they left her alone. One of them threw a rock at her in a moment of rash courage, hitting her in the arm and leaving her with a large bruise, but that was all they dared.

When the muttering stopped and a frightened silence came over the room, Annah looked up hopefully. Her eyes filled with tears as Kelkh stepped into the room with the copper skinned Slave Master fawning behind him, apologising for the unworthiness of the slave quarters for such a great warrior. Annah almost ran forward, only stopping when her senses kicked in and reminded her of the proper decorum. She slowed to a fast walk as she approached and knelt in front of him. Kelkh looked down and saw the bruises on her face and arm straight away.

'By The Dragon, girl, what happened to you? Are you all right?'

'Please, Master, it's nothing,' she replied.

Kelkh glowered at the copper skinned Slave Master, who lowered his head, and he snarled at the slaves who paled and scattered, but he honoured Annah's request to let it be.

'Come on, girl,' he said gently. 'It's time to go home.'

Kelkh swept from the room and Annah followed close behind, sighing in heartfelt relief. Kelkh stayed close to her as they hurried through the courtyard, keeping his watchful eye on her. Annah felt safe under that gaze, which was something she knew she would never get from her own race.

'Did your party go well, Master?'

'Better than I expected,' he smiled. 'And worse. I wasn't bombarded with talk of our new creations, for which I will be eternally grateful. But unfortunately, that was only because the gossips now talk of war. The Cat-Men are attacking our southern borders and I've been ordered to put my energy back to making weapons for the army officers. I'm sorry, Annah, but for now our other creations will have to wait.'

'I understand, Master,' she replied, trying to hide her disappointment.

'But don't worry,' he smiled. 'That just means you'll have more time to spend with Ishkal on your training.'

For the first time that evening, Annah smiled happily.

CHAPTER 8

Aerik peeled back his filthy black robes and dropped them in a pile by his locker. He was bone tired and he was losing the struggle against the exhaustion that came from too much adrenaline. He'd fought a running battle with a Samurai and somehow managed to duck into an alleyway while the Samurai caught his sword in a garbage bin with a blow that was meant for Aerik's head. By the time the Samurai freed his weapon, Aerik was long gone into the streets of the slave city.

Two of his men weren't so lucky. They had left themselves exposed and the Drakes caught them in the open with nowhere to run. The Samurai did them the honour of fighting one on one, but it took them only moments to defeat the untrained slaves. By the time Aerik found his way back to them, the only thing he could do was sneak up and take their bodies home.

It was one of Aerik's suggestions, to take the bodies of their dead, and one that Ebon quickly agreed to. Half the Drake Samurais thought the slaves in black were actually evil spirits sent from the underworld to kill them, and Aerik knew that their fear was one of the few weapons they had in their arsenal. If the Drakes recovered one of the black clad bodies and proved that they were just human slaves, then that small advantage was gone.

If the bodies just disappeared, then the myth of evil spirits would grow stronger.

But even though he knew what he was doing was right, carrying the body of a former comrade through the streets tore at the gentle core of his soul. It took a part of him away that would be forever numb, but he consoled himself with the thought that they died free men, fighting for what they believed in.

'Rough night, I take it?'

Aerik opened his eyes and saw Ebon standing in front of him, smiling wearily. 'I lost Griff and Torp. They never had a chance.'

'Be free brothers,' Ebon sighed.

'It's all we can say, isn't it?' Aerik muttered. 'They're dead because we convinced them to join us, and all we can say is 'lucky them, be free'. It just seems ... unfair.'

'They died free men, fighting for a better life, not just some slave dead on a Drake's whim,' Ebon said. 'Would you rob them of that?'

'No, of course not,' Aerik replied. 'It just hurts.'

'Good. As soon as it stops hurting to have someone under your command die, you should stop being a leader.'

Aerik nodded and wearily started to wipe himself clean with a shabby rag and a bowl of water. 'What happened while I was away?'

'We lost Dean and Ekler,' Ebon grimaced. 'The Drakes caught them with knives hidden under their tunics. They were executed then and there.'

'Damn it, I keep telling you that having knives on us while we're not on missions is too dangerous,' Aerik snapped. 'We need to think of something less conspicuous.'

'Well you're going to get the chance to come up with an idea and put it into practice,' Ebon shrugged.

'What do you mean?'

'I'm turning over command of this cell to you, Aerik,' Ebon said. 'I've seen you plan and lead enough attacks that I can tell you have the skill and the heart to do it justice.'

'But why me?' Aerik asked. 'You're the one with all the experience. Why don't you just keep leading us?'

'Because I'm not staying here, Aerik,' Ebon replied. 'I've done what I came here to do — I've set up a resistance cell in this ghetto and given you all the training I can. Now you can take over here and I'll move to the next ghetto and do the same thing there. I'll stay with you for a few weeks to smooth the transition from me to you, but the rest of my team will return to their homes to renew their fight there.'

'So you're putting me in charge, just like that?' Aerik asked.

'Just like that,' Ebon smiled.

'I don't have to see an elder or get some slave council approval or anything?'

'Come on, Aerik, you've seen how we operate,' Ebon said. 'There's no leadership and no elders. There's just a few people like me who travel around trying to start up enough cells that we might be able to build a real revolution.'

'So what am I meant to do?'

'That, my friend, is up to you now.'

'Alright, fine,' Aerik growled. 'But if I'm in charge, then I'm going to do things *my* way.'

'As long as you follow the few laws we've established, you're free to do whatever you want. If your ideas turn out to be a success,

I'll even pass them on to the other resistance cells.'

Aerik sighed and closed his eyes. All he felt like doing was going back to his quarters and playing with Rebecca until it was time for her to sleep, but he knew that wasn't going to happen. Lysa wasn't going to be happy, but she wouldn't argue too much. She knew why he fought the Drakes and she was behind him all the way, but she still worried that something might happen to him.

'So you're my second in command now, that right?' he asked.

'That's right,' Ebon nodded. 'For a few weeks until you're settled in, anyway.'

'Good, then get everyone gathered in the meeting hall in two hours — and I mean everyone.'

The revolutionaries were all gathered in the meeting hall several minutes before the appointed time. They were ten ragged former slaves, physically and emotionally scarred from their ordeals with the Drakes and now fiercely committed to exacting their revenge. They shuffled anxiously as they waited for Aerik to arrive, still a little nervous under Ebon's watchful gaze. They all jumped when the door finally opened and Aerik swept inside.

'I take it you all know why we're here,' he said, walking to the front of the room to stand next to Ebon.

'I've told them,' Ebon said. 'They know you're our new leader.'

'Then I can move straight into telling you about the changes I'm making as of right now,' he nodded. 'First and most important for my mind, I've decided that each of us will begin training three times a week. Every second day should be enough, but that might be increased or decreased based on the experience and skill of the individual.'

A chorus of groans erupted from the troops and Ebon coughed politely into his hand.

'Does someone have a problem with that?' Aerik looked each person in the face, all of them people he had recruited — with Ebon's blessing, of course — and all of them people whose life he had saved more than once. None of them could meet his gaze, and in the end the muttering stopped.

'Are you sure that's wise?' Ebon asked when it was clear no one else would say anything. 'If we ease the pressure on the Drakes, people might forget who we are and what we do. The Drake's fear of us and our support in the slave community are the only advantages we have. Can we afford the loss of status?'

'Today we lost four people,' Aerik said. 'Four, out of fifteen. Two of them died because they were too inexperienced to prevent themselves being manoeuvred into an inescapable position. Can we afford this loss of life?'

Aerik stared around the room, daring someone to say he was wrong. Ebon bowed in apology for speaking out of turn and motioned Aerik to continue.

'Our status will increase as we get more recruits and as the people we already have get better at what they do. My second order is that no member of this cell will carry a dagger, sword or any other conspicuous weapon on their person unless they're on a mission and wearing their black uniforms.'

This time the outcry was more forceful, as all the revolutionaries, Ebon included, voiced their opposition. Aerik stood calmly in the face of it all, until the noise subsided.

'Are you finished?' he asked finally. 'Two men were executed today because the Drakes found them carrying knives. These men were picked for a random search and they died for it.'

'They were unlucky,' Ebon said.

'No,' Aerik replied. 'We were stupid to ever give them something that could get them killed.'

'Then what do you suggest?' one man asked. 'That we fight the Drakes with our bare hands?'

'No,' Aerik smiled. 'I suggest that we start using our brains.'

Aerik walked across the room to a pair of buckets that had been hooked onto a thick staff. Aerik deftly lifted the staff and settled it across his shoulders with a bucket on either side.

'What's this?' he asked. 'Anyone?'

'Two buckets of water,' someone said. 'So what?'

Aerik punched sideways with an open palm, knocking one bucket off the end of the staff. The weight of the second bucket unbalanced the staff as it too slid off and fell to the ground. Aerik caught the staff as it dropped and, grasping it in both hands, smashed it into a nearby practice dummy. The crack of wood on wood made everyone wince, and from where they stood, everyone could see the thick dent in the Drake shaped dummy.

'*Now* tell me what this is,' Aerik said, puffing slightly. 'Is this any less a weapon than a dagger? Is it?'

The room was silent as everyone considered the possibilities Aerik was suggesting.

'A Drake searches a slave carrying a dagger and he sees a dead man in the making,' Aerik said. 'A Drake searches a man with this staff and he sees a man carrying two buckets of water. I want all of you to come up with other ideas for weapons, but they're all to be every day items that won't raise any suspicion if you're searched. You might think differently, but I think it's more valuable to our cause to have you all alive and well.'

A murmur of laughter rippled through the troops, which eased the nervous knot in Aerik's stomach. He had won them over in this at least, and if it worked they would more readily follow his other ideas.

'Training will start tomorrow morning,' he said. 'I want to start putting scouts and support men on the streets during our missions, but not until you know how to use these new weapons and not until you don't look so damned conspicuous. Some of you stand in the street so aggressively, you might as well have "search me for weapons" written on your foreheads.'

More laughter went through the group, but Aerik saw more than one head hang low in embarrassment. From the corner of his eye he saw Ebon nodding in agreement, a simple movement that gave Aerik the confidence that he was on the right track.

'I have one more thing to discuss and then you can all get some sleep,' he said finally. 'I want all of the money we've taken from the Drakes, down to the last copper Shill. And I want all the armour we've captured melted down and cast into ingots. I'm sure we can steal a few moulds from the furnaces ...'

The copper skinned Drake pulled open the gates to his manor and stared grumpily out onto the street. It was early in the morning, and even though people were already moving about on their business, the sun wasn't up yet and the night chill still dominated the air. He was already annoyed at being pulled from his warm bed and his anger flared when he saw the human slave kneeling nervously on the cobblestones.

'What do you want?' he asked menacingly.

'Noble Dragon, I'm here at the order of my master,' the slave said. 'He has recently acquired interests in this part of the city and wishes to purchase your manor so that he might have a home worthy of him nearby.'

'Your master wishes to buy *this* house?' the Drake asked.

'Yes, Noble Dragon,' the slave replied.

The Drake frowned and stamped his feet to ward off the chill. He had been a mediocre merchant when he was younger, with a taste for the finer things in life. His home was a beautiful building, finely designed, well made and built on a large block of land with a thick border of trees and hedges to ensure privacy. The reason the Drake had been able to afford it was because it was built on the very edge of a human slave ghetto at the outskirts of the Imperial city. Beautiful as it was, no self respecting Drake would want a house that was in sight of humans, let alone one that backed onto a whole town of them.

'How much does your master offer?' the Drake asked suspiciously. 'And why doesn't he come to see me himself?'

'My master means no offence,' the slave said hurriedly, bowing to hide his suddenly pale face. 'He's a private person who values his solitude. It is his path to enlightenment.'

'A fine philosophy,' the Drake grunted — it was a common excuse used by young Drake Nobles who wanted to impress their friends by 'slumming' near the slave pens. The Drake decided not to push any further, just in case he discovered too much about the slave's mysterious master. 'How much does your master offer?'

'One thousand gold Shills and twenty steel ingots,' the slave replied.

The Drake's eye's widened as the years of merchant trading automatically took over. One thousand gold Shills was a good price for his property, and twenty steel ingots would net him a further two hundred gold Shills if he found the right buyer. The blazing light of greed burned deep in the Drake's eyes and he rubbed his hands together unconsciously.

'What are the terms?'

'My master asks that you vacate the property within five days and that you hand the deed and keys over to me for delivery.'

'To you?' the Drake sneered — whether this human's master was a Noble or not, he could at least show the courtesy of having a Drake finish the transaction. Dealing with a human was demeaning.

'My master wished me to convey his regrets that your most worthy personage must be put through this process and he asked me to offer you a further two steel ingots as compensation for this grievous breach of etiquette.'

The Drake's tongue flicked in and out of his mouth rapidly as he started to calculate what he would do with his new found wealth. So what if he was forced to deal with a human, they were just an intermediary to a Drake of high standing and they were offering a large sum of money. With his honour assuaged by that reasoning, the Drake rubbed his hands together anxiously.

'I accept,' he hissed. 'Do you have a contract or do you need me to have one drawn up?'

'I have one here, ready for your signature, Noble Dragon.'

The slave held two rolled parchments in one hand and an ink

quill in the other. He shuffled forward on his knees until both items were in easy reach of the Drake.

The Drake took the quill with a superior sneer and scanned through the parchments to ensure that the details were all correct. The slave remained motionless until the Drake grunted in satisfaction and signed his name at the bottom.

'Now get off my land,' he growled, throwing one of the parchments at the slave's feet. 'I have a lot to do if I'm going to leave this house in five days.'

'Yes, Noble Dragon,' the slave bowed, retrieving the parchment and walking backwards, still bowing, into the street.

As the gates to the manor slammed shut, Aerik straightened and smiled in satisfaction. It had all gone according to plan, and in five days they would have a base of operations that they could live and train in; one that wasn't a decrepit building one storm away from being demolished. Turning his back on the manor, he disappeared into the crowded streets and was lost from sight.

CHAPTER 9

'Tell me what happened,' Ishkal said, calmly following through his Kata as Annah told him about her encounter with the slave at the previous night's dinner party.

'It was strange, my Lord,' she replied. 'I moved my arm to block without even thinking about what I was doing. Then the man struck again and I started moving through my Kata, blocking his attacks again and again just by doing the steps that you showed me.'

'And tell me, Annah, what do you think we've been doing all these mornings?' Ishkal asked. 'What do you think these Kata are?'

'I don't know, my Lord,' she replied. 'I thought ... I thought they were a beautiful dance.'

'That they are,' he laughed. 'But they're also much more. They're the steps of combat, the dance of the melee. They're the most basic lessons taught to a warrior monk of the Order of the Gold Dragon.'

Annah stopped mid-step, completely forgetting her next movements as she realised what Ishkal had said.

'You taught me to fight?' she gasped. 'But, Lord Ishkal, why would you put yourself in such danger for me? I'm just a slave!'

'Oh, I'm in no danger,' he grinned. 'I'm a monk of the Gold Dragon — the highest rank of Drakes. Not even the Imperial Nobles would dare harm me; that would risk an uprising from the Empire and undermine the caste society that has kept them as the ruling class for centuries. No, I am safe, but you could be in danger. A Drake who discovers that you know our Order's ways might kill you out of spite, so keep that knowledge to yourself.'

'Yes, my Lord,' she said, belatedly jumping back into step and continuing her Kata.

'And as for you being just a slave, I think you know that's not true,' he continued. 'You're a smart, skilled young woman and you mean a great deal to both Kelkh and I, whether he will admit it or not.'

'Thank you, my Lord,' she sighed. She lapsed into an embarrassed silence as she completed her exercises. When she heard Ishkal softly singing the song of creation, she happily closed her eyes and lost herself in the soul lifting power of the song.

Weeks passed by quickly, as Annah trained day after day with Ishkal. Happy with the speed of her achievements, he quickly introduced more and more advanced lessons into her routine, keeping her busy and working her to the limits of her endurance. Every night she struggled to complete her stretches before she flopped into bed, and every morning she woke up aching all over, but even with all that discomfort, she was as happy as she had ever been in her life. Her one disappointment was that she saw Kelkh less and less as the days went by.

With the talk of war changing from rumour to fact, Kelkh had been commissioned by the Emperor himself to work on weapons for the army's officers — at least those who didn't already wield family heirlooms of similar power. The commission was delivered by a patrol of royal guards, twelve Iron Drakes dressed in the high livery of the palace, who almost frightened Annah to death when they arrived. Kelkh had been forced to spend every waking moment in his forge. The only time he ever emerged was to have breakfast and dinner, which he usually wolfed down as quickly as possible so he could return to his work.

Annah found that she missed seeing her master and she missed the time they shared designing the beautiful artwork that was still the toast of the Drake nobility. Though she loved her training with Ishkal and she would be forever indebted to him for the lessons he taught her, she looked forward to the day that Kelkh would be free to work with her once again. It was almost a month later when her prayers were answered.

'Strike!'

Annah lashed out with her clenched fist, wincing as she hit the wooden board with a dull thud. The board remained whole, mocking her as she wringed her hand and glared at it.

'Remember, Annah, you must harness your energy and release it when you're at peace,' Ishkal said. 'Find a tranquil place inside yourself and gather your power there, then release it in a single strike at the board.'

Annah nodded dutifully, took a deep breath and closed her

eyes. She thought of a number of places that she hoped would be tranquil — her room, Mange's pen where she spent so much time feeding and petting the giant Rock Dragon, a tree in the garden where she sometimes enjoyed her rare time off — but nothing seemed to make her feel any different. They were places of comfort, but they didn't inspire anything inside. She heard Ishkal pacing around her and she desperately tried to think of a place, somewhere that would give her peace.

An image of the forge sprung to her mind, drifting at the edge of her thoughts as she grew more and more frustrated. She sighed angrily and tried to sweep the thought aside — she could dream of working the forge later, but for now there were other things to concentrate on. But the thought grew stronger, filling her senses with familiar sensations. She could smell the tang of raw steel being shaped and forged by Kelkh's magic, she could see the bright glimmer of the winter sun glinting off the molten metal, and she could hear Kelkh's song, filling her with the joy and power of creation.

For that instant, Annah forgot herself, forgot where she was and what she was doing and lost herself to the power of the song. She was soaring through the vast dome of the heavens, lifted high upon notes that were clearer and more pure than anything she had imagined. She felt as if she had been caught in a storm and was being whisked away, thrown into the air and left to fly. Most strangely of all, she felt as if she had come home.

'Strike!'

Before she even realised what she was doing, Annah reacted to Ishkal's command and punched forward. The storm abated and the powerful memory of the forge fled back to the realms of imagination, leaving Annah staring at a shattered pine board.

'Excellent work, Annah,' Ishkal said, clapping heartily. 'It normally takes our novices weeks and many cracked knuckle scales to break their first board. If it was within my power to do so, I would award you the brown belt, a sign that you have passed your first stage of training. As it is, I will pass a request on to my Abbott and see if he will grant me permission to do so.'

'At least in the meantime, I'll know who to call if I am attacked by board wielding Ronin.'

Annah jumped when she heard Kelkh's gruff voice behind her and she immediately spun and dropped to her knees. 'Master, I apologise. I didn't hear you approach.'

'Oh, get up, girl,' Kelkh huffed. 'And don't apologise either. You were busy with your lessons and I expect you to give Ishkal your full attention.'

'Yes, master,' she said, touching her forehead to the ground then scrambling to her feet.

'It seems I have a small contract that I need your assistance with,' Kelkh said. 'The Duchess Inral wants me to make her daughter a set of wedding rings for her imminent marriage to Samurai General Saad and she won't take no for an answer.'

Ishkal raised his eyebrows and looked sceptically at Kelkh. 'I thought you had been ordered by the Emperor to divert all your energy towards making weapons.'

'Duchess Inral has obtained special dispensation for this work to be done,' Kelkh shrugged. 'So I'll have to interrupt your training, girl, so we can get this done.'

'Of course, master,' Annah bowed. 'Lord Ishkal?'

'You may go, Annah,' Ishkal smiled. 'But remember what

you've learned and we will pick it up where we left off.'

Annah bowed to Ishkal and then hurried after Kelkh as the old forger limped back to the cottage. They spent the next hour in the lounge room while Annah drew sketch after sketch of wedding ring ideas. In the end they settled on an elegant design, with a band fashioned as a Dragon's claw clutching an egg carved from a flawless pearl. That was the banner of the Duchy of Inral, and Kelkh thought it fitting that it should be the design of the wedding rings for a scion of that house. It was another half hour before Annah had the rings drawn to Kelkh's exacting specifications and they finally moved to the forge to begin work.

Annah knelt in her usual position just in front of the door and watched Kelkh follow his ritual for forging. He inspected the block of gold carefully, looking for any signs that it was unsuitable for his needs, and then did the same for the two white pearls he took from a pouch in his material locker. When he was satisfied, he set the pearls aside, placed the gold block on his anvil and started to sing.

Annah smiled as the Forgesong washed over her, welcoming it after a month's forced absence. She closed her eyes as she felt the power lift her spirits and carry her away, and she thought briefly of her earlier lesson with Ishkal. This was her tranquil place, but it was no memory — it was real, and the music flowed through her soul, not from her mind.

She thought of the words that Ishkal had tried to teach her, the basics of the Forgesong that the Order of the Gold Dragon used to reach enlightenment, and she thought how limited such things were. The Forgesong was a flowing, liquid thing that couldn't be written down and memorised no matter how hard the Gold

Monks tried. Annah started to hum along with the song, forgetting Ishkal's words and losing herself in the music.

Suddenly, Annah found herself at the eye of a storm, with music and raw magic swirling past at dizzying speed. The song no longer flowed through her and around her, but flowed *from* her. She could feel the power of the notes as they poured from her mouth and she knew that somehow it was possible to shape it to her will, but the necessary control wasn't within her power yet. For now, she just sang and revelled in the exhilaration of the magic.

Then as suddenly as it had started, the flowing river slowed and the magic came sluggishly to Annah's call. Before she could wonder at the change, fatigue hit her like a battering ram and jolted her back to reality. She knelt unsteadily in the forge, right where she had always been, but it was no longer the middle of the day. The sun was almost hidden behind the tall mountain peaks outside the window and long shadows dominated the room.

Kelkh stood in the last of the waning light, staring at her in open mouthed amazement with Ishkal by his side. Kelkh must have left the room at some stage to fetch his friend, but Annah had no recollection of him leaving — all she remembered was the magic of the Song.

'Annah,' Kelkh gaped. 'Are you alright, girl?'

'I ... feel tired, mast...'

She fell forward as exhaustion overtook her, and the last thing she felt was Kelkh's arms catch her before she hit the floor.

'How could such a thing happen, Ishkal?' Kelkh asked. 'The

legends tell us that humans can't use the Forgesong. No human has ever been able to use it.'

'So we've been told,' Ishkal said. 'Yet Annah seems proof that the stories were wrong.'

'It's incredible,' Kelkh sighed. 'I could train her as my apprentice. With her skill she could be the toast of the Nobility — all of them would want something made by her.'

'She would be a novelty,' Ishkal said distastefully. 'A trained monkey that amused them by doing their bidding. That is, assuming they even let her live.'

Kelkh bared his fangs angrily to show what he thought of that idea. 'So what do we do?'

'I suggest you train Annah the best that you can,' Ishkal said. 'With power like that at her command I think it's important that she learn how to properly wield it. In the meantime, I will travel back to the Monastery and see what I can find out about this in our archives.'

'You're joking, aren't you?' Kelkh replied. 'You can't go, I need you! I know weapons, I know fighting and I know how to do what I do with the Forgesong, but I'm no teacher of the mystical. If you were asking me to drill the girl as a swordsman, then I'm your Drake, but magic is instinctive to me, not something I've learned. I don't know how to teach someone. You do.'

Ishkal flicked a talon against his teeth as he thought about what he would do. Staying here would mean a long delay in finding out what was going on, but it would probably be better for Annah in the end.

'Please, Ishkal?' Kelkh asked gruffly.

'All right, Kelkh,' Ishkal sighed. 'I will stay.'

CHAPTER 10

Two black clad figures dropped into the courtyard, slipping silently over the walls into the thick shadows of the tree lined garden. They wore flowing black outfits with long daggers and short swords at their side, painted matte black to blend into the night. They took only an instant to scout the area before they set off towards the door at the far end of the courtyard, their entry point to the manor where their target waited.

They moved swiftly from tree to tree until they were opposite the door, where they broke free from cover and crossed over the pavestones. For those few heartbeats, they were in the open and vulnerable to attack without escape, but they thought it was worth the risk. There was no one about, they could clearly see that, and it was a much faster way to complete their mission.

The crash of a gong split the air and the revolutionaries knew with a sudden horrific clarity that they had walked into a trap. The doorway swung open and four armoured Samurai poured out into the courtyard. Two of them charged straight at the black pair, while the other two moved to cut off any escape. One revolutionary bellowed a challenge and charged the Samurai with sword and dagger held clumsily in each hand. The Samurai watched impassively as the revolutionary approached, then dropped to one knee and scythed his blade across their midriff as they passed. The air flew from the revolutionary's lungs and they fell to the ground with an agonised groan.

That was enough for the second revolutionary who jolted into action and fled the oncoming Samurai. He turned and ran back through the courtyard the way he had come, hoping to climb back up the wall and disappear into the night. But the Samurai had already anticipated such a move — he was cut down before he was even half way there.

A blaze of torches flared to life as Aerik strode through the open doorway from the manor, his face a mixture of disappointment and frustration. He patted one of the Samurai on the shoulder as he crossed the courtyard, the same Samurai who had cut down the first figure. The Samurai took a step back, allowing Aerik room to kneel next to the black figure and help her to her feet. At the far end of courtyard, two Samurai were helping the second figure stand and walk back to Aerik.

After a sharp command from the Samurai leader, the two black clad figures pulled back their hoods and face masks to reveal a sheepish looking young man and an angry young woman. Behind them, the Samurais removed their helmets to let the night air brush against their faces, the faces of Aerik's slave revolutionaries, not Drakes.

'What did you do wrong?' Aerik asked.

'Nothing,' the girl growled. 'They set a trap for us. There was nothing we could do.'

'Is that right, Saera?' Aerik asked coldly. 'When you crossed the courtyard, you left yourself completely vulnerable to attack. Why did you do that?'

'I'd scouted the area and there was no danger that I could see,' the girl, Saera, said.

'So instead of playing it safe and walking the long way around the courtyard, you decided to save time and just cut across,' Aerik finished. 'If you had stayed in the shadows, you could have jumped the fence and escaped when the trap was sprung. Or perhaps you would have seen the trap *before* it was sprung.'

Saera said nothing, but her glare spoke volumes.

'Why did you run at the Samurai?' Aerik asked.

'Because they were trying to kill us,' she said.

'So instead of running away, saving your life and the life of your companion, you decided to attack a Drake Samurai that's bigger, stronger and faster than you are, *and* has been training in weapons craft since the age of ten,' Aerik said sarcastically.

'Someone has to stand up to them,' Saera spat.

'And someone is,' Aerik replied. 'But I've seen too many friends die already to just throw lives at the Drakes. We will fight them, but on *our* terms and at a time of *our* choosing. Eamon did the right thing by running away. His only mistake was that he fled without giving any thought to the defensibility of his escape.'

'I'm sorry, master,' the young man stammered, dropping to his knees.

Aerik sighed bent down to the young man. 'Stand up, Eamon,' he said gently. 'You have no master; not any more. You're free and you don't have to kneel to anyone.'

'Yes, mast... my Lord,' Eamon said uncertainly.

Aerik smothered another exasperated sigh and rubbed his eyes. Revolutionaries like Eamon were difficult to train; people who had become so accustomed to life as a slave that they had no idea how to act when they were given their freedom. They learned, in time, but it was a hard road.

'You're dismissed,' Aerik said. 'All of you go and get some rest. Tomorrow will be busy enough.'

The gathered revolutionaries all shuffled off under Ebon's watchful eye, leaving Aerik and Saera alone in the courtyard.

'Can I help you, Saera?' Aerik asked wearily.

'I want to be included in the mission tomorrow,' she said.

'After such a beating in training, I would have thought you'd want to wait before you put your life at actual risk.'

'I'm a better fighter than half the crew going with you,' Saera protested. 'And what happened here was a fluke — it would never happen in a real operation.'

'Is that so? Tell me, Saera, where do you think I got the idea for this test?'

Saera looked at Aerik sullenly for a moment as she thought of a new argument, but he didn't allow her the time.

'Saera, you're a gifted fighter, but compared to a Drake Samurai your skills are that of a child. I know you hate the Drakes for what they did to your family; we all have our reasons for being here, but we can't let that anger control our actions. If that had been a real mission and you'd acted with your emotions instead of your brain, it wouldn't just have been your life that was lost.'

Saera's face screwed up as she prepared to argue, then she paused and the frown lines cleared. She nodded slowly as some small understanding dawned upon her. 'I think I understand, my Lord.'

'Good,' he sighed. 'Then you can accompany us as a reserve scout on tomorrow's mission.' Saera's face broke into an eager grin that faltered as Aerik raised a finger in warning. 'But understand, if you put the mission or your comrades in danger by your actions, I will follow our laws. Blood for blood.'

'I understand, my Lord,' she said solemnly.

'Then go and get some rest,' he ordered. She nodded and ran from the room; Aerik watched her go and wondered if he had made the right choice.

He pondered it as he walked through the halls of the manor back to his bedroom. It was something he saw more and more often as they recruited slaves to their cause. Men and women who had suffered under the iron heel of the Drakes who let the anger simmering in their hearts explode in a fit of rage. It was dangerous both to the person in question and their companions, and it brought up many questions that Aerik had been trying to avoid.

He reached the door to his living quarters and stepped inside. Lysa was in the large living room, nursing a gurgling Rebecca on her knee. Rebecca squealed when she saw Aerik, and Lysa looked up at him and smiled, but her smile faded when she saw his tired expression.

'Is everything all right?' she asked. 'You look terrible.'

'Lysa, I need to ask you something and I want you to be completely honest with me.'

'Of course,' she said. 'You can ask me anything, you know that.'

He closed the door and sat down next to her, and when Rebecca held out her pudgy arms, he gathered her up and cradled her in the crook of his elbow. 'Did I do the right thing?' he asked finally. 'Am I still doing the right thing?'

'Of course,' Lysa replied immediately. 'You did what you were forced to do. The Drakes killed our family and tried to kill you – if you'd done nothing you would be dead.'

'But the Drakes who killed Monta and Tisa are dead, so why do I keep fighting?'

Lysa reached out and tickled Rebecca under her little arms, while Aerik bounced her on his knee.

'You fight so that Rebecca can be free,' Lysa said. 'So that our little girl can live her life however she likes, without being afraid that someone she's never met will make her a widow or an orphan for the second time.'

Aerik hoisted Rebecca up into the air where she hung laughing in his hands.

'But you know that already,' Lysa said. 'What's really on your mind?'

He lowered Rebecca back down and bounced her gently on his knee. 'If our mission goes as planned tomorrow, we'll have enough money to buy dozens of slaves from the markets and set them free.'

'I know, it's a brilliant plan,' Lysa smiled. 'And it will swell the ranks of your revolutionaries.'

'That's what I'm afraid of,' he replied. 'I'm frightened that what I'm building here has nothing to do with freedom. So many of the slaves I've freed don't *want* freedom, they want revenge. If the Drakes gave in and freed all the humans tomorrow, some of these people would keep fighting because their hate is all that keeps them going.'

'Aerik, the Drakes have hurt all of us in some way. These people are entitled to their pain; your job is to guide them, not to run their lives for them. You're fighting a war and you can't be choosy about who helps you.'

Aerik sighed and handed Rebecca back to Lysa. The baby was almost asleep, and from the look of Aerik, he wasn't too far behind.

'Come on, Aerik,' Lysa smiled. 'I heard you were a pretty good bard once and I've got a little girl here who would love a bedtime song.'

The Drake caravan rumbled down the street, a single heavy wagon drawn by two stocky ponies. A pair of Emerald Drakes sat on a bench at the front, one driving while the other watched the road. Six more Emerald Samurai walked beside the wagon, one at every corner and two in the middle. They expected no trouble, but they remained watchful for it nonetheless. The wagon's route had been specially planned to run through the slave sector, where the chances of attack were considered almost non existent and collateral damage was not an issue.

The wagon turned the corner and moved into the main thoroughfare of the slave town. The street looked like all the others before it, although there were more humans wandering around than there had been previously. It was the middle of the day when most slaves should have either been in the mines or working in the ro-khill fields, but at least a dozen humans were walking the streets. The Samurai on the wagon raised his hand and halted the caravan.

'Sergeant,' the Drake called. 'There are too many humans here for my liking and too many rumours of Samurai disappearing in these slave towns. Search them all and report anything unusual.'

The Sergeant saluted and motioned to three of his men who

followed him into the street. Leaving two Drakes on the ground and two on the wagon to guard their cargo, the four Drakes marched into the street, shouting at the top of their voices for the slaves to remain where they were. The humans dropped to their knees immediately and submitted themselves to the search without a murmur of protest.

The Drakes searched all twelve slaves in the street but found no weapons on them. There was a pair of men carrying water buckets, three women carrying sacks of grain with the aid of an old fashioned hook and rope sling, and a crippled man with a walking stick, but nothing incriminating. The sergeant waved at the officer on the wagon and the caravan rumbled forward once more.

The lumbering wagon barely moved five meters when the dull thud of wood on wood echoed into the air. The Drake officer stared dumbly at the arrow shaft protruding from the seat next to him, until his mind finally caught up with what his eyes were seeing.

'Attack,' he screamed. 'We're under attack.'

A flurry of five arrows quickly followed the first, but luckily for the Drakes, those firing them were either very inexperienced or just clumsy in the extreme. He looked up and saw six black clad figures crouching on the rooftops with Samurai short bows poached from the bodies of his dead comrades.

'They're on the rooftops,' the officer yelled. 'Get up the access ladders before they figure out how to aim those bows!'

The Sergeant leapt into action, roaring at his troops and directing them towards the closest four ladders. He almost had the defence formation under control when the air was blasted from his lungs by a heavy object crashing against his back. He hit the ground and rolled instinctively to avoid the follow up attack. A heavy staff hit the cobblestones where his head had been and the Drake lashed out at his attacker.

His hand hit a man's leg and he quickly sunk his claws into the fleshy calf as he fumbled with his sword buckle. The man, a water carrier that the sergeant had searched just minutes earlier, screamed in pain and would have been easy prey for a quick sword thrust to the belly, but one of the man's companion's stepped forward and brought his walking stick down heavily on the Drake's head. The Sergeant's vision went black and he knew no more.

The element of surprise had carried the humans a long way in the battle — the Drake Sergeant was knocked to the ground with one of his men following quickly after. The other two Samurai reached for their swords as they each saw three women stepping towards them. The women dropped their sacks of grain and wielded the hook and rope sling like a weapon. The rope had a heavy weight attached to one end, which the women swung like a ball and chain, ready to strike. With more humans on the way, the two Samurai stood back to back and prepared to meet the rabble.

One woman made a feint to the side, which the Samurai discouraged with a swift thrust forward. Another woman flung out her weighted rope, wrapping it around the Samurai's blade and tangling it completely. Moving quickly, she dropped to a crouch and clipped the hook onto a street water drain, so the Samurai couldn't use his superior strength to wrench the blade free.

Caught completely off guard by this unorthodox tactic, the Samurai yanked twice at his sword before he realised what had been done. He grabbed a dagger from his belt and pulled it free, but those seconds of vulnerability cost him dearly. A man with a staff and another with a walking stick took the opportunity to move within striking distance and attack his unprotected flank. The Samurai accepted a blow to the ribs from the walking stick and used his forearm to block the staff blow aimed at his head. He winced as he heard the crack of bone, but he ignored the pain and lashed out with his dagger.

An angry red line appeared on the man holding the staff and he jumped back holding his arm while his eyes widened in pain. His staff clattered to the ground, leaving the Drake with one less thing to worry about. Unfortunately, the man with the walking stick proved more dangerous than the Drake expected. Before he had recovered from his dagger strike, the man caught him on the side of the head with a heavy blow.

The Drake stumbled forward a step before he had his dagger back up in defence, but the human wasn't following — in fact, the human was looking past him, at someone behind him.

Agony exploded in the Samurai's chest and he looked down to see a sword hilt sticking out from his side. One of the human women, the one who had entangled his sword, had cut the weapon free while the human male manoeuvred him into a spot where the sword could be brought to bear. The Drake dropped to his knees, his mind still whirling in disbelief. Weapons and tactics — who would have thought these stupid slaves would be so resourceful?

Ebon swung his walking stick hard on the back of the other Samurai's head — the Drake hadn't realised that his companion was no longer watching his back. Saera stepped in quickly at Ebon's side and put her newly acquired sword to use once again. The Drake bellowed in pain and spun to see who had struck him, whipping his sword around in an arc as he turned.

The blade should have taken Saera's head from her shoulders, but she found herself jerked backwards by a strong grip on the back of her shirt. She hit the ground heavily and saw Ebon standing above her, using his walking stick to block the weakened strikes of the Samurai. Seconds later, the Drake seemed to realise there was three feet of steel embedded through his back and he crumpled to the ground. Ebon stepped backwards and gripped Saera by the arm, helping her to her feet.

'Thanks. I didn't think that lizard would have any strength left.' She spat on the ground next to the body to emphasise her disgust.

'No thanks necessary,' Ebon replied. 'You helped me with my fight, so I helped you with yours — remember our aim is to finish our mission and keep our people alive. We're not here on a killing spree or a revenge bout.'

'So Lord Aerik told me,' Saera replied dryly.

'Then you'd better listen,' Ebon said. 'And you'd better remember that Drakes are stronger and tougher than humans, so don't ever underestimate them. They do rule an empire, you know.'

'Can I go and help my comrades now, sir?' she asked.

Ebon sighed and waved her away, shaking his head as he followed her back to the battle. He and Aerik were going to have to have a stern talk with some of these newer revolutionaries. They were too bloodthirsty for their own good and it would put a lot of people at risk. Shelving that thought for another time, Ebon hefted his walking stick and charged the Drake wagon.

While Ebon led the attack on the streets, Aerik led his black clad 'elite' unit against the main wagon. They fired short bows that they had stripped off dead Samurai and stolen from raided barracks, but unfortunately their skill with the weapon was poor despite their attempts at training. For the most part, they considered it a major achievement when they even hit the wagon. The Samurai had no bows to return fire, so they hunkered down under their shields and waited for the humans to run out of ammunition.

When Aerik realised that the other Drakes in the street were dead or unconscious, he took his force down the ladders onto the streets to face the remaining Samurai. He had no fear that they would flee with the wagon — fleeing combat was a dishonour that no Drake Samurai would ever contemplate. It was far better to die in battle and dwell with honour in heaven. When the Drakes saw the six black clad figures on the street approaching them, they cautiously lowered their shields and drew their swords to meet the spirits in combat.

The four Drakes moved forward cautiously, gaining speed when it became obvious that no one was going to fire arrows at them. Aerik stood at the front of the formation and shouted an order, and his comrades each pulled three metal discs from their belts and hurled them at the Drakes. The discs were cut in star shapes, weighted for throwing and barbed to cause as much damage as possible on impact. Two Drakes shouted in pain and surprise as the stars hit them, one in the forearm and one in the snout.

Aerik let the Drakes recover and move forward once more, before calling out the same command again. Once more, the humans dug into their belts and pulled free a throwing weapon, but this time the Drakes were ready. As the six objects arced towards them, the Drakes raised their shields to block the missiles, just as Aerik had hoped they would. Instead of sharpened stars, they had thrown hollowed chicken eggs filled with itching powder and metal shavings that exploded into a white cloud as it hit the shields.

Aerik had used the powder in many childhood pranks, but now it served a far more deadly purpose. Before they knew it, the Drakes were almost blinded as their eyes watered and itched despite all their best efforts to blink away the distraction. Aerik shouted a third command and they charged forward to engage the Drakes.

With his greater numbers and tactical advantage, Aerik finished the Drakes while receiving only minor wounds to two of his comrades. When the last wagon guard was dead, Aerik quickly ordered his men to take control of the cargo.

'Ebon, what do we have?' he asked as his Lieutenant jumped up on the wagon and pulled the coverings open.

'More than we ever dreamed,' Ebon grinned. 'Close to ten thousand gold Shills at a guess.'

'Ten thousand?' Aerik asked. 'By the gods, that must be a whole region's taxes. That will buy ...' Aerik tried to calculate quickly how many slaves he could buy off the blocks with that much money, but the numbers were too much for him.

'It will buy many people's freedom,' Ebon finished. 'But we still need to get it out of here.'

'Of course,' Aerik nodded. 'Load the Drakes and their weapons onto the wagon and get it out of sight. Take it to the warehouse and strip it down to lumber, then move everything back to the Manor. Make sure no one notices you shifting the cargo or we can be sure they'll report it to the Drakes in hope of a trustee placement.'

Ebon nodded and jumped swiftly into action. Aerik glanced around at his companions in black, who were reclaiming any arrows that could be reused. He gave a sharp whistle and they all left what they were doing and clambered up the ladders onto the rooftops, quickly disappearing from sight. Minutes later, Ebon cracked a whip and the wagon lumbered from view, leaving the street empty and deserted. The only signs that a battle had taken place were the blood stains on the cobblestones which the coming storm would wash clean away, leaving the Drakes to wonder what had happened to their caravan.

Chapter 11

Annah sung softly as she finished the delicate scrollwork on her latest commission. It was a long curving katana, designed for a company Commander who led his troops from the thick of battle. It was elegant and beautiful, but it was also well balanced, light and deadly. Kelkh had designed it well, and his trust in Annah and her skills had grown to such a level that he knew she would make it flawlessly. She lost herself to the room around her, forgot the smells and the sights and just concentrated on the music that flowed through her mind with barely a conscious thought.

'It truly is a beautiful weapon.'

Annah's eyes snapped open at the sound of the voice, a human voice not a Drake's. She looked around for the person who had spoken, but saw no one. As her head swept from side to side, it dawned on her that the room she was in wasn't familiar. The simple forge that she was so accustomed to had gone, replaced by a room of crystal and stone. With another nervous glance around her for the source of the voice, Annah scrambled to her feet and went to inspect the unfamiliar surroundings.

Built with unnatural skill, the stone and crystal had been fashioned into a single seamless wall, carved with elegant scrollwork and alien writing. Annah looked out the crystal window and saw nothing outside but heavy grey mist. For a moment she thought she saw something hovering in the mist, a vague outline of a face, but it was gone too quickly for her to be sure.

'Ah, yes, a beautiful weapon.'

Annah jumped and spun around to see a tall, human male, wearing long robes woven in a rainbow of colours. He stood in the middle of the room, holding the sword Annah had just finished, turning it in his hands to see how it caught the light.

'Nothing to say, my dear girl?' he asked.

'Who are you?' she stammered finally. 'Where am I? How did I get here?'

'My, my,' he sighed, putting the sword back down with a regretful pat. 'From nothing at all to a flood of questions — we will have to work on that. I am Taan and you are in my home, such as it is. You're here because I brought you here to serve my purpose.'

'I serve Master Kelkh Ironbound and no other unless he sells my contract,' Annah replied. 'When he realises that I'm not on his property, he will come looking for me.'

'Oh, but you are on his property,' Taan grinned. 'You are at this very moment asleep in your room, happily burrowed into your blankets. But your mind ... ah, your mind is in a different place altogether.'

Annah frowned as she tried to understand. 'You mean this is a dream?'

'In a way, yes,' Taan laughed. 'But this is far more powerful than those petty imaginings you call dreams.'

'Why am I here?' Annah asked. For some indefinable reason the old man frightened her.

'You're here because you are special,' he said. 'You have a power inside you that you cannot begin to understand and you need my help to control it.'

'I already have teachers,' Annah replied, backing away from him. 'Master Kelkh teaches me to use the Forgesong and Lord Ishkal teaches me to master my physical body.'

'Bah, Drake teachers,' Taan scoffed. 'How much can you learn from a race that threw you into slavery and forbade you your most basic rights? They will use you to their own ends and then throw you away once they're finished.'

'No, they wouldn't,' Annah said. 'Not Master Kelkh and not Lord Ishkal.'

Taan looked at her for a long time, his gaze becoming hard and merciless. Annah took another step backwards as she watched the sudden transformation. 'One last chance, girl,' he said. 'Learn from me willingly and I will teach you what I know. Defy me, and face the consequences.'

'Get away from me,' she cried. 'Take me back home!'

Taan's eyes narrowed dangerously. 'Very well, you can go home. But I will call on you again and you *will* learn.'

Taan waved his hand and the world in front of Annah's eyes swam and blurred until it was unrecognisable. The world swirled grey one last time, then she was floating away on endless black.

Annah sat bolt upright in her bed, ignoring the cold chill as the bed sheets slipped away. She couldn't remember what had woken her, just that it was a dream and it had been disturbing. She tried desperately to grasp the memory of the nightmare, but it danced mockingly out of her reach. With a frustrated sigh, she swung herself out of bed and grabbed her clothes from the wardrobe.

It was close enough to morning that she knew she couldn't go back to sleep, so she finished getting dressed and started the morning exercises that Ishkal had shown her. She took her time, leisurely completing the circuit in an hour when it usually took her half that. When she was finished, she headed to the kitchen to make breakfast.

She had just put the boar steaks in the frypan when Kelkh stepped bleary eyed from his room. Ever since the war with the Cat-Men had begun in earnest, he had been forced to abandon his late mornings and start forging early. He walked over to the table and sat heavily on the closest chair. Annah turned the heat down on the food and lifted a pot of thick garshk, a Drake coffee that made most humans violently ill. She placed the steaming pot and a large mug on the table in easy reach of Kelkh, who smiled tiredly.

Amidst the slurp of garshk and the sizzle of food on the stove, the door swung open and Ishkal stepped inside. He was dusted around the shoulders by a light sprinkling of snow, but otherwise he showed no sign of the exertions that Annah knew he had just finished. He nodded to her and sat next to Kelkh while she dished up breakfast.

'I've got a new order in for you this morning, girl,' Kelkh said, stuffing the last piece of steak into his mouth and tearing off a hunk of bread. 'A battle halberd for Count Arai's son, Captain Illik of the fifth Legion.'

'Of course, master,' Annah replied, curtsying lightly.

'The specifications are on my drawing board in the forge,' he said. 'You can get started after you and Ishkal have finished your lessons.'

Annah curtsied again and sat down to her own breakfast. She sat quietly at the table, still not completely used to eating with her master but enjoying it nonetheless. She listened to Ishkal and Kelkh talk about the war with the Cat-Men, understanding little but trying to follow as best she could. When she was finished, she tidied away the food and cleaned the dishes while Kelkh set up his forge and Ishkal stepped outside to prepare her next lesson.

The morning flew by as it always did, with Ishkal working her to the best of her abilities and beyond. As well as her usual training, he gave her a new tool called a palah that looked like a child's toy. It was a pair of balls made of woven reeds, joined by a length of string. Annah stood in the cold morning air for almost an hour, twirling one of these palah in each hand and trying to follow the patterns that Ishkal showed her. She held one of the balls in one hand while she twirled the other in circles and attempted to keep it moving in a fluid pattern, while at the same time making sure it didn't get tangled up with the palah in her other hand. She decided after an hour that she wasn't very good at it.

According to Ishkal, the palah were warrior weapons of his ancestors, designed to strengthen the muscles in the wrists for fighting and improve coordination. They forced the warrior to concentrate equally on each hand and not to forget what one hand was doing because they were concentrating too much on the other. Annah nodded wearily and tried to look attentive, despite the array of bruises on her body where a misdirected palah ball had hit her.

When her time with Ishkal was up, Annah hurried back to the

house, stopping only to dunk her head in a water barrel to wash off some of the morning's accumulated grime, and headed for Kelkh's forge. She heard the joyous notes of the Forgesong well before she entered the room, but she knew better than to disturb Kelkh when he was deep in his forging. Following his instructions, she found the specifications for her day's commission on his workbench and took them to her corner of the forge, where Kelkh had set up a small anvil for her own use.

For the next hour, Annah leafed through the specifications, making notes of the measurements and the weighting requirements that Kelkh wanted. When she was certain that she had all the information memorised, she walked to the storage bins at the back of the forge. Having honed her muscles under Ishkal's tutelage, Annah had no trouble hefting the metal bricks from the bins and carrying them to the anvil, where she set them side by side in preparation for forging.

The halberd was to have a burnished bronze handle the colour of stained wood and a broad silver blade with gold inlay. Looking at the specifications, Annah could tell it would be a work of art — provided she did her job properly. Picking up the first bronze brick, Annah closed her eyes and looked inside herself for the spark of magic that Kelkh had taught her to use. Before she even realised her mouth had opened, the Forgesong came flowing out and a second tune of magic joined Kelkh's in the warm stones of the forge.

Time lost all meaning as Annah gave herself completely to the magic of her creation. The bronze bricks melted into liquid blobs on the anvil, still cool but easily malleable in Annah's hands. Using the exacting standards of the Song and her own sense of perfection, she shaped the molten bronze into a metal shaft six feet long.

It was impossibly straight, perfectly round and imbued with a strength that was available to only the minute few in every generation who claimed the honour of being named a Forger. Dark veins of metal shot through the lighter bronze, giving the halberd shaft the swirling grain look of polished darkwood, and Annah allowed herself a swell of pride as her creation took form.

She quickly put her pride aside as she finished the halberd shaft, adding the final touches, smoothing any rough patches and polishing the metal until it shone. She could feel the power swell inside her, stronger than anything she had ever felt before and she knew that this weapon would be her finest work yet. Placing the completed shaft back on the anvil, she picked up a brick of silver and started work on the halberd blade.

Lost in a dream of magic and imagination, Annah barely even noticed as her hands flowed and moulded the weapon blade. She wasn't even aware that she had picked up the gold brick until she looked down and saw the roaring dragon inlay that she had moulded into the blade. As she brought the blade and shaft of the weapon together, she felt the power of the Forgesong swell to a crescendo of magic. The blade moulded to the shaft as though they were meant for each other, creations of metal that were destined to become a single creation of power.

Annah cried out as the Forgesong reached its pinnacle and for the briefest of moments she thought she heard another voice singing along with hers. Had she stopped to consider it, she might have been curious, but she was too far lost in the Song.

When her creation was finished and the Forgesong faded, the

room came slowly back into focus. Kelkh stood proudly at the far end of the forge, watching as his protégée finished her latest creation. He smiled at her and she smiled back while she let the Forgesong fade into nothing. She held the halberd out, looking at the beautiful weapon she had created. She still heard the Forgesong echoing in her head, but for some reason it wasn't her own voice that was singing.

'You were warned,' the voice whispered. 'Now, you will learn.'

Annah felt dread form like ice in her stomach, and in that instant of fright she let her creation fall. Time slowed as the halberd dropped towards the ground, and it seemed to Annah as though her body was moving through honey when she tried to reach out and catch the shaft. With agonizing slowness she forced her body to move, positioning her knees underneath the weapon so it would hit her rather than the floor.

It was an irrational fear, born of instinct rather than any real thought; the halberd was created and strengthened by the Forgesong and could never be damaged by something as mundane as being dropped on the floor. But Annah tried to save it nonetheless. The halberd touched her legs and time sped up in a rush, much to Annah's dismay.

As soon as it touched her, the halberd lost all shape and form, melting and falling all over her arms and lap. She cried in agony as the metal sank through her skin and ran like fire in her veins, burning its way into her body in seconds. Annah felt Kelkh's arms wrap around her and she heard his deep voice speaking to her in panicked tones, but she couldn't understand the words. All she knew was the fire under her skin and the pain in her mind.

Darkness crowded in around the edges of her consciousness,

and she almost welcomed its approach. The pain was so real, she longed for any release she could find. She surrendered herself to the dark and as the familiar sound of Kelkh's voice faded away, she heard the mocking sound of laughter ringing in her ears.

CHAPTER 12

'I've got some news you need to hear.'

Aerik looked up from his desk as Ebon stepped into his office. Since the attacks on the Drakes had become more organised and the spoils of those attacks had become more worthwhile, Aerik had set up one of the empty manor rooms as his office and command centre. Papers and crude reports were spread out over a large granite topped desk that had been too large for the manor's former owner to bother moving, and Aerik almost looked lost as he sat in the midst of it all.

'I suppose I could do with a break from all this for a few minutes,' Aerik sighed. 'What have you got for me?'

'I'm not going back to command my resistance cell.'

Aerik stared up at him in surprise — that wasn't what he had expected. To be honest, Aerik had expected Ebon to leave weeks ago and return to the men under his own command.

'Why?' he asked, realising as he said it that a more enthusiastic response might have been called for.

'Because I've found what I've been looking for,' Ebon smiled. 'I've been preparing our people for years, hoping to find a leader who could unite us and rally our cause.'

'But you—'

'I'm no great leader,' Ebon said, cutting short Aerik's protest. 'I've been building and training resistance cells for five years, and not once did I consider smelting our stolen equipment and selling it at the markets. I never thought we had the time or resources to train our people. Dear gods, I never thought of stealing *Drake money* and using it to buy our people's freedom from the slave block! But you did. In only a few months, you did all that.'

'I'm no great leader either, Ebon,' Aerik said. 'I am a bard slave who saw his brother and sister-in-law killed by Drake cruelty.'

'But look at what you've accomplished.'

Ebon spread his arms out wide, encompassing the whole manor and all that it symbolised. It was their headquarters, their training ground, their safe-house and their home. It was a reality that Aerik had built when no one else had even dreamed it was possible. Looking around at everything Ebon indicated, Aerik was torn between pride at his creation and fear at having the responsibility of another group of resistance fighters.

'But this isn't how we do things,' Aerik said. 'Each cell has its own leader and is answerable to no one else. The other cells won't follow me.'

'Things change, Aerik,' Ebon said. 'The cells are joining together and leaders are starting to appear. There are four men and two women so far who command two or more fighting cells. You'll make it seven.'

'Why not let them take the leadership,' Aerik replied. 'If they want the responsibility then they can damn well have it.'

'They're not you, Aerik,' Ebon said. 'They're tough slaves, brutes and thugs made into leaders by circumstance. They're the fittest out of all those who have died in our cause, but they don't have the skill and cunning you show in your plans. They think with their blades and they'll eventually get us all killed.'

Aerik put his head in his hands and groaned. He'd created a runaway cart that was carrying him along in its wake. When he started, his one goal was revenge for his brother. He had killed Drakes for that purpose, but in time his rage and hurt had subsided. What did he fight for now?

To keep his people alive and to make the future a better place for Rebecca to live. He had built this resistance cell into something more than Ebon had hoped, and now his creation was carrying him along whether he wanted it or not.

'I wouldn't give my faith or my men to just anyone,' Ebon said.

Aerik looked up at him and nodded. 'You stay on the cart until the end of the line,' he said, quoting an old slave proverb from the mine shafts.

'Yes, you do,' Ebon nodded. 'Does that mean you accept?'

'I do,' Aerik said. 'Gods give me strength, I do.'

Ebon just nodded, happy that Aerik had accepted and willing to leave things at that. Besides, he had more news he was not looking forward to delivering — but he couldn't put it off any longer. 'I've got something else you need to hear.'

Aerik heard something in Ebon's voice and he looked hard at his friend's grim face. 'Ebon, what's happened?'

'The Drakes have liquidated the Mirin ghetto,' Ebon said softly.

Aerik's face turned ashen. 'All of them?'

'All of them.'

'Two hundred people,' Aerik said in a strangled voice. 'Why would the Drakes kill two hundred people?'

'The resistance cell for that ghetto was led by a man called

Umbar. I didn't train him personally, but I know the type — strong and mean but not too bright. He led one too many botched raids and the Drakes caught on. They weren't sure how much of the slave population was part of or sympathetic to the 'uprising', and two hundred humans is an insignificant part of their overall slave force. So they decided it was easier just to kill everyone.'

For the next few minutes, Aerik just sat, staring into space as he thought about the casual murder of two hundred people. He thought of the complete disregard that the Drakes had for the human race and he thought once again about the night that Monta and Tisa were killed. He hadn't thought about that night for many weeks, but now it hung before him like a banner, reminding him what he was doing and why he fought. All his doubt and all his second-guessing was buried beneath a fire of rage. It would be back, he knew — it would always be there, the gnawing doubt that he was leading people to their deaths for no good reason, but right now it was a tiny voice in the back of his mind.

'What are the Drakes doing with Mirin now that there are no slaves left to live in it?' he asked.

'They're shipping a hundred and fifty new slaves in from the provinces,' Ebon replied. 'They'll be here in a week.'

'I want you to gather a team to meet them on the first day and set up a resistance cell there. That town uses the same ro-khill paddies and mine shafts as we do, and I want our teams to run both slave towns.'

Ebon blinked in surprise; he'd expected Aerik to be devastated, angry and emotional, but this cold calculation was completely unexpected. 'Of course, I'll get on it right away,' he said when he realised Aerik was waiting for a response.

'You've got something to say?' Aerik asked.

Ebon winced, realising he hadn't covered his surprise at all. 'I guess I just hadn't expected you to move so quickly, that's all.'

'As you've already pointed out, Ebon, there are other resistance cells out there who are expanding their influence. A completely new ghetto full of slaves is an opportunity they won't miss.'

'I understand that,' Ebon said. 'But why do you want this all of a sudden? Five minutes ago you didn't want to take over my team, let alone want to start up a new one somewhere else.'

'Five minutes ago I had no idea that two hundred people were dead,' Aerik said grimly. 'You've reminded me that I have a responsibility to see what I've started through to the end, and now you've given me a vivid example of *why* I have to see it through. If there'd been a trained and component resistance cell in that town, the Drakes would have had no idea what was going on and two hundred people might still be alive. I won't let that happen again while I can do something to avoid it.'

'I understand,' Ebon said. He turned and started towards the door so he could make the necessary preparations, stopping short when Aerik called out to him.

'Ebon, I want you to get teams one and five ready to go out tonight. We're going to make the Drakes pay for this.'

Ebon nodded and hurried from the room. Aerik stared at the door until Ebon's footsteps had disappeared down the corridor, and when he was certain that he was alone, he put his head in his hands and let the tears flow unheeded down his face.

'Good evening, Sergeant Dankin.'

Dankin leapt to his feet and snapped to attention, nearly dislodging the carved pipe sticking out of his snout. He made a desperate snap at it and caught it firmly between his teeth before it dropped to the walkway and he risked losing it to the murky waters of the ro-khill paddies. When the Samurai Captain stepped into view, Dankin almost wished he had just let the pipe drop.

'You may be at ease, Sergeant,' the Captain said.

Dankin breathed a quiet sigh of relief and took the pipe from his mouth. The Captain had only been assigned to the ro-khill paddies for a week and Dankin didn't yet have a feel for how strict the officer was with minor matters of protocol.

'Can I help you with anything, sir?' he asked.

'Perhaps you can,' the Captain replied. 'How long have you been stationed here?'

'Ten years, sir,' Dankin said. 'Just after I was injured in the battle of Karendale.'

'Ten years is a long time, Sergeant,' the Captain said. 'A soldier could learn a great deal about a place in ten years.'

'Yes, sir,' Dankin agreed dutifully.

The Captain nodded and moved to the edge of the walkway where he stood and stared out into the growing darkness. The sounds of night washed over him; the gurgle of the water in the ro-khill paddies, the soft lap of the ripples against the walkway support posts, and the shrill buzzing of mosquitoes as they searched for something softer than a Drake's scales to feed on.

'Tell me something, Sergeant,' the Captain said finally. 'In your ten years here, have you battled many foes?'

'Not unless you count boredom and solitude, sir,' Dankin snorted.

'Dangerous foes, they are,' the Captain nodded. 'They can kill a Drake quicker than a pitched battle, and I have seen the effects of it in this garrison since I first arrived here.'

'How do you mean, sir?'

'Don't play innocent, Sergeant. I know you must see the laxity that has crept into your troops.'

'They're Drakes of action, sir,' Dankin mumbled defensively. 'They're good, honourable Samurai, skilled at any and every task I give them — but this lack of danger or challenge blunts their edge. No soldier can stay at peak readiness when there's no enemy to defend against.'

'But there is an enemy, Sergeant,' the Captain said. 'These humans are our enemy. They bow and scrape in front of us, while they plot to kill us behind our backs.'

Dankin grimaced at the Captain's words. So he was one of *those* ones — one of the few Drakes who thought that humans were the ones responsible for the disappearance of every missing Drake in the Empire.

'Sir, with all due respect, these humans are no enemy. They're a weak, cowardly breed and none too bright. They don't have the organisation to be any threat.'

'They did once, Sergeant. Once, long ago, they were our greatest threat. They were a power even greater than the Cat-Men and we fought them for supremacy of this world.'

'That's just legend, sir,' Dankin laughed. 'Made up by some Drake who wanted to romanticise the origins of his house slaves.'

'I take it that you have never seen Darendall then?' the Captain asked. 'Humans still hold sway there, you know. Their Empire remains independent, despite the best efforts of our armies.'

Dankin sighed heavily, sorry that he'd ever entered into this conversation. All he really wanted to do was finish his pipe and keep on with his patrol, but the Captain seemed content to look out into the shadowy ro-khill paddies and listen to the steady lap of water.

'Sir, the humans of Darendall remain independent because our armies have been busy fighting the Cat-Men.'

Dankin paused, knowing that wasn't entirely true. Originally, the increase in Cat-Men raids had been the reason why the war on Darendall had stopped, but that was nearly three hundred years ago according to the histories. The humans had been inexplicably determined in keeping the Drakes out of their land ever since, and Dankin expected the Captain to say just that in response.

But the Captain was no longer listening. He stood at the edge of the walkway, staring at the water's surface six inches from his feet.

'Is something wrong, sir?' Dankin asked.

'I've never seen the water bubble like that, Sergeant,' the Captain murmured. 'Why would it be doing that, do you think?'

Dankin never had a chance to reply. The water erupted as two black figures burst upwards and grappled the startled Captain. The first figure drove a knife into the Captain's neck, while the second grabbed his belt and yanked him into the water. Dankin drew his sword and charged forward to help, but it was too late. The Captain lay motionless under the three foot deep water, barely visible in the flickering torchlight of the guard post. The weight of his armour kept his body on the muddy lake floor after the black clad figures slipped out of sight; but as he stared into the murky water, Dankin knew the Shadows were there somewhere.

Dankin was suddenly gripped by a surge of fear and he jumped away from the water. He was a swordsman of many years experience and had fought bravely in wars for decades. He feared no living being and understood that death in battle was an honour to aspire to — but to fight a Shadow, that was another thing altogether. How did one fight an evil spirit with nothing but plain steel? His mind raced as he tried to think of some possible way that he could kill a Demon, some way that he could even the odds against him.

Frantically, he dredged up every myth that his grandmother had spun about the Shadows, looking for any hint to what might save him. SongForged metal was rumoured to harm supernatural creatures, but that was little help — Dankin had neither the money nor the influence to buy such a magical weapon. But the Captain did. He was the youngest son born of wealthy nobility and he wore his SongForged, gold gilded katana with pride.

Dankin was seconds from diving into the water after the sword when a black painted arrow thudded into the walkway not three feet from him. Acting on years of experience, he tracked the arrow's path back to its source and found another black figure standing on the walkway with a bow in hand, knocking another arrow.

Dankin knew right away that he would never reach the Captain's sword, not with two Shadows in the water and another with a bow pointed at him. Drawing his own sword, he charged down the walkway to reach the Shadow before it could fire another arrow.

The Shadow fired the arrow hastily, sacrificing aim for speed as Dankin hurtled along the walkway. The arrow glanced off the Drake's shoulder, doing little more than scratching his painted armour. The Shadow muttered a very mortal curse and dropped the bow in favour of a black short sword. Priming his mind for battle, Dankin sized up his opponent and formulated a strategy for fighting on the slick walkway — his fear was momentarily forgotten as his instinct took over and he fell under the sway of battle rage.

The black figure did not charge, nor did it run. It just stood, with sword drawn, waiting for Dankin to approach. The old Sergeant sneered at his opponent's stupidity and wondered why the Shadow didn't take advantage of his lack of mobility. With his crippled foot, Dankin would have had a harder time fighting out in the open, but on the walkway that drawback was removed. He screamed a battle roar and quickly closed the gap, effortlessly breaking through the concealed wire that ran across the walkway.

Dankin never realised his mistake; as soon as the wire snapped, it released a catch that held the trap in place. A supple tree branch was bent into a U shape with a dagger tied to one end. When the catch was released, the branch swung out like a spring and the dagger hit Dankin's chest with enough force to knock him backwards onto the walkway.

Dankin lay on the wooden slats, looking in disbelief at the tiny hole in his armour that was rapidly filling with red. As his vision dimmed, he saw the black clad figure walk towards him, sword drawn and bow slung over its shoulder.

Aerik stood in the shadows, watching the guardhouse and waiting for the time to strike. He heard a whisper of movement behind him and turned to see Ebon creeping towards him.

'Is the perimeter clear?'

'All guards accounted for,' Ebon nodded. 'With an extra bonus. The guard Captain was out on patrol with the watch Sergeant. We got 'em both.'

'Good work,' Aerik said. 'That means one less Drake than we thought in the guardhouse.'

'There's more,' Ebon smiled. 'The guard Captain was a noble. He was wearing gilded full plate and I think his sword is magic.'

Ebon held up a long bladed katana for Aerik's inspection. It was a work of art in every possible aspect. The hilt was chased in gold and the pommel carefully sculpted in the shape of a wolf's head. The silver blade was polished to a high shine, with lines of some black metal running through it to create images that danced and moved in front of their eyes. It weighed almost nothing, but Aerik knew it was probably stronger than steel. No Drake would ever carry a sword that would break under battle conditions, as such a thing would be a devastating blow to their honour.

'Very impressive,' Aerik said.

'I thought you'd be pleased,' Ebon replied.

'It'll look good on you,' Aerik nodded, handing the blade back.

'Me?' Ebon asked. 'But I though you should ...'

'You lead more field sorties than I do, Ebon,' Aerik smiled. 'I'm more for planning than execution. That sword will do more damage in your hands than mine.'

'Thank you,' Ebon grinned. 'Sir.'

Aerik frowned in mock fury and jabbed a finger at Ebon's chest. 'You 'sir' me one more time, Ebon, and I'm going to take that sword off you and give it to Saera!'

'I'll be good, I promise,' Ebon chuckled, holding up his hands in surrender. 'Speaking of Saera, has there been any improvement?'

'She seems less anxious to kill every Drake she sees,' Aerik replied. 'I'd say that counts as improvement. And she hasn't let her rage direct her battle movements for a week or so.'

'That's good,' Ebon nodded. 'I still worry about her, though.'

'Amongst others,' Aerik sighed. 'But this is a discussion for another time. Are we ready to move on the guard house?'

Ebon cupped his hands around his mouth and gave a single loud owl hoot. It was returned three times a moment later and Ebon nodded to Aerik. 'We're ready.'

'Good, then let's finish this. Lead the way, Ebon.'

Ebon hooted again, then moved towards the guardhouse with Aerik and two other figures trailing behind him. Clad in their usual clothes, hoods and face masks, they were just another piece of shadow in a night landscape. Even they couldn't spot the other three teams moving towards their targets in the complex, and they knew that their comrades were out there. The Drakes, cocooned in their sense of superiority, were completely oblivious.

Ebon reached the corner of the barracks, near a thick trunked tree and as far away from any windows as possible. Aerik boosted Ebon into the lower branches and from there Ebon climbed the rest of the way with the aid of some bent-nail climbing gloves.

When he reached the barracks roof, Ebon found a thick bough that was sturdy enough to hold a man's weight and tied a knotted rope to it. He dropped the other end of the rope down to Aerik and saw him lift a long bundle back up. Ebon grabbed the bundle, shifting position in the tree to account for the new weight, then swung it over his shoulder and stepped lightly onto the roof.

By the time Aerik and the other two revolutionaries climbed up the rope and stepped onto the roof, Ebon had already removed a number of tiles to open an access hole into the roof cavity. On his silent order, they crawled into the dark, cramped ceiling of the Drake barracks.

The Drakes built all their barracks along the same traditional lines — the walls were stone for the first meter off the ground, with wooden pillars set at regular intervals that supported the roof. Between each pillar were walls made of thick bamboo and woven matting. The roof was triangular and supported by beams a foot in diameter, with an internal ceiling made of tightly bundled straw.

Ebon, Aerik and their companions crept across the beams, making sure that they stayed off the straw. One misstep and they would have fallen through the straw ceiling and landed on the laps of some very irate Drakes.

They followed Aerik's directions until they reached the sleeping quarters. Ebon carefully lifted the straw ceiling bundles and passed them to Aerik who stacked them carefully on a beam. Taking a firm grip on Ebon's forearm, Aerik lowered him into the dark room, listening to the rhythmic sounds of breathing for any change in tempo or depth that might indicate that the Drakes had woken up and been alerted to Ebon's presence. But there was none, and in barely a minute Ebon returned to the hole where Aerik pulled him back up. They replaced the straw bundles and moved back towards the main barracks, the sound of breathing conspicuously silent behind them.

They moved swiftly through the roof cavity towards the common room, in case the bodies of the dead Drakes were discovered before their work was complete. They slowed when they heard the low rumble of Drake voices and saw the flicker of firelight through the gaps in the ceiling. Aerik pushed the ceiling bundles apart until he had a small opening, and with Ebon gripping him firmly by the back of his shirt, he knelt over and looked through the peephole. He counted how many Drakes were in the room and motioned each of his comrades to a position above them.

At Ebon's command, they moved a straw bundle so they could see their targets, and readied the fire hardened spears that he had carried in the material bundle. He held up his hand and counted down to one on his fingers and all four of them dropped in unison, spears held firmly in their hands.

The Drakes were dead before they even realised what had happened.

'What do we do now?' Ebon asked, looking around the sparse guardhouse.

'Strip the bodies and take anything of value,' Aerik said. 'Then empty the warehouse and get me every sack of ro-khill you can find. We'll sell it on the black market once the price spikes.'

'What about the paddies and the facility?'

Aerik looked around grimly, remembering the years of slavery he'd spent in these very paddies. He imagined himself as a child, wading through the murky water, trying desperately to keep his ro-khill sack dry. And he imagined Rebecca, his brother's beautiful girl and now his ward, wading through the muck with nothing but death waiting as a reward.

'Burn it,' he said. 'Burn it all.'

Chapter 13

Annah stood on top of a hill, looking down at the world around her. The hill and the surroundings were unknown to her, but as she looked out at the scenery she could not help but be stirred by its beauty under the twilight sky. Her clothing was different as well, she realised finally; she was dressed in boiled leather armour, dyed a rich violet with matching clothes underneath. A violet cloak was draped over her shoulders and in her hands she held the halberd she had created in Kelkh's forge.

'The halberd,' she thought, looking at it curiously. The halberd had become one with her, become a part of her when she finished its forging — but if that was the case, then how could it also be here in her hands? Had she been dreaming, dreaming that she had forged this weapon and it had melted into her? Was she dreaming now?

A peal of thunder broke the still night and bolts of lightning struck up a dance on the horizon. Annah watched them dully, not certain enough of anything to know what she should be doing.

'Greetings, Annah.'

She looked around to see Taan standing five feet from her, staring at her with a sinister glint in his eyes. Annah stepped back and held her halberd up warily.

'You shouldn't wave that around, my dear,' Taan said. 'Someone might get hurt. Think of all the damage you've caused with it already.'

'What are you talking about?' she asked.

'Why, look for yourself.'

Taan waved a gloved hand at something behind her, and with a wary look at the strange man, she looked in that direction.

'Oh, by The Dragon, no,' she moaned. 'No, please.'

Lying on the hill, eyes open to stare eternally at the grey sky, lay Kelkh and Ishkal. Mange was a crumpled heap lying further down the slope and beyond him lay more shadows cloaked in darkness.

'Tsk, tsk, tsk,' Taan sighed. 'The things you do when you're in a temper, my dear.'

'No, it wasn't me. It couldn't have been — I could never …'

But then the memories flooded back to her, horrifying in their clarity and detail. She had done it, she had killed them all and many others who had stumbled across her path. She was a monster, a remorseless killer who had spawned chaos across the Empire. Her legs buckled underneath her and she fell to the ground in a heap, stomach roiling at the memory of her actions. She had enough clarity of mind to hang her head over the hill while she was sick.

In the distance, the thunder rolled and lightning flashed, and as if in response to Annah's tears, the skies opened and rained down on her.

'What have I done?' she sobbed.

'What you were born to do, nothing more,' Taan said. 'You are beast, my dear, a creature of rage and instinct. If you don't do what I tell you to, then this vision will become reality.'

'No, I won't,' she replied automatically.

'Look at what you have done here and think carefully about your answer,' Taan snarled. 'I will not be denied this!'

'No,' she screamed.

The rage and pain burst from her like a flood, and before she realised what she was doing, she jumped to her feet and swung her halberd at Taan with all of her might. Taan looked surprised for a moment, then his expression changed to anger. A stream of metal flowed from his body like water, forming a mesh shield which effortlessly blocked Annah's attack.

'Insolent girl,' he snarled. 'You will learn to do my bidding, or you will learn to expect the punishment I shall inflict on you!'

Taan's shield warped, twisting into a dozen mesh fists that lunged forward and attacked her. She dodged most of the first wave through skill and instinct born of Ishkal's training, but there were simply too many fists to avoid them all. One caught her a vicious blow to the hip, spinning her around and knocking her to her knees. She lashed out with her halberd, slicing another in half down the middle, but it quickly reformed and struck back with a vengeance.

Annah lost her grip on the halberd and threw both arms above her head, trying to fend off the worst of the beating. Taan stood to the side, indifferent to the rain and lightning that played around him, watching the punishment that his magic exacted. She saw his mouth move and she tried desperately to focus on what he was saying, but the darkness of sleep was rushing to save her from the nightmare. As she drifted away, she heard his voice echoing in her mind.

'You will learn.'

'I don't care how it happened, I just want to know what it's done to her!'

Ishkal sighed and took a long drink of scalett, then picked up the half empty bottle and refilled both his and Kelkh's glasses.

'Knowing how this happened will give us a better grasp on what it has done to her,' he said. 'For the moment, at least, she seems to be fine.'

'Fine for someone who has six foot of halberd fused into her body,' Kelkh snapped.

'All the more reason for me to go to the monastery and see if I can find out what's happened to her,' Ishkal replied. 'I let you talk me out of going once, Kelkh, but this time there's nothing you can say that will convince me. I must seek the wisdom of my Order and she must come with me. You know it's for the best.'

Kelkh glared at his friend, but it was a look filled with frustration at his own helplessness and Ishkal knew it.

'Fine, you do what you have to,' he said ungraciously. 'You just make sure the girl is given the best care, or your Order will have *me* to answer to.'

'A situation to be avoided at all costs,' Ishkal replied. 'Where is she?'

'You're leaving now?' Kelkh asked.

'The sooner the better,' Ishkal said. 'She's strong enough to travel and we need to get her quickly to people who can help her if something more goes wrong.'

Kelkh sighed and dropped into a chair, feeling impossibly tired. 'She's feeding Mange. Her things are in a chest at the foot of her bed — I don't think her last master liked her having ornaments and I've never been able to convince her it's all right to put things around her room.'

Ishkal nodded and pushed away from the table. 'My things are in my room — it won't take me long to pack. Will you come and say goodbye?'

'No,' Kelkh said, shaking his head. 'I've too much work to do.'

After a moment's hesitation he dug into his pocket and pulled out a small package, carefully wrapped in paper and tied with thin ribbon. He stared at it for a moment, then handed it to Ishkal.

'I made it for her as a summer festival present. Give it to her when you go, and tell her ...' Kelkh paused and looked out the window towards Mange's pen. 'Just tell her.'

'I will,' Ishkal smiled. 'She will be safe and back be fore you know it.'

Kelkh grunted and drained his scalett in a single swallow. He dropped the glass back on the table, then walked into his forge and quietly closed the door.

Annah sat with her back against the stable wall, teasing Mange with a lump of metal laced ro-khill. The rock dragon's head moved from side to side as she waved her hand, eyes always watching the ro-khill in her fingers. With a smile, she tossed the black lump into the air and Mange leaped forward to snap it up before it hit the floor. He flopped to the ground happily and Annah heard contented crunching sounds from him moments later.

She closed her eyes as her smile faded and she tried to relax. She was exhausted and she had no idea why. She wondered if it had anything to do with her accident in the forge, but she couldn't imagine how that was possible. Then again, she had no idea how it was possible for a six-foot halberd to melt in her hands and flow into her body either.

She opened her eyes again and picked up a lump of ro-khill, studying the spider webs of silver running through it. What had she done different that time? What had she done wrong? She knew in her heart that she hadn't done anything out of the ordinary, but her head insisted that something must have changed. Before she even realised what she was doing, she started singing and working her magic on the metal laced into the ro-khill. She had to know if she could ever forge again, or if everything she sang to would melt in her hands.

The ro-khill glowed bright gold but otherwise didn't change. It did exactly what it was meant to and Annah breathed a sigh of relief that her new found talent wasn't lost forever. But what had happened in the forge and how could she make sure that it didn't happen again?

Her thoughts were interrupted when Mange's head nuzzled into her stomach, desperately trying to push past her to reach the ro-khill in her hand. Mange stretched his tongue out as far as it would reach, desperate to grab the food.

'Be gentle, big dragon,' Annah laughed, stroking Mange's neck. 'You don't have to be so forceful; you'll get it in a minute.'

Mange looked up at her mournfully, then stretched out his tongue again. Annah laughed and moved the ro-khill into his reach. Mange quickly snatched it away and gobbled it down.

'A stranger might think you were never fed,' Annah said. 'I've never seen you so eager to get a piece of ro-khill, especially when there's a whole bag of it next to me.'

Mange looked up at her hopefully, then sniffed around the stable looking for more. Annah just shook her head and grabbed another lump from the sack.

'Here you are,' she said, holding it out.

Mange hopped over eagerly and sniffed the ro-khill, then looked up at Annah sadly. If Rock Dragons possessed vocal cords, Annah knew Mange would have been whining.

'What's the matter?' Annah asked. 'You've never turned down ro-khill before.'

Mange sniffed around one more time, then dropped to the ground on his belly with a clatter like a dropped sack of pebbles. Confused, Annah replayed the events of the last few seconds until understanding slowly dawned on her. Singing softly to herself, she used the power of the Forgesong to enchant the metal laced through the ro-khill, making it glow golden in the palm of her hand. Mange's head immediately rose from the ground, and when Annah's voice dropped to a whisper he darted forward, wrapped his tongue gently around the ro-khill and tugged at it.

'Here you are,' Annah said, releasing the ro-khill with a smile. Mange pulled the ro-khill into his mouth and crunched it contentedly as he lay back on the ground.

'He has an insatiable appetite, that one.'

Annah jumped at the unexpected sound and turned to see Ishkal walking into the stable with a small backpack slung across his shoulders. He was wearing his plain travel garb and he carried his favourite walking stick in his hands.

'Are you leaving, Master Ishkal?' Annah asked, forcing down the lump that had suddenly formed in her throat.

'We are both leaving, Annah,' Ishkal smiled. 'Kelkh and I have decided it would be in your best interests to come with me to the Golden Monastery, the home of my Order. No one in the entire Drake Empire knows more about magic and magical history than the Abbot. With his wisdom, we will find out why these things have been happening to you and what it means.'

'Is Master Kelkh coming with us?' she asked anxiously.

'No, he won't be able to,' Ishkal replied. 'He's under orders from the Emperor himself to forge weapons for the war. If he left his post, he would be declared Ronin and sentenced to death for treason.'

'Will he say goodbye?'

'Kelkh has never been one for goodbyes,' Ishkal sighed. 'I think he finds them too difficult. But I know he will miss you terribly while you are away. He gave me this to give to you, so that you have something to remember him by until we return.'

Ishkal reached into his backpack and pulled out a small package, as long as Annah's forearm and as wide as her hand. It was wrapped carefully in paper and tied with ribbon, the way that Kelkh wrapped all of his work when he had them delivered to a customer. She reached out and took it from Ishkal's waiting hands, staring at the paper as she tried to deal with the sudden upheaval of her life.

'You can open that later, Annah,' Ishkal said. 'When you're alone and you need something to cheer you up. But for now, we should get going.'

'Shall I gather my things, Master Ishkal?'

'I've already done that,' he said. 'Your trunk is outside the door. Go and put your present away, then I'll strap the trunk to Mange.'

At the sound of his name, Mange looked up sleepily from the

ground to see if he was needed. Ishkal looked at him, curled into a tight ball, like some giant, lethal cat, and chuckled to himself.

'On second thought, perhaps we'll leave your trunk here and have Mange meet us outside the city walls,' Ishkal said. 'He looks ready for a nap, and it's always a rough ride when you fly a grumpy Keldarkan.'

'How will we get to the gates, Master Ishkal?' Annah asked. 'Do you need me to call for a carriage?'

Ishkal scratched his chin thoughtfully and looked through the open section of the stable roof at the cloudless sky. 'It's the first truly nice day we've had in a long time. I think it would do us good to walk.'

They left almost immediately, waiting only long enough for Ishkal to instruct Mange when and where to meet them and ensure that the sleepy Rock Dragon understood. Ishkal set a brisk pace, but after all the training Annah had done with him she was able to keep up without any difficulty.

It wasn't until midday that they finally stopped, and by then they were almost at the city centre. Ishkal bought them each a bowl of hot broth and some fresh bread from a street vendor while Annah stared in disbelief at the bustling city. A slave for most of her life, she had only ever caught the briefest glimpses of the city as she passed through, and even then they were the less reputable parts. The city centre, with its gleaming marble buildings, parks and wide open plazas, seemed like a realm of the gods that Drakes from all the clans claimed as their birthright.

As far as she could see, she was the only human in sight, and if the looks on the faces of the passing Drakes were any indication, she was not in any way welcome. If it hadn't been for Ishkal's calm presence, Annah was certain that some of the Drakes would have killed her for her presumption. She gulped down the broth as quickly as she could, burning her tongue in the process, but she was too anxious to care. Ishkal sensed her discomfort, though, and they were on the move again quickly — much to Annah's relief.

The city swept past in a blur of magnificent buildings, too numerous for Annah to take in any of them completely, but all so very Drake in design. It wasn't until they reached one of the slave ghettos at the outskirts of the city that Annah finally started to relax. The surroundings were depressing, but at the same time comfortingly familiar.

The buildings, while cramped, drab and decrepit, were uniquely human and appealed to Annah's nature more than any Drake built mansion. Ishkal pushed ahead, while Annah lagged behind to soak up the atmosphere. When Ishkal stopped in the street, Annah didn't even realise until she walked into the back of him.

'Annah, is it normal for there to be so many people on the streets of a slave ghetto during the day?' he asked.

Annah looked around, studying the people this time and not the buildings. There were three men carrying water buckets on thick poles over their shoulders, several women carrying sacks of grain using an old fashioned hook and sling, and a man walking up the street with the aid of a walking stick. There was nothing incriminating about any of them, except the fact that all able bodied slaves were required to be at their daytime duties unless they had special dispensation.

'No, Master Ishkal,' she said. 'It's very unusual to have so many slaves not at work.'

'Then be alert,' Ishkal replied. 'There's something very wrong here.'

They moved slowly through the street and Annah's relief at being away from the city centre quickly evaporated. They approached the end of the block without incident; the slaves ignored them and Ishkal pretended that he wasn't interested at all in his surroundings. If it wasn't for the naked fear in Annah's expression, it would have looked like a perfectly normal scene — but everyone involved in the dance knew how it was going to end.

As they reached the last house on the block, the slaves made their move. One man carrying the water buckets punched out to the side with an open palm, knocking a bucket off his pole. The weight of the other bucket tipped the pole into a vertical position and the man snatched it as it fell, leaving the second bucket to fall to the ground as he pulled the pole into a quarterstaff position. It was all done so quickly that Annah hadn't even realised what had happened until the man swung a vicious strike at Ishkal — but Ishkal was never going to be surprised.

Shouting a chant that seemed strangely melodic for the opening of a battle, Ishkal dropped his pack to the ground and raised his forearm to block the staff. The enchanted bands that crisscrossed his body reacted instantly to his call, forming a mesh shield that knocked the staff harmlessly wide.

Before the man could figure out what had gone wrong, Ishkal stepped inside his guard and punched him hard in the stomach.

The man stumbled back, retching and gasping for air, and preparing himself for the blow that would end his life. Luckily for him, Ishkal had no intention of killing anyone and wasn't about to strike again. Unluckily for Ishkal, the other humans were closing in and they had every intention of killing him.

A tall, stocky man with dark brown hair darted out from the shadows and grabbed Annah in a firm hug, lifting her off her feet and carrying her swiftly out of harm's way. Her scream of surprise was Ishkal's only warning, but with her gone the other humans charged and left Ishkal with no chance to help her.

The man with the walking stick reached Ishkal first, swinging a vicious overhead blow. Ishkal stepped forward, coming under the man's arm and grabbing his wrist. Before the surprised man could react, Ishkal yanked his arm down and twisted. The man shouted in pain and dropped the walking stick to the ground, while Ishkal grabbed him by the shirt collar, spun around on his heel and bent at the waist. The man flew over Ishkal's shoulder and landed flat on his back on the cobblestones. A quick blow to the temple knocked him unconscious, but left him otherwise unharmed.

As much as he hated to hurt these people, Ishkal knew that he had to incapacitate his enemies or he would be overwhelmed by sheer numbers, and that would mean losing Annah, which was something he would not allow.

The pitch and volume of Ishkal's voice changed as the other humans advanced warily, and the bands crossing his body jumped to his command. He formed a mesh web one centimetre above his scales that acted like armour against the blunt weapons of the humans. They could still jab at him through the mesh gaps, but the power of their strikes would be reduced and a heavy swinging strike wouldn't do much at all. Confident in his mesh armour, Ishkal sprang forward and took the fight to his enemy.

'Easy, sister, we're here to rescue you,' Ebon said, carrying the struggling girl to the safety of the street edge.

'But Ishkal—' the girl started.

'Ishkal won't harm you any more,' he promised. 'We'll protect you from him. You're free now.'

'You don't understand,' she shouted. 'He wouldn't hurt me; he's trying to help me. He's my *friend*.'

Ebon dropped her gently to the ground, where two of his companions took charge of her welfare. He turned back to fight and was aghast at how badly they were doing. They hadn't taken so many injuries in a single fight since Aerik had taken control of this resistance cell; through both weight of numbers and superior planning they'd lost almost no lives at all. But watching this Gold Drake at work, Ebon realised how far they still had to come.

The Drake pivoted on one leg and kicked forward, knocking down one of his best quarterstaff fighters, and at the same time caught Saera a glancing blow to the head with his tail as she tried to flank him.

'Griff, go find Aerik and tell him that we need all the reinforcements he can muster,' Ebon shouted. 'This one's taking us apart!'

Griff nodded and sprinted into the alley, and Ebon turned back to the fight just in time to see the Drake leap two metres into the air and deliver a split kick to two men, who both hit the ground hard. Ebon shook his head in grudging admiration, then drew his sword and charged into the battle.

His last companion was knocked to the ground as he ran in and the gold scaled Drake turned his full attention to him. Ebon was a veteran of many battles and he knew better than to attack head on; he reached into his belt and tossed two egg shells full of blinding powder. The Drake gasped in surprise as the shells broke in a shower of white and immediately shut his eyes against the stinging pain.

Ebon took the advantage and swung a heavy blow at the Drake's head. He almost over-balanced when he hit nothing but air, and had to drop flat on the street to avoid catching a return blow between the eyes. He jabbed out several times with his sword as he rolled away and jumped back to his feet, but the Drake somehow managed to knock them all aside without serious damage to himself. Ebon weighed his options and decided it was be best to wait until Griff returned with reinforcements.

'You fight well when you're blind,' he said grudgingly.

'Thank you,' the Drake replied. 'It took many years of training and many painful sparring bouts, I assure you.'

'It's a shame all that time's been wasted.'

'Is this really necessary?' the Drake asked. 'I've tried very hard not to kill any of your comrades, yet you seem determined to do away with me. Why not let me pass before you or one of your friends get permanently injured?'

'Because you've seen too much,' Ebon replied.

'True, I suppose,' the Drake sighed. 'Your attack was rather ingenious, and I suppose seeing a human with a SongForged blade would shout 'revolution' to most Drakes.'

'How did you know I have a SongForged sword?' Ebon asked. Out of the corner of his eye he saw Griff returning with five more men.

'It calls to me,' the Drake replied. 'Louder than you do and louder than the footsteps of your friends approaching behind me. So there's no way for us to solve this amicably?'

'I'm afraid not,' Ebon shrugged. He waved his comrades over and raised his own sword to strike. 'For what it's worth, you're more noble than most of your kind — but I'll understand if that's not much consolation.'

Annah sat in a petrified huddle while one of the women tried to calm her down by talking gibberish in soothing tones. She watched Ishkal take the first wave of attackers apart in minutes, but the man who then charged into the fray was a far better calibre of fighter. When Griff arrived with five more revolutionaries, her worst fears came to vivid life in her mind.

'You can't do this,' she said. 'He's my friend. I won't let you.'

The woman looked anxiously to the man by her side who started to say something comforting, but Annah was beyond their words.

'I won't let you hurt him,' she said, jumping to her feet and running towards Ishkal.

The man stood to block her way, but Annah ducked underneath his arms and thrust out with an open palm strike that Ishkal had taught her. She blasted the air from his lungs and knocked him to the ground, but the woman was faster than she had expected;

she caught Annah around the shoulders and wrapped her arms around her in a bear hug.

'Let me go,' Annah screamed, but the woman held on with all of her might.

Annah saw the new wave of fighters join the battle against Ishkal, who was still hampered by the itching powder, and she saw the man she had knocked down approach with a length of rope to tie her hands. She struggled against the woman holding her and succeeded in getting one arm mostly free, but she knew her feeble efforts would be too little to help her friend.

She screamed in frustration and her vision turned red as she heard the notes of the Forgesong playing at the edge of her consciousness. She knew somehow that those notes were her salvation, but at the same time she knew that they were horribly wrong. She hesitated for just a moment, not certain that she wanted to set the magic loose but the music seemed to be guided by another power. It changed from a soft lullaby to a thundering crescendo, too powerful for her mind to contain. It burst from her mouth like water from a broken dam and the world around her disappeared.

A stream of liquid metal burst from her outstretched hand, forming into a halberd blade and shaft as it sped through the air. It struck the man approaching with the rope and stabbed deep into his shoulder. Annah swung the halberd backwards, catching the woman behind her in the stomach with the butt of the shaft, and then she was free. She stood at the side of the street, looking in distain at the weaklings around her. She was powerful, magical, a force that only the great wizards of the Empire would dare oppose, and those around her were mere pack animals.

She strode across the street towards the knot of humans surrounding the battered Ishkal. A man had his back to her, the skilled one who carried her away from the fight. She raised her halberd high and stabbed down with all her strength. At the last moment she felt a sense of revulsion at killing a man unnecessarily and she changed the angle of her attack just slightly to catch him square in the back with the flat of her blade.

The man dropped to the ground and rolled around groggily, the magic of the halberd strong enough to land a powerful blow even with just the flat of the blade. The other humans looked at her in surprise, but they had seen enough to know she was no friend of theirs. Two of them broke off their attack on Ishkal and charged. Annah laughed cruelly and prepared to meet them; all revulsion at killing was gone, buried beneath a mountain of hate and vengeance. She wouldn't use the flat of her blade this time — this time, they would die for daring to attack her.

'Hold!'

The voice cut across the battlefield in an instant. The human fighters stopped and stepped back immediately. Ishkal, still half blind, ceased his attacks but remained prepared for the fighting to resume. Annah, lost in her magic, tried to ignore the voice, but something about it cut through the haze clouding her mind. The magic fled back to wherever it came from and Annah was suddenly herself again, a young, frightened slave girl.

A man stepped into the street, striding purposefully towards Annah and Ishkal. He was short and slight, with close cropped hair and an intense but youthful face. Given the respect that the other humans showed him, Annah guessed he was some sort of leader. He stopped in front of her and waved his men back.

'Who are you?'

'My name is Annah Tress,' she replied nervously.

'You performed magic, Annah. How did you do that? I was always told humans couldn't use magic.'

'I don't know how I can use it,' she replied. 'I only found out I could do it by accident.'

'And what accident made you find out?'

'It doesn't matter,' Ishkal interrupted. 'She doesn't know how she inherited this gift, which is why we're on our way to the Abbey of the Gold Dragon. Her magic has unusual side effects that could prove dangerous. We intend to discover why.'

A low murmur passed through the humans as they shuffled uncomfortably in her presence. 'She's cursed,' one muttered. 'Look at her hair and her skin!'

'The colour of a person's hair doesn't mean they're cursed,' the leader said sharply. 'Neither does the shade of their skin. You should know better than that, Mannon.'

The crowd fell into an abashed silence, but they watched Annah with a sullen intensity that made her fearful. The young leader studied her for a few moments before coming to a decision.

'My name is Aerik,' he said. 'I'm the leader of the human resistance in this part of the Imperial City.'

'I am Ishkal the Gold,' Ishkal said. 'Drake of the Order of the Golden Dragon.'

Aerik nodded absently, but otherwise ignored Ishkal completely. He stared intensely at Annah, as if sizing her worth.

'Tell me, Annah, what will you do with your power when you learn to control it?'

'I suppose I'll keep doing what I've always done with it,' she replied, confused. 'I will assist my master, Kelkh Ironbound, in creating weapons and ornaments from the forge.'

'I see,' Aerik replied. 'You don't want freedom? No desire to receive some gain for your work?'

'I don't understand what you mean,' she stammered.

'Let me put it another way,' Aerik said, his voice hardening. 'Every day, dozens of your people are put to death by the Drakes through overwork, dangerous conditions, sloppy safety practice or plain sadistic pleasure. One town over from here, the Drakes put two hundred humans to death — an entire slave ghetto — because they found a small resistance cell. They wanted to make those deaths an example. Those humans only wanted the freedom to live their own lives their own way, and they died because they had no way to fight back. And here you are with powerful magic inside you, waiting for your command. So I ask again, what will you do with it? Will you use it to gain your own freedom and perhaps gain freedom for other humans as well?'

Annah stood agape as she struggled with the grim reality that most human slaves lived by every day. Aerik waited for her response, but she was too tired and shocked to think properly. It was Ishkal who finally broke the silence.

'I don't think Annah has ever had to contemplate that question,' he said, placing his hands protectively on her shoulders. 'She hasn't endured the hardships you have, and she might need some time to think over what you have said.'

Annah nodded quickly, relieved that she didn't have to answer. Aerik scratched his chin thoughtfully, though exactly what he was thinking was a mystery. He came to a decision quickly, running one hand through his hair and dropping the other to his dagger pommel.

'I agree, you need time to think,' Aerik said. 'So you can go free and you can have that time. I hope you understand the size of this gift, Annah Tress. I hope you understand just how wonderful a thing it is to be given your freedom, to walk away from a place with your fate in your own hands, not subject to the whims of others. Think about it.'

Annah sagged in relief, falling back onto Ishkal as he steadied her on her feet. She saw surprise on the faces of the other humans, but strangely she saw no anger. These men and women trusted Aerik, and she was glad that none of them would break his orders.

'There's just one problem we need to resolve before you go,' Aerik said. Annah felt Ishkal stiffen and she suddenly felt afraid again. 'You've injured a fellow human, Annah Tress, and that wrong must be punished. Blood for blood, that's our law.'

'You will not touch her,' Ishkal said. 'You claim to offer her the gift of freedom and the chance to leave here free from the whims of others, yet you impose your own will upon her. Is this the honour you abide by?'

It was the closest to angry that Annah had ever heard him, and that steely reassurance was all that kept her on her feet. Aerik, too, sensed Ishkal's anger, but he wasn't intimidated by it in the least. He listened to Ishkal carefully and Annah was certain that he was mentally recording every word.

'She is free, Ishkal the Gold, but freedom must be constrained by laws, otherwise her choices might restrict the freedom of others. We don't have many laws in the ghettos, but this is one that we hold sacred. The Drakes are our enemy, not each other, and if we fight amongst ourselves then we'll never be free. Nor would we deserve to be. The Drakes have a similar law, am I right?'

'They do,' Ishkal nodded. 'We are all considered children of The Dragon, and to kill a fellow Drake is a crime against The Dragon itself. Such a crime is punishable by death.'

'Then you understand,' Aerik said. 'We're one family under the yoke of the Drakes, and we won't allow fighting within our family.'

'I understand,' Ishkal replied. 'But I don't accept. You will not harm Annah, and I will fight to my last breath to stop you.'

'Then we have a stalemate,' Aerik sighed. 'I can't let that law be broken — it's all we have to bind us together.'

'You wouldn't allow mitigating circumstances?' Ishkal asked, cocking one eyebrow.

'I would, if there were any,' Aerik replied. 'But unfortunately, the truth is clear. Annah was in no danger; in fact, we took great lengths to keep her safe. She stabbed Petra in the shoulder even though there were no weapons near her. Not much to mitigate.'

'Then we truly are at an impasse,' Ishkal said.

With blinding speed, Ishkal lashed out at the two closest humans, catching them in the solar plexus. One fell to the ground gasping for breath, while the other fell to his knees and was sick on the street. The other humans belatedly brought their weapons to bear and Ishkal knew that good as he was, he couldn't defeat them all. Behind him, Ishkal heard Annah gasp for breath and start to sing the words of the Forgesong.

'Hold!'

The humans immediately backed up several steps, though there was definitely irritation on their faces this time. Annah stopped singing with a sudden croak and silence once again descended on the street.

'If you keep fighting, Ishkal the Gold, you will die,' Aerik said.

'I will fight to the last,' Ishkal growled. 'You will not harm her.'

Aerik's face broke into a bemused smile, an expression that's comforting aspect was offset by the dagger he tapped against his shoulder.

'You'd give your life for a human? I'd never have thought it possible for a Drake to offer his life to save a slave. Such honour should be rewarded. I can't pardon the crime, but as it's not a charge of murder, I can allow another to take the punishment in her place.'

'You want me to take this punishment?' Ishkal asked. 'And then you will leave Annah alone?'

'What — injure an honourable Drake?' Aerik laughed. 'And end any chance that Annah might join our cause? Besides, the laws of human slaves don't apply to you, even if you offered to take the punishment. No, that's not what I had in mind.'

Moving with a swiftness that rivalled Ishkal's, Aerik reversed his dagger blade and drove it hard into his own shoulder. He staggered slightly and gasped in pain, but remained on his feet.

'Blood for blood,' he said through clenched teeth as he pulled the dagger free. 'The law has been satisfied. You're free to go. Remember what you have learned here, Annah Tress.'

Aerik motioned to his companions and they disappeared swiftly into the alleyway, leaving Ishkal and Annah alone on the dismal street.

Chapter 14

'Of all the ideas you've had, that was the stupidest.'

Aerik held up one hand to forestall Ebon's lecture — his other arm was firmly in Lysa's grip, who was busy stitching the wound in his shoulder.

'Ebon, I've already had an earful from Lysa; I don't need it from you, too.'

He grimaced as Lysa tugged at the last stitch and tied it off. 'You deserve another lecture, Aerik,' Lysa said. 'You won't be able to lift Rebecca for a month at least.'

'I can still sing to her,' he smiled.

'And you will,' she frowned. 'Every night until you're better, and more if I decide she needs it — I don't care how busy you are!'

She snatched up her sewing needles and packed them away in a basket, then left the room to give Ebon and Aerik some privacy.

'She's just angry that I did this to myself,' Aerik sighed. 'And frightened that it could have been worse.'

'She's already lost two family members,' Ebon said. 'She doesn't want to lose you, too.'

'I know. Sometimes I wonder if I was right in dragging her into this. She should be out there flirting with some young man, dancing and drinking at The Stable, not here fighting a revolution.'

'First, you had no choice about dragging her into this; that was the Drakes' fault when they killed your family. And second, if you even hinted to Lysa that she should think about her own future instead of looking after you and Rebecca, I think she'd take to you with a broom handle.'

Aerik laughed at the thought of Lysa swinging her broom at him, but the mirth was short lived.

'Would you ever consider joining with her?' Ebon asked.

'Me?' Aerik asked, surprised. 'No, I couldn't — I don't think either of us could. We'd remind each other too much of the siblings we lost. Besides, she's too much a sister to me for her to be anything else — we're the only family either of us has left, and we love each other like family, but nothing more.'

Several emotions flitted across Ebon's face, as though he had a number of questions he wanted to ask, but wasn't really sure that it was his place to ask any of them. Finally, he settled on one.

'Aerik, I have to know — why did you do this to yourself? And why let the girl go with a Drake who knows our secret?'

'The Drake won't betray us,' Aerik said. 'There's honour in him, I sensed it. And as for the girl ... tell me, Ebon, how many humans do you know who can wield magic?'

'None.'

'And why is that?'

'Because humans can't wield magic; they've never been able to.'

'But she can!'

'Aerik, I didn't want to disagree with you in front of the others, but Mannon was right — she's cursed.'

'Why — because she looks different?'

'The legends say that any human bearing the colour of a Dragon on their bodies has been touched by The Dragon and cursed for all time!'

'And where did that legend come from?'

'I don't know,' Ebon admitted. 'Does it matter?'

'Of course it matters. If the legend came from the Drakes, then it's immediately suspect! What if they started the rumour because they knew that the greatest threat to their rule was humans who could use magic — and what better way to neutralise that threat than by turning their own people against them.'

Ebon conceded the point but didn't look convinced.

'Ebon, think about what having magic on our side could do for our cause,' Aerik said. 'Think of the lives we could save if we all had SongForged weapons like yours.'

'All right, Aerik, I admit that magic could really help us,' Ebon replied. 'But I still think you need be more careful. Losing you isn't going to help our cause either!'

'If Annah Tress ever comes back to see us then I will be, I promise,' Aerik smiled. 'Now what else do we have on our agenda today?'

Ebon pulled a battered sheet of parchment out of his pocket and scanned his own crude handwriting until he found an item that he hadn' t crossed out yet.

'You wanted to talk about getting slaves out of the city, and I also have a report for you on all Drake movements since the attack on the Mirin ghetto. Which do you want first?'

'It's best to take the bitter medicine first, so you'd better give me the Mirin report,' Aerik said.

'Since the Drakes liquidated the Mirin ghetto, they've been wary of other human insurrections in the other ghettos as well,'

Ebon said grimly. 'Some of the resistance leaders, like yourself, have reduced the number of missions so the Drakes don't realise there's a resistance cell in their area, and to our knowledge, this has worked. The Drakes don't know there's a cell in this ghetto, or in the new Mirin ghetto, or in my old stomping grounds. They still mark down any losses to sightings of evil spirits and Ronin raids.'

'You say some of the resistance leaders have cut back on missions,' Aerik said. 'Who hasn't?'

'Kebble from the Argus ghetto has stepped up his attacks — he calls it a crusade to make the Drakes pay. He's deliberately hitting highly visible targets whose loss would hurt the Drakes badly.'

'In other words, the ones that are best defended,' Aerik said. 'What losses has he taken?'

'Thirty percent dead and closer to forty percent wounded,' Ebon replied. 'But he has managed to destroy two auxiliary barracks and a foundry.'

Aerik ran his hand over his eyes and shook his head in dismay. 'That man runs three resistance cells—'

'Four,' Ebon interrupted. 'Elba from the Daeng ghetto joined him after Mirin.'

'Four resistance cells, even worse,' Aerik sighed. 'And he's killed thirty percent of them just to destroy a foundry and two *auxiliary* barracks? What if he's seen?'

Ebon's eyes dropped to the floor and Aerik felt his heart plummet.

'Oh, no,' he whispered. 'No, not again. Where were they seen?'

'Running from the foundry fire back into the Argus ghetto,' Ebon said.

'And what are the Drakes doing about it?' Aerik asked, dreading the answer.

'The Argus ghetto is too large to destroy, which is our only good news,' Ebon said. 'It's almost three times the size of Mirin. The Drakes can't afford to kill all the slaves; the drop in production would be too big.'

'Thank the gods for that.'

'But they're scouring the ghetto from top to bottom,' Ebon continued. 'House searches, trade restrictions and harsher curfews. They're even escorting people in groups to the work camps and back again. Kebble has lost more men to the searches then he did on the raids.'

'Is there any way we can smuggle him and his teams out of there?'

'Possibly, if he was willing to leave.'

'And if we're willing to take a chance that he won't foul up again and make us a target, too,' Aerik sighed. 'Gods, why did he have to be so stupid?'

'There is one good thing that's come of it,' Ebon said. 'Some of the resistance leaders have finally agreed to a meeting. They want to form a council or some sort of organised leadership amongst the resistance; something that can stop this kind of thing from happening or react to it if it does. They've sent a messenger asking for you to join them.'

'It's about time,' Aerik said. 'I wish it didn't take something like this to get it going, but at least it has.'

'So you're accepting the invitation?'

'Yes,' Aerik nodded. 'Tell me when and where.'

'When — one week from yesterday. Where — that hasn't been decided yet. They'll pick a place the day before, when they know what the Drakes are up to.'

'Sensible,' Aerik nodded. 'Maybe they're learning a thing or two.'

'Maybe.'

Aerik sighed and dropped his head into his hands. Yes, they had learned something — some of the lessons Aerik taught his own men had filtered down to the other resistance groups, but it was painfully slow. Every day that passed by without those lessons being taught meant more and more slave fighters were losing their lives. But with a council of resistance leaders pooling their efforts and passing their training on to everyone, they could really make a difference.

Aerik was startled out of his thoughts as Ebon cleared his throat subtly. 'You wanted to talk to me about something else?'

'Yes, yes I do,' Aerik replied. 'We need to find a way to get slaves out of the city. I mean really out of here.'

'Why?' Ebon asked bluntly.

'Two reasons, my friend. One, because with all the money we're making selling Drake horses and supplies, we can buy more and more slaves off the block. With the way our fighters are surviving missions lately, we've lost almost no one for the past few months and we just can't find spots for all the new slaves coming in.'

'True,' Ebon sighed. 'We're pretty stretched in the training yards at the moment. What's the second reason?'

'The second reason is even more important. Some of the people we set free don't want to fight.'

'I know that,' Ebon said. 'But we *do* give them a choice — a choice we gave you as well from memory.'

'I remember, Ebon, but what future do they have if they don't join us? They can't go back to their homes because the Drakes will find them, and they don't want to stay and fight with us — what other options do they have? Stay here, out of sight and just hope that one day they'll be truly free?'

Ebon shrugged helplessly. 'I don't know what else we can do. We don't know anything about the land outside the city limits.'

'I know, I know,' Aerik sighed. 'That's what we need to work out. Maybe we can send an emissary to the humans in Darendall, see if we can smuggle people there.'

'It'd be tough, but not impossible,' Ebon said. 'You can't save them all you know.'

'I can try,' Aerik replied.

Ebon nodded and walked thoughtfully out of the room. Aerik turned back to the pile of papers on his desk and tried to plan where the weakest point would be for his next attack. He looked up when he heard a knock on his door and saw Ebon's head sticking back into the room.

'Are you sure there's nothing between you and Lysa?'

'I'm sure, Ebon, and so is she.'

Ebon nodded and looked at the floor in something resembling embarrassment. 'Would you mind if I asked her to dinner?'

Aerik's jaw dropped and for one of the few times in his life he was completely speechless.

'A bard with nothing to say,' Ebon said uncomfortably. 'I don't think I've ever seen that.'

'You just caught me by surprise, that's all.'

'So, is that a yes?'

'That's a yes, Ebon,' Aerik smiled. 'You have my blessing. Make her happy for me.'

Ebon grinned like a schoolboy and disappeared from sight.

Aerik leaned back in his chair with his hands behind his head, humming happily to himself. Ebon could make Lysa happy, he knew that — despite his rough manner, Ebon was a caring man when given the opportunity. The Samurai serving in the slave sector might disagree, as might some of the resistance fighters Ebon had trained, but Aerik knew he would treat Lysa with care and respect.

Aerik took one more look at the papers on his desk and decided he really didn't feel like planning a raid that might cost the life of a friend or colleague. Dropping his charcoal stick, he walked out of the room and headed for Rebecca's crib.

'A bard lost for words,' he muttered. 'I must be out of practice. I'm going to have to do something about that.'

He picked up his lyre and walked into Rebecca's room, already humming the tune he was going to play for his little girl.

Chapter 15

The great oak doors swung open on oiled hinges, revealing a huge audience chamber with a great carved chair at one end. Annah walked nervously down the hall until she was only metres from the chair, then dropped to her knees and pressed her forehead to the floor. While she knelt on the soft carpet, filled with the smell of incense that permeated the wool, she tried desperately to remain calm but she found it difficult.

It had been a long trip from the Imperial City, one made even longer by the encounter with Aerik in the slums and the unexplained transformation that had shaken her to the core. They had flown on Mange's back for a full day before they reached the lower mountains of the Golden Range, home of the Gold Drake Clan. The bastion of the most powerful clan was not a castle or a keep, as the other clans had built, but a magnificent monastery nestled at the foot of the mountain range. Annah had seen it from miles away but didn't truly comprehend the sheer size of it until they approached its doors.

The monastery was built of wood and stone like most Drake structures, but was designed to enhance meditation and inner peace rather than looking to defence. Annah followed Ishkal through a dozen courtyards, ranging from private bonsai gardens to huge training courtyards paved with stone slabs. The courtyards were lightly dusted with the last snows of winter and filled with young golden scaled acolytes moving through their flowing kata, while older monks walked between them, watching their every move.

The buildings were just as impressive; their huge open spaces held up with thick red columns that Annah couldn't have stretched her arms around. The walls were covered in tapestries depicting all facets of life, and incense burned in wall sconces at regular intervals. It was almost impossible to believe that the place could become more amazing, but when she finally approached the Abbot's chambers and saw the sheer passionate beauty of the artefacts and tapestries in his private collection, she was proved wrong. And now she knelt on the carpeted floor, in the presence of one of the most powerful Drakes in the Empire and leader of the greatest Drake Clan, the Abbot of the Golden Monastery.

'Rise.'

Annah lifted her head but remained kneeling, and looked into the face of the wizened Abbot. Ishkal sat cross-legged on the floor in front of the old Drake, and he winked at her reassuringly to calm her nerves. She started to smile back at him, then she remembered where she was and looked back respectfully at the Abbot.

'I greet you, Great Abbot of the Golden Order,' she said, her voice wavering only slightly. 'I humbly pay homage to your great person and bring honour—'

'Yes, yes, honours and respects and all that guff,' the Abbot huffed. 'You know, when I was a young Drake I used to love all this talk about my greatness, and how privileged people were to meet me. But the older I get, the less time I have, and I'll be darned if I'm going to squander my final years listening to people tell me how honoured they are to see me instead of getting to the point.'

Annah sat in a stunned silence as she tried to think of the right thing to say. The words of her carefully prepared introduction flew from her head and she could only gape stupidly under the Abbot's gaze. From the corner of her eye she saw Ishkal's mouth twitch as he tried to suppress a smile, and she felt some of the tightness in her chest ease — unfortunately, she still couldn't think of something to say.

'What's the matter, girl?' the Abbot asked. 'Cat got your tongue?'

'No, your Grace,' Annah stammered. 'I'm sorry, your Grace.'

'Oh, good,' the Abbot said. 'Now young Ishkal has told me all sorts of stories about you, and I wanted to ask you a thing or two to clarify things, if that's all right.'

'Of course, your Grace. I'll do everything I can to assist you.'

'Just answering the questions will do for a start,' he laughed, slapping his hand on his thigh at his own joke. 'Now, I hear that you have the gift of the Forgesong, is that correct?'

'It is, your Grace.'

'And I also hear that you've been trained by Ishkal here as a Monk of the Gold Dragon.'

'Yes, your Grace.'

The Abbot scratched his chin thoughtfully and smiled. He opened a small compartment set into the arm of his chair and pulled out two fist sized lead balls. With strength that belied his age, the Abbot tossed the balls to Annah, who caught them with experienced grace.

'You have used these before, Annah Tress?'

'Yes, your Grace.'

'Then I want you to show me the Kata of the Flying Dragon.'

Ishkal rose on unspoken command and walked to the side of the hall. He reached behind one of the banners draping the walls and pulled a stout, waist high post from a hidden alcove. He placed it on the ground in front of Annah, then returned to the Abbot's side and knelt once more.

Annah tentatively climbed to her feet and stepped up to the post. She knew how to do the Kata of the Flying Dragon; she had done it countless times with Ishkal in the gardens of Kelkh's home. But back then she had only used one lead ball and the post she stood on was planted firmly in the ground. If she overbalanced on Kelkh's post, she had the chance to regain her balance before she fell, but if she overbalanced here, the unsecured post would topple leaving her no room for error.

Taking a steadying breath, she climbed on top of the post and fell into the meditative trance that Ishkal had taught her. Steady breathing, in and out, the rhythmic beating of the heart, the relaxed state of the muscles and the total exclusion of all outside distractions.

Her hands started moving automatically, reacting on instinct as she reached the point of absolute calm. Her hands rose and fell, and her feet twisted in perfect harmony as she performed the monk art. Time lost its meaning and in what Annah would have sworn was only a few seconds, her arms drooped and she hopped off the unstable post.

'My, my, my,' the Abbot sighed. 'And all without even a wobble. I'm impressed — I wish some of my own Acolytes were as proficient.'

'Thank you, your Grace,' Annah replied, kneeling and bowing her head.

'Now, let's try something else.'

The Abbot reached back into his chair compartment and pulled out a large wooden board. He handed it to Ishkal, who bowed and rose to his feet, then stood in front of Annah. He held the board in front of him with both hands, keeping it as far away from his snout as possible.

'I think you know the rest,' the Abbot said.

Annah touched her forehead to the floor once again and jumped to her feet. She had practiced this manoeuvre with Ishkal and had almost perfected the art of breaking the board with a single punch. As she fell into her trance, she wondered briefly if the Abbot would add an extra layer of difficulty to this test as he had done with the last one.

She closed her eyes and fell into a soothing rhythm. The sounds and smells of Kelkh's forge filled her senses and the power of the Forgesong tingled in her limbs. From the depths of her mind, she heard Ishkal's voice whisper 'strike' and her fist lashed out.

There was a loud crack as her fist shattered the board into two equal halves. Ishkal smiled as he placed one half on top of the other and presented them to the Abbot. Annah saw the backs of the board briefly as Ishkal presented them, and she noticed that the wood was set on a backing of stone — the Abbot had strengthened the board as a test of her abilities, and Annah breathed a sigh of relief that she had passed.

'Well, Annah Tress, it appears that you've been an apt pupil,' the Abbot said. 'And Ishkal, you still have a knack for teaching.'

'Thank you, your Grace,' Ishkal bowed.

'Thank you, your Grace,' Annah echoed, touching her forehead to the ground.

'Yes, yes, yes,' the Abbot sighed. 'But what am I to do now, young Annah? You've passed every test required to become an Acolyte of the Order — do you want to become one?'

Annah's eyes opened wide as she realised what the Abbot was asking. 'Your Grace, I … I …'

'I believe Annah is worried about the reaction other Drakes might have to her wearing the robes of a Drake Monk,' Ishkal said. 'She is considered a slave by the other clans, and they might take badly to what they see as her presumption.'

'I see,' the Abbot replied. 'Ignorant louts. Then I'll give her a golden signet. I think that should fix any problems we have there, don't you Ishkal?'

Ishkal nodded dumbly, now looking as stunned as Annah. The Abbot looked from one to the other and burst into gales of laughter.

'It is good to know that I can still surprise people,' he laughed. 'Annah, do you know what the golden signet is?'

'No, your Grace, I do not.'

'It's a gold ring forged in the shape of a dragon. More importantly, it's a sign that you're under the protection of the Order of the Gold Dragon, and any Drake who harms you is answerable to us.'

Annah's eyes grew wider still and she turned chalk white as she struggled to take everything in.

'Ishkal, I think Annah's had just about enough excitement for one day,' the Abbot said. 'Show her to the outer chamber and then come back here. We have things to discuss.'

Ishkal nodded and helped Annah up from the floor. He led her to the luxurious chamber just outside the main audience hall and took a few minutes to make her comfortable, then hurried back to the Abbot. He would have liked to spend more time with Annah, to talk to her about what had just happened, but it would never do to keep the Abbot waiting.

He walked back into the audience hall and found the Abbot leafing through an old, leather bound book. Without a sound, Ishkal knelt in front of the Abbot's chair and waited until the old Drake was ready to speak.

'So what do you think?' the Abbot asked.

'About what in particular, your Grace?'

'Oh, drop the formality, Ishkal,' the Abbot snapped. 'We're alone now. What do you think of my decision to make Annah a monk?'

'I think it will anger the Emperor rather badly, your Grace.'

'Yes, that's one of the best things about it.'

'Your Grace, I should remind you that one of your duties is to ensure that the relationship between our clan and the Royal Clan remains amicable.'

'You're no fun, Ishkal,' the Abbot sighed. 'A Major Domo with no sense of humour, how on earth did I ever let that happen?'

Ishkal smiled thinly, but he knew the Abbot too well to think that this had simply been a prank on the Emperor. He waited on his knees for the Abbot to speak in his own time.

'You're worried for her safety?' he asked finally.

'I am, your Grace,' Ishkal replied. 'I think this could make her a target for other Drakes' anger.'

'No, the Golden Signet will prevent that,' the Abbot said. 'But I agree, it will gain her more than her fair share of animosity.'

'Then why do it, your Grace?'

'Let me ask you a question, Ishkal. Why did you train Annah as a monk if you never intended for her to join the Order?'

'I don't know, your Grace,' Ishkal admitted. 'I would have to say, because she showed an interest in what I did. Our clan has never believed that humans should be slaves and I wanted to prove that we honestly believe in those principals.'

'And I could reply to your question by saying that I agree with you. Annah passed all the tests for entry to our Order, and we have no limitations preventing humans becoming one of us. That would be a valid answer, just as yours was, but it wouldn't be the whole truth from either of us, would it?'

'No, your Grace,' Ishkal said. 'I ... when I spoke to her, when I was around her, there was just something about her, something in her presence that was just ...'

'Special.'

'Yes. Something I couldn't place. And when I learned she could perform magic, it seemed even more important for me to train her, to guide her.'

The Abbot nodded sagely and turned the pages of the leather bound book.

'This is the 'Chronicle of Abbots',' he said. 'It holds the wisdom and experience of the generations of Abbots who have come before me, from the dry speeches of Abbot Ysek, to the rather emotive memoirs of Abbot Unis. It also contains the dozens of true visions that were granted to these Abbots by The Dragon during the purest of meditation.'

Ishkal looked in awe at the book in the Abbot's hands, feeling humbled by the knowledge contained in its plain leather covers.

'I was deep in meditation last night, Ishkal, when The Dragon gave me a vision of my own. In my vision, I walked through the halls of this monastery to search out this book. I took it from my own bookshelf and looked through the pages until I found what I was looking for. At that point my vision ended and I opened my eyes to find that I had indeed walked through the monastery, and this book was open in front of me at this page.'

The Abbot passed the book to Ishkal who took it reverently and laid it on the floor. Ishkal leaned forward to read the small, neat writing on the page.

'And a child shall rise from the ranks of the oppressed,
Marked by The Dragon,
Called cursed by masters and peers.
A child of The Dragon,
They will have magic greater than any seen in an age.
They will be the key to the future of The Dragon's children.
Great evil, great good
The child will bring one to the world.'

Ishkal sat back on his heels as the last piece of the day's puzzle fell into place. The Abbot believed that Annah might be the child of this prophecy, not definitely, but possibly. If it wasn't her, then the Order of the Gold Dragon lost a small amount of prestige, which was something they cared little for in any case. But if it *was* her, the potential consequences of their inactions would be disastrous.

'She has risen from the ranks of the oppressed,' Ishkal said. 'She is certainly called cursed by both masters and peers, and that curse is said to be a mark of The Dragon.'

'She fits most of the criteria,' the Abbot agreed. 'Except one; she's a human, not a Drake, and humans are not children of The Dragon.'

'I still think it's more than mere coincidence.'

'I agree,' the Abbot nodded. 'And between my vision and the links in this prophecy, I'm not willing to take chances. You will continue to train her, Ishkal, and she will be free to advance in the ranks of our Order. If we're right, we *must* guide her to the path of good, or our entire world will suffer for it.'

Ishkal nodded and, after touching his head to the floor in respect, rose from his knees and turned to leave the room.

'And if we're wrong,' the Abbot called after him, 'we will have angered the Emperor. That alone ensures that it won't be a total waste of time.'

Ishkal laughed quietly to himself as he walked out the doors.

Annah stood in a cobbled street, lined with crowded, shabby houses that were visible for ten meters in each direction before the street disappeared in a swirl of grey mist. People moved around her, fighting with each other as they charged back and forth across the cobblestones, but Annah ignored them — they were insects to her, unimportant specks on her future plan. She could crush them with a thought, but she wouldn't. That would be wrong, wouldn't it?

'I can feel your struggle, Annah. Why do you fight against what you are?'

She spun around to see a single solid human step through the ill defined blobs that fought around the street. She knew him; she had met him before and struggled against the offers and moralities that he had tried to enforce. Taan, her self-proclaimed teacher and mysterious dark master.

'Why won't you embrace your power, use it as you see fit?' he said. 'You could right so many wrongs in this world. You felt it when you were fighting for that Drake's life against those petty humans; you felt the power calling for release. You should have set it free and swept your enemies from the earth.'

'No,' she replied, shaking her head. 'I didn't need to. The fight was finished without any deaths. Why would I kill if I don't need to?'

'Because they should learn to fear you, to know what it means to dare attack you!'

'No. No, that's not right — I don't want anyone to fear me.'

'Don't lie to me, Annah,' Taan snarled. 'I know who you are, even if you deny it to yourself. You want people to fear you, the way the Drakes and other human slaves make you fear them!'

Annah buried her head in her hands, trying to block Taan's words from her mind. 'No. I don't want anything you say.'

'You lie!' Taan shouted. 'When that red haze came down, you felt the power and you wanted it.'

Annah screamed inside her mind that it wasn't true, but a growing part of her resisted the denial. It agreed with Taan, it revelled in the promise of destruction and it cried out for vengeance against everyone who had pushed her around.

'You want to embrace the power,' Taan said. 'To learn what it can do.'

'Yes.'

It was barely a whisper but as soon as she said it, the floodgates opened; a red haze dropped in front of her eyes and the power of magic surged through her limbs. Liquid metal flowed from her fingertips, forming into a now familiar halberd, and Annah knew she was complete. A tiny voice of compassion and reason screamed at her that this was wrong, but the red haze was strong enough to push that voice into insignificance.

'You will learn from me,' Taan said. 'You will become my apprentice.'

'Yes,' Annah replied.

'No.'

That single word was like a slap in the face, shattering the red haze in an instant. The halberd melted and ran back inside her, and she fell to her knees coughing and retching. The street setting exploded in a cloud of grey smoke and the light around her dimmed rapidly leaving only Taan, looking shocked and angry at the sudden turn of events.

As the darkness closed in around her, Annah focused on the voice that had saved her sanity. She recognised it, she knew she did, but she had no idea where she had heard it before.

As the last light disappeared and Annah felt herself floating away, she remembered how she knew that voice. It wasn't one voice, but a combination of two. Ishkal. Aerik. Then the darkness closed in and she knew no more.

'Annah, Annah wake up.'

Annah opened her eyes to see Ishkal staring at her, a curious expression on his face. She sat up quickly, flushing red as she realised she'd fallen asleep in the Abbot's outer chamber.

'I'm sorry, Master Ishkal,' she said, scrambling out of her chair and dropping to her knees.

'There's no need to be sorry, Annah,' Ishkal smiled. 'It's been a long day and it's been tiring for us both. Come, I will take you to your room.'

'Thank you,' she said, standing shakily.

'Are you all right?' he asked. 'You seem upset.'

Annah frowned as she fought through the haze of sleep on her memory. There was something, something she was dreaming about that had frightened her. It was something important that she should tell Ishkal, but it was as illusive as smoke, slipping through her fingers as she tried to grasp at it.

'No, there's nothing wrong, Master Ishkal,' she said finally. 'Just a bad dream, I think.'

'You should be wary of dreams, Annah,' Ishkal said. 'They can be windows to the soul or visions of the future, especially when you have such powerful magic at your disposal.'

'Yes, Master Ishkal,' Annah said, stifling a yawn. 'I'll try and remember it next time, I promise.'

Ishkal nodded, and realising that there was nothing more to be gained pursuing the conversation, he led Annah to the door, but his face was grim as he left the room. He had sensed something when he woke her, something ancient and powerful. Perhaps it was only paranoia after his discussion with the Abbot, but on the other hand perhaps it wasn't. As he walked Annah back to her room, he decided that he would stop in on the Dream Master of the Monastery before he went to bed himself.

CHAPTER 16

Aerik looked around the shabby room at the nine other resistance leaders seated near him, watching their reactions at the suggestions put forth. He ignored the aides that each leader had behind them, trusting Ebon to watch them and learn what he could. One of the leaders, a great bear of a man called Kebble, tapped his dagger hilt on the table to call an end to what he referred to as 'consideration time' for this particular proposal.

'It's time to vote,' Kebble said. 'All who agree that we should launch a full blown attack on the Drakes raise your hands.'

Aerik watched the group ripple with uncertainty and he knew it was finally his moment to speak. He had kept his mouth closed for most of the proceedings, judging the crowd until he decided it was time for him to step in. It was a knack he'd always had, ever since he was a young boy stepping up onto The Stable's stage for the first time. Several years as a bard had only honed that instinct, and now it served him well in ways he'd never imagined.

'I have something to say before the vote,' he said, leaning forward over the table and raising his hand.

Kebble looked annoyed at the break in his momentum, but he had no way of refusing another leader their time. He nodded ungraciously and sat back down. Aerik stood slowly, waiting as Ebon shuffled back to give him space to stand in the crowded room.

'It seems to me that we're voting on how to split the scrum before we've brewed the batch,' Aerik said. 'We haven't even decided on what powers this council will have to control each of our resistance cells, but we're going to plan a joint attack? That's a recipe for disaster. The first thing we need to do is decide what to place under the jurisdiction of this council and what to leave under the control of the individual cell leaders.'

Kebble slid to his feet and Aerik noticed that the room had been arranged so that he had enough room to stand without anyone else having to shuffle out of his way. Aerik felt the hairs at the back of his neck tingle in warning as he wondered just how subtle Kebble was, and wondered whether that had been a deliberate ploy or just a fortuitous coincidence.

'The cells will remain as individual groups under the control of their current leaders,' Kebble said. 'This council is just a forum to decide when and where we might need to combine forces in a unified assault. The council will also decide what specific targets we should destroy with our combined attacks.'

'So we're just a pool of resources, nothing more,' Aerik replied. 'What about training regimes? I know each of us has certain styles of fighting and each of us has knowledge that the others don't have — why not pool our talents and work out how to train our men better? There's nothing to lose and everything to gain.'

It was such a simple request with such clear scope for benefit, but Aerik could already see the scowls on some of the other leaders' faces. He had expected nothing less, but deep down he had hoped.

'Very well, Aerik,' Kebble conceded with a thin smile. 'Training assistance will be allowed across cells for any who want it. I'll leave it up to each individual leader to decide if they want their cell to have it or not.'

'A good proposal,' Aerik nodded. 'I call for it to be brought to a vote. All in favour?'

There was no mistaking the flash of anger in Kebble's eyes. He hid it well, but Aerik knew how to see such things. Kebble had meant his offer as an order, a law to be laid in the council without a vote, cementing his position of leadership amongst leaders. But Aerik had no intention of letting Kebble make a power grab. After seeing the disaster this man had caused with only his own cells, Aerik knew the death and destruction that would result if he came to power over the whole resistance.

'It's unanimous then,' Kebble growled. 'Training will be available for everyone, but it will be at the discretion of each cell leader. Now, on to more important matters — where to direct our attacks against the Drakes. There are a number of emplacements that I've targeted for our initial attack ...'

Aerik watched the proceedings grimly, listening to Kebble weave his spell and thinking of the best way to break it. For all his unsubtle ways, Kebble was smarter than Aerik had given him credit for. By wording his training proposal just right, he had pandered to Aerik but also put the final decision for what to do in the hands of the resistance leaders. Those that wanted training could have it, and those that didn't want to relinquish their grip on power enough to let someone else help them didn't have to. And they all owed it to Kebble and his ideas. Aerik wondered if any of the leaders realised just how well they were being manoeuvred.

'One moment, Kebble,' he said, breaking the big man's verbal hold. 'I wasn't aware that we'd agreed to an attack on the Drakes, so I think that deciding on a target would be a bit premature.'

'What do you think we're here for, Aerik?' Kebble growled. 'Scrum and honey cake? We're here to plan the downfall of the Drake Empire!'

'Actually, I thought we were here to plan for the freedom of all human slaves,' Aerik replied. 'And to learn from and support each other so that we can keep as many of our people alive as we can in the process.'

'We need to destroy the Drakes before we can ever be free,' Kebble said.

'Kebble, if you think that, then you're a fool,' Aerik replied bluntly. Kebble's eyes widened in anger, but Aerik pushed on before he could say anything. 'The Drake Empire has more land, equipment and troops than we can ever hope to muster, and they're trained to be warriors from the time they can hold a weapon. As a race, they're stronger, faster and more resilient than us, so we can't hope to fight them one on one. We're not soldiers and we don't have an army, so we should stop trying to pretend that we do.'

'Are you a coward, Aerik? Is that your problem?' Kebble asked. 'You're afraid to die for this cause and see your children free? Because if you think that the Drakes are just going to hand over our freedom to us, then you're sorely mistaken.'

'I'd be happy to die in this cause, Kebble, but I want my death to mean something. I object to throwing anyone's life away in a useless, prideful gesture. We're thieves and assassins, not soldiers, and we should be acting like it! A full scale assault on a heavily defended barracks will only get us killed, but a subtle attack would be just as devastating and would keep more people alive.'

Kebble looked like he would jump across the table and throttle Aerik, but another voice spoke up from across the room. Aerik tentatively identified it as belonging to Pan of the Hokkin ghetto.

'So you're saying that Kebble's attack plan on the Drake barracks is a bad one,' Pan said. 'Let's hear your plan of attack.'

'I'd rather not attack anything with such a high profile just yet,' Aerik sighed. 'But if you're determined to do it, then there are better ways than a full frontal assault.'

'Such as?' Pan persisted.

Aerik turned to one of the other cell leaders, a man named Jink who was seated at the far end of the table.

'Jink, I've heard that your men have discovered the recipe for making Drake black powder, is that right?'

'Yeah, that's right,' Jink replied, taken by surprise by the change in topic.

'Can you tell us what it is?'

'It's powerful stuff,' Jink shrugged. 'The Drakes use it in their fireworks and sometimes they use it to blast rocks apart in the mines.'

'Could it take down a building, if you placed it at the right spots?'

'Like if you put it on the foundations?' Jink asked. 'Yeah sure — but you'd never be able to do that.'

'Why not?'

'Because you'd never get enough of it,' Jink said. 'The ingredients are expensive and closely guarded. We don't have any money to buy it and not enough manpower to steal it, so the recipe's pretty much useless to us.'

'But I do,' Aerik said. 'I have the finances and the merchant contacts to get what you need; I just need you to tell me what the ingredients are.'

Jink looked around the table, fidgeting as he tried to decide whether he wanted to give up the secret of making black powder. His was one of the smaller resistance cells, and that recipe was the only advantage he had over the other leaders. Aerik picked up on Jink's hesitation faster than the others, except perhaps Kebble, and sighed in frustration.

'Listen, Jink, you don't have the contacts we need to buy these goods without arousing suspicion,' Aerik said. 'If you did, I'd give you the money and let you buy it, but you don't. We have to trust each other here, or we'll be so busy snapping at each other and protecting our own petty slices of power that we'll never be a threat to the Drakes. We'll probably just get ourselves killed!'

Jink looked sheepish at his own selfishness and at the same time angry at Aerik's presumption, but he was still wavering on giving Aerik the list of supplies he needed.

'What if I guaranteed that your cell alone would produce black powder for us, Jink?' Kebble said. 'Would that set your mind at ease?'

'If I had the council's word, then yes,' Jink nodded.

Aerik was surprised at Kebble's subtlety, both at putting himself back into a position of authority and by increasing his hold on the Council. Jink was in his debt because Kebble had just given him a win-win situation, and the other leaders saw him as a conciliator — but Aerik hadn't missed Kebble's use of 'I guarantee' not 'we guarantee', and he knew Kebble's thirst for revenge. If Kebble was given free reign, the resistance would end in a very short, very bloody affair.

'The proposal has been put forward that Jink's cell alone produce all our black powder,' Aerik said. 'All in favour?'

'I've already *guaranteed* Jink that right,' Kebble said softly, a hint of menace in his voice.

'Yes, you have,' Aerik replied. 'And now the council will guarantee that. If it's not voted on by the council then it's not binding, your guarantee or not. All in favour?'

Aerik raised his hand, and around the table eight other hands followed his with all the hesitance of a child caught between two bickering parents. The last hand raised was Kebble's, and Aerik saw a grudging respect flicker in his eyes. He knew now that Aerik wasn't going to be bullied aside, though Aerik knew that didn't mean Kebble was going to give up trying.

'The council has voted,' Aerik said. 'Jink, the black powder rights are yours. If you give me a list of materials, I'll get them to you as soon as I can. I'll need enough black powder to destroy the foundations of an inner city barracks.'

'I'll get right onto it,' Jink promised.

'My proposed alternative to a full frontal assault should be obvious by now,' Aerik said. 'But in case it's not, here's the outline. We'll need to get a layout of the barracks, from the access points to the roof lines, load bearing walls and foundation locations.'

'I can get them for you,' Kebble said.

'Good. With that layout we can approach the attack from two angles. Option one, we sneak into the barracks at night and plant the black powder on the building's foundations. We then set timed fuses and blow the building once we're clear.'

'That's risky,' Pan said. 'It's not really much safer than a full frontal assault.'

From the corner of his eye, Aerik saw a smug grin creep across Kebble's face; he was glad that his second option would wipe that smirk away.

'I agree, it's really too risky,' Aerik said, though he still thought his own men could have pulled it off. 'My second option is this; the Drakes use human slaves to do the cleaning and grubby maintenance of the barracks. They empty the slop buckets, clean the latrines and bilge them when they're too full, they clean the dirty dishes — all the jobs that the Drakes would never dream of stooping to do themselves. What we need to do is get our people into the slave cleaning crews and plant the black powder while we're in plain sight of the Drakes.'

'Are you insane?' Kebble asked. 'How the hell is that safer than a full assault? At least then if I die, I'll die fighting!'

'Hold on a moment, Kebble, I think I see where Aerik's going with this,' Pan said. 'If we disguise the black powder somehow or put it in places that the Drakes would never look, like the bottom of a latrine, we could plant it all without the Drakes ever knowing.'

'That's the plan,' Aerik nodded. 'Now I know the details still need to be ironed out, but I think we have enough of an outline to put it to a vote. All in favour of running with this plan over a frontal assault?'

Aerik raised his hand, as did Pan and four others. To Aerik's surprise, Kebble also raised his hand, which quickly prompted the last three to give in as well.

'The council has voted,' Aerik said. 'I'll finish up the details and bring them for approval at the next meeting.'

'And now on to our next order of business,' Kebble said loudly.

Aerik sat down and settled in to watch. It had been a long meeting already and he knew that it was only going to get longer.

'So what do you think?'

Aerik took a long drink of water, then refilled his mug and poured it over his head. It had been an exhausting day, filled with frustration and dashed hopes.

'I don't know, Ebon,' he sighed. 'That council has the potential to be so good for us, but the people on it have to change first.'

'They will,' Ebon replied. 'When they realise the benefits, they will.'

'Maybe. Some of them are so protective of the cells they've built they resent the thought of someone taking control away from them.'

'I guess you can't really blame them,' Ebon said. 'They grew up as slaves with nothing. Everything they have, they earned through hard work and horrible loss. They have something now, something that they can call their own, and they don't want to give it up to anyone.'

'Then none of us will ever be any more than what we are now — split groups of slaves with dreams of being free,' Aerik sighed. 'How can we fight the Drakes when we're too busy fighting ourselves for the scraps of this resistance.'

'Would you give up your resistance cell then, Aerik? If it was for the greater good?'

Aerik and Ebon both looked up as the new voice echoed in the room. Pan stepped out from the shadows, looking thoughtful and completely unabashed at having eavesdropped.

'Absolutely,' Aerik nodded. 'But only to someone who'd make it into something greater and strive for freedom, not to someone who'd use it as a tool for revenge and most likely kill the people currently under my protection.'

'And let me guess which category Kebble falls under.'

'Pan, if the Drakes freed us all tomorrow, he'd keep fighting because his anger is all that drives him. He wants revenge for past wrongs; he doesn't look to a future for our people.'

'And if the Drakes freed us tomorrow, what would *you* do, Aerik?' Pan asked.

'I'd find a home out of the city, perhaps a farm near Darendall where my daughter could live her life free from fear and hate.'

'You have a daughter?' Pan asked. 'You never struck me as someone who would settle down long enough to have children.'

'I ... I misspoke,' Aerik blushed. 'She's actually my brother's daughter, but he was killed by the Drakes just after her birth. I look after her with her mother's sister, but she's as much a child to the two of us as anyone.'

Pan smiled and nodded, leaving it that. She wasn't trying to pry into any one topic; she just wanted a feel for who Aerik really was. With subtle grace she moved the conversation to more important matters.

'So what are your thoughts on Kebble?'

'For all of his fierce appearance and bloodthirsty tactics, he's amazingly deft at manipulating people,' Aerik replied. 'He knows what each leader's weaknesses are and he's ready to exploit them — but he does it in a way that people don't even realise he's doing it.'

'He's polarising the council, that's for sure,' Pan nodded. 'Those who want to keep control of their resistance cells are supporting him and those who see the benefit of joining together are looking for another to lead them. Your ideas of joint co-operation between resistance cells are scaring people into Kebble's court.'

'They oppose me to try and keep their freedom, and by doing so they hand control over to Kebble,' Aerik sighed. 'I wonder if they appreciate the irony of that.'

'Most of them think it will only be temporary,' Pan agreed. 'That once things are settled, Kebble will leave them to their own ways with only minor interruption from the council.'

'And what do you think?' Aerik asked. 'Do you want independence, or do you support unity?'

Pan got to her feet with a mischievous smile on her face and headed to the door as silently as she had arrived. She turned around as she left the room, looking over her shoulder at them.

'You really should consider putting yourself forward for leadership of the council,' she said. 'You might be surprised how many people follow you instead of Kebble.'

'The purpose of a council is to have many people choosing a direction, not a single leader,' Aerik said.

'That's nice for a central government but we're a revolution,' Pan said. 'We can't afford the delays that debating things in a council will bring, not if we're going to survive.'

'Then why did you join the council if you don't believe in it?'

Pan shrugged and walked out of the room, leaving Aerik and Ebon alone with much to ponder.

Chapter 17

Annah opened her eyes to the soft sunlight filtering through her thin curtains and the crisp air drifting through the open window. It took a moment for her to realise that she wasn't at home with Kelkh, and she didn't need to prepare breakfast or complete her chores — though she did still have to complete her exercises, especially as she was now an Acolyte of the Order.

Stifling a yawn with the back of her hand, she sat up from her pallet and stretched out her stiff arms. She had slept well, in fact better than she had for a long time. She hadn't been disturbed by the illusive nightmares that seemed to trouble her mercilessly and were forgotten as soon as she woke. Perhaps it was the serene setting of the monastery or the tiring journey to reach it, or even the draining meeting with the Abbot — but whatever it was, she was happy and not inclined to question her good fortune.

She shrugged and dropped her hands to the floor to push herself up, and her fingers brushed against a small turquoise stone. She looked at it in confusion and noticed that there were eleven more of them placed in a circle around her. Perhaps her unbroken sleep was due to something else.

'The Pecwae of the wild lands believe that turquoise is a magic stone, capable of warding away powerful evil spirits. The legends say that they sing these stones out of the ground with the magic of their voices alone.'

Annah jumped at the unexpected voice but settled quickly as she recognised it as Ishkal's. She looked over her shoulder and saw him lying on the floor, eyes closed and his cloak rolled up under his head.

'I don't know how many of those legends I believe,' he continued, 'but they do seem to stop the nightmares.'

'They did indeed, Master,' Annah replied.

'I'm glad,' he smiled, finally opening his eyes and looking at her. 'Because I think your new training regime will be such that you can't afford to be unrested.'

'New training regime, Master?'

'Of course! You're an Acolyte of the Order now, Annah Tress, and you must be trained accordingly. And equipped accordingly, too.'

'Equipped, Master?'

Ishkal pulled a small package out from under his bundled cloak, wrapped carefully in paper and tied with ribbon. Annah recognised it immediately as the parting gift Kelkh had made for her, and her hands trembled with a sudden desire to see her grouchy master once more. She reached out unsteadily and took the package from Ishkal's hands, then carefully unwrapped it and opened the box to see two shining silver bracers, made of thick metal bands woven to a mesh and embossed with Kelkh's family crest. Annah looked at Ishkal, who raised his arm to show an almost identical bracer on his own forearm.

'They're called The Bracers of Illaed,' Ishkal said. 'They're the first SongForged piece that any Acolyte is allowed to wear. Kelkh had no doubt that you would join the Order; he knew before I even intended to bring you here. He asked me once why I trained you if I wasn't going to try and make you a monk. I always thought I was the one who saw things in *him* that he didn't realise.'

He chuckled to himself about Kelkh's unlikely insight then looked back to Annah, who sat staring at the beautiful bracers on her lap, tracing the engraving of Kelkh's family crest.

'He added the crest for you especially,' Ishkal smiled. 'I have my own family crest on my bracers, but as you have no Drake lineage, Kelkh wanted to give you one. It's his way of saying that he considers you a part of his family.'

Annah sat in silence, holding the bracers and fighting back tears as she thought about her Master, her friend. Ishkal closed his eyes again, leaving Annah some privacy for her emotions. He lay in quiet meditation until he heard her take three deep breaths, then he opened his eyes and climbed to his feet.

'Come, young Acolyte,' he said. 'It's time we found you some robes to wear and got you to your training. You have much to learn and your classes start in less than an hour. Bring your bracers, you're going to need them.'

Annah hopped off the pallet, bracers in hand, and followed Ishkal out of the room. She knew nothing of the great monastery and she relied on Ishkal for his directions. He looked back at her as they turned into the next corridor, his mouth open in a toothy smile.

'And later this afternoon, you'll need to go and see Mange,' he said. 'Apparently that Rock Dragon has taken a liking to you and won't be fed by anyone else.'

Annah just smiled and kept walking behind him. It seemed she was being welcomed by another member of her family.

The day was as exciting as it was exhausting, but Annah found that her rigors as a slave had prepared her better than most other new Acolytes, even ones who had been training for weeks longer than she had.

Ishkal had hurried her to the tailor, where she was given a plain brown robe to replace her slave kimono. She was only a little embarrassed that they had to delve into the children's sizes to find one small enough for her — Drakes were larger than humans at the best of times, and Annah was small even by slave standards. Once she was robed, Ishkal showed her how to slip on her bracers then led her to her first training session.

She stepped into the padded training room, weaving a path through the groups of sparring Acolytes. Her mind raced as she tried to imagine what her training would be like. She imagined her teacher to be like Ishkal, calm and fair, but she was frightened that they would be somewhat less accepting. The last thing she expected was a young, female Drake who looked barely out of her teens. She flashed a toothy smile at Ishkal and batted her gold eyelids, making him blush a tarnished bronze, then turned her attention to Annah.

'Greetings, Acolyte,' she said. 'I am Dala and I will be your group's trainer.'

Annah fought the impulse to drop to her knees and bow her head — Ishkal had told her that it wasn't necessary in the monastery, as Acolytes were not required to kneel to their masters. But she did bow her head, showing all the respect required for a Master of the Order.

'I'm told that you have particular skill in the use of the Forgesong,' Dala said. 'Is that right?'

'I'm told so, Master,' Annah replied.

'Then let's find out.' Dala held up a small bar of metal for Annah to take. 'Hum something for me, Annah Tress, something to make this metal extraordinary.'

Annah resisted the urge to look over to Ishkal for confirmation, and reached out with a trembling hand to take the bar from Dala's hand. She closed her eyes and sent her mind racing back to the forge, remembering the acrid smells of metal and the baritone notes of Kelkh's voice as he forged his craft. The Song sprang from her lips easily, caressing her with familiar warmth and carrying her away on a wave of joy and power. The metal glowed in her hand, shedding light that she could see even through her closed eyelids.

'Amazing,' Dala murmured.

Annah opened her eyes as the glow faded, looking from the metal bar in her hand to Dala's fascinated face.

'You certainly have a gift, Annah,' Dala said. 'And I see that you know how to use it to forge items of skill and magic. Now it's up to me to teach you how we use this power in the Order of the Gold Dragon.'

Annah reached out and pushed open the door to Mange's stable with her last remaining strength. It had been an exhausting day, and one that had challenged her physical and magical skills in ways she never imagined possible. She had learned from Kelkh to use her magic to forge metal, but the Monks of the Order used it in a manner that was totally unfamiliar to her. She was taught to manipulate metal, to force it to obey her command and move wherever her voice told it. It required immense concentration and a fine control that she hadn't yet acquired, but she was confident she would gain it in time.

Mange looked up expectantly as she stepped inside, jumping to his feet and nuzzling his head against her shoulder almost immediately. Annah took a step back to adjust to the unexpected push of the big dragon's head, but she smiled at his affection and wrapped her arms around his neck.

'What is this I hear about you not eating, Mange?' she asked.

Mange's head dropped sheepishly and he looked up at her with his big brown eyes. If Annah didn't know better, she would have sworn he was looking ashamed about something.

'You're not coming down with something, are you?' she asked. 'I've never known you to say no to food before.'

Mange leaned forward and nuzzled Annah again, snuffling loudly at her tunic. Annah's brow furrowed in confusion until she slipped her hand into her pocket and pulled out the small metal bar that she had enchanted for Dala earlier that day. As soon as he saw it, Mange leaned forward and wrapped his tongue around it eagerly. Annah laughed and tugged back at the bar to tease Mange, who stared mournfully at the metal gripped in his rocky tongue, but only for a moment. She let him have the metal bar and he flopped happily onto his stomach to chew on his new snack.

'There's something about the magic, isn't there?' she murmured, listening to the crunch of metal in his rocky teeth. 'Anything that can make you turn your snout up at food has got to be pretty special.'

Mange looked up at her, his eyes half shut as he savoured the taste. Annah had to laugh and she reached out to scratch the big dragon behind his horns.

'Well if you're not going to eat anything else, then you're going to have to learn to wait until I have time to come feed you.'

Mange looked up and nuzzled her eagerly, making Annah laugh again and roll her eyes. She shifted Mange's heavy head off her lap and walked out of the stable in search of a sack of ro-khill for his dinner. She'd almost given up when she heard the shuffle of footsteps behind her. She turned quickly, years of experience taking control as she prepared to kneel if the newcomer was a Drake.

Standing three meters away, staring at her intently and leaning on a battered shovel, was a human slave. He was tall and broad, with the corded muscles that came hand in hand with a lifetime of hard slavery. Annah wondered briefly where the man had come from, given that the Drakes of the Order didn't keep slaves of their own. They considered it character building for aspiring Acolytes to learn what hard labour was like, giving them a sense of humility and an appreciation of the often unnoticed people in life.

Annah assumed the man was a personal slave of some visiting dignitary, brought along to slop out the horse stables — the Keldarkan Rock Dragons were looked after by the Drakes themselves. It was a sign of Kelkh's immense trust in Annah for him to allow her to look after Mange.

The man stepped forward, jolting Annah from her immaterial thoughts. It didn't really matter where he had come from, only that he was here and he wasn't looking at her in a friendly way. He took another step forward and Annah was hit by the stench of manure coming off him; she could see the grit under his fingernails and the calluses on his hands, she could see where his stubble was buried by ingrained dirt and she could smell his rank breath.

She felt the urge to sprint from the stables, but her only path out was past the man. She felt trapped and afraid, and deep down in the shadows of her mind she felt the urge to strike the man down and brutally silence her fears.

'Well, look at you, girl,' he growled. 'All dolled up like a Drake. I wonder what you had to offer them to get that under your belt. What could you do for them that would make them forget you's a cursed girl?'

'I don't know what you mean,' Annah said, trying hard not to tremble. The thought sped through her mind that with all her training she could easily strike this man dead, but true as it was, the thought revolted her.

'What I mean is that you're cursed, marked by The Dragon for all to see,' he replied. 'But somehow you've wormed your way into an Order full of *them*. I want to know what you did for them that got you such a cushy post.'

Annah opened her mouth to reply, then shut it again slowly. Something in the man's tone told her that he'd already made up his mind what she had done and he didn't really expect her to answer.

'I think you should show me what you did,' he growled, taking another step forward. 'Show me what you were willing to do to betray your race and sell yourself to the Drakes!'

The man lunged forward, covering the remaining distance

between them in an instant. Annah reacted without thinking, ducking under his outstretched arms and twisting out of his reach. She darted towards the door, looking to find Ishkal or Dala or anyone who would make this man back down.

She got two steps away from him when she felt a burst of pain in her ankle and fell to the ground, her scream cut short as the air was blasted from her lungs by the impact. She looked back dazedly at her feet and saw a jagged mark where the spade blade had hit her foot. The man dropped the spade to the cobblestones with a loud clatter and walked slowly towards her, his expression caught somewhere between satisfaction, anger and disgust.

Annah thought desperately of what to do. It was no use screaming, there was no one nearby who could hear her. She knew in her heart that she could overpower this man, her training had given her those skills, but her entire lifetime had been spent in servitude, learning how to obey others and accept pain without complaint. It was a mental block that prevented her from hurting anyone, no matter her situation.

Just this once, she prayed that the red haze that had consumed her on the streets of the slave town would return and break through her fear. Deep inside her mind she heard a voice laughing, mocking her and her fear.

You see what you are without me, the voice whispered. *Now bear the consequences. See what happens when you're powerless and weak. Perhaps then you will join me and you will never be powerless again.*

Annah had no time to wonder where the voice came from, as the man finally approached her. She screamed then, and to her surprise the man screamed back, his eyes focused on something past her. There was a whoosh of air and the man was knocked clear across the other side of the street. A huge clawed leg cracked against the cobblestones as it dropped protectively over Annah, and she realised with a sob of relief what had saved her.

Standing over her, jaws open in his silent cry of rage, was Mange. Annah had only ever known Mange as the docile, almost puppy-like mount from Kelkh's stable, but seeing him above her with his fangs bared and barbed tail swishing from side to side, she realised why the Keldarkan Rock Dragon was considered the most fearsome Drake mount ever seen on the battlefield. The man screamed in terror and ran into the monastery, fleeing from the terrifying apparition.

Annah watched Mange's claws dig jagged rents in the cobblestones as he tensed to chase the man down, and with a desperate shout she threw her arms around the huge rock leg.

'No, Mange,' she cried. 'Please, don't leave me.'

The big Rock Dragon looked down at her in surprise, then up at the fleeing man. Annah squeezed his leg harder and Mange finally lowered his head to nuzzle her cheek. Annah collapsed in relief and burst into tears, letting go of his leg and clutching his huge head. Mange dropped carefully to the ground, wrapping his body protectively around her.

Between sobs, Annah's mind raced and spun. She thought of Aerik and his offer to help human kind, but why should she? Because of the colour of her eyes and hair, Annah had been shunned by her own people, and after what had almost happened she had to ask if humans were really worth saving.

CHAPTER 18

Kelkh lost himself to the power of the Forge, letting the Song guide his hands and his mind as he created his next commission. What was it? he wondered. Deep down in the most creative part of his mind he knew what he was making, but like the Song that sprang from his lips, that part of his mind seemed to operate all by itself. His thoughts were not on what he was making, or even on the soul lifting joy that the Forgesong offered, but on the young girl Ishkal had taken with him to the Order.

He missed her more than he had ever expected; her quiet presence and her awestruck wonder at simple things that he didn't give a second thought. He found himself wondering when she would come back home.

He caught the mistake a moment before it happened; a slip of the tongue and a flick of the talon that would have rendered the day's work useless. Snarling to himself, he poured all of his attention back to his craft. He never made mistakes, never took lightly the charge that had been thrown upon him. He may not have asked for or even wanted this position, but he would do it to the utmost of his considerable skills. His honour demanded no less. He would not let his feelings for Annah impair his work.

'She's just a girl, anyway,' he muttered. But he was wrong and he felt ashamed of the words before he'd even finished them. She was far more than 'just a girl' and she was worthy of more than that from him. He sighed in frustration and wrenched his thoughts back to his forging.

Time passed unnoticed as he gave everything to his creation, and when he finally opened his eyes to the real world, he found that he wasn't disappointed. Even with the aura of the Forgesong still fading away, he could feel the power of the weapon he had created.

It was a dagger, long and slender, crafted in the shape of a human girl. The legs were outstretched with toes pointing downwards to create the blade and tip. The body made the grip with the arms resting on the hips to fashion the hilt and finger guard, and the head made the pommel. He knew at a glance whose face was carved on the pommel, staring up at him from sapphire eyes that he couldn't even remember adding. It even wore the same clothes that she did, carved in exquisite detail down to the boot buckles.

It was a thing of art and beauty made in Annah's likeness, but it was also completely useless. No Drake would ever use a dagger shaped like a human no matter how powerful it was, which meant that he had just fallen even further behind in his work. He sighed heavily and placed the dagger down on his anvil, rubbing his eyes to remove the burning weariness.

He looked up as he heard someone respectfully clearing their throat, and for the first time he noticed two Drakes standing on either side of the forge entry. From their gilded armour and iron scales, Kelkh saw that they were members of the Royal Guard attached to one of the major nobles, and from their stance he realised that they had been waiting for some time.

'Forgemaster Kelkh?' one of the guards asked.

Kelkh flinched at the title, still not used to it after all this time. 'I am Kelkh.'

'Prince Dragath asked us not to disturb your work, Forgemaster,' the guard said, bowing low. 'He wishes to meet with you at your convenience. He is waiting for you in the dining room.'

Kelkh flushed, turning his scales an ugly tarnish at the thought that anyone would presume to take such liberties in his home, but he kept his mouth clamped firmly shut. Dragath was a Prince of the Royal Family, a direct descendant of the Emperor. It wouldn't do to upset him. Not again.

'I'll see him immediately,' Kelkh muttered, stepping between the two Drakes and through the doors. The Drakes snapped to attention as he passed, but Kelkh's trained eye noticed the sloppiness in their movements — nothing overtly wrong, just not as fluid as he would have expected. If he was still Guard Captain, he would have had that seen to.

But he wasn't. Sighing heavily, he shoved that thought as far back into his mind as he could, burying it with his other unwanted memories, and limped towards the dining room. Perhaps it was just the lingering cold from winter, but his old leg wound seemed to hurt more today than usual.

He entered the room to see Prince Dragath sprawled across one of his couches, ruby scales glittering in the sun as he peeled the rock fruit he had liberated from Kelkh's pantry. Judging from the rind lying on the couch and the floor, this one wasn't his first.

'Ah, Forgemaster Kelkh,' he said, smiling tightly. 'So nice to see you.'

'Prince Dragath,' Kelkh bowed, 'an honour, as always.'

Dragath looked past Kelkh's shoulder at the soldiers behind him. 'You may leave us,' he said. 'Take up post outside the room, but no further.' The guards saluted and disappeared out the door, leaving Kelkh and Dragath alone.

'You approve of my guards?' Dragath asked.

'They are ... adequate, your Majesty.'

'But not up to your high standards, Kelkh.'

'I would give them more training, your Majesty,' Kelkh replied. 'They've got the skill in them, I can see it. They just need to be drilled harder.'

'Yes, I agree. I can see why you didn't put Captain Baaru's name forward to take over your post when you left.'

'I considered the men I recommended to be better suited.'

'Indeed,' Dragath sighed. 'Unfortunately, the Emperor seemed to agree with you and each of those men have been placed in charge of battalions in his personal retinue.'

'Then it is their honour.'

'Yes, it is,' Dragath said, his tone implying anything but.

Kelkh bowed his head to keep his look of contempt hidden. He knew Dragath well enough to understand that the Prince wanted to be the most powerful individual in the Empire. He wanted the best trained men, the most loyal followers and he wanted the Emperor's crown when he died. That the current Emperor was able to pick the best men for his own guard would have irked Dragath incredibly.

'But enough talk of politics and soldiers,' Dragath said. 'That's not why I am here and it's no longer your area of expertise in any case.' Kelkh ignored the jibe and stayed silent, waiting for Dragath to continue. 'I am here for two reasons, the first of which is to ask why the number of weapons coming from your forge has dropped in the past few weeks.'

Kelkh winced unconsciously; he had hoped to keep Annah completely from the conversation. Dragath leaned forward, tossing the remains of the rock fruit over his shoulder. He knew he had hit on something, but he had no idea what.

'Your forge experienced an inexplicable increase in productivity for several months, then just as inexplicably, your productivity has dropped below even your usual standards. As one of the only two SongForgers in the entire Empire, the Emperor is understandably concerned. Your problems are our problems, and we must see them resolved so you can get back to forging weapons for the war.'

Kelkh flicked his tongue nervously across his scaled lips as he tried to decide what to say. He knew he would have to mention Annah, but how much he revealed was the question he wrestled with.

'You recall some time ago you told me to hire an assistant,' he said eventually.

'I recall telling you to buy a slave,' Dragath snorted. 'Are we talking about the same thing?'

'We are, your Majesty,' Kelkh sighed. 'I did so, acquiring the services of a young human girl to aid me in the forge. It was due to her assistance that my output was increased. Her services were lost to me three weeks ago.'

'Her services were lost to you?' Dragath asked, raising his eyebrows. 'What happened to her, Kelkh? Did she die? Just buy another one and be done with it.'

Kelkh gritted his teeth and bit back a caustic reply at the thought that anything had happened to Annah. He would gain nothing by it, and probably lose more than he was willing to give up.

'She hasn't died, Your Majesty. She fell ill and was taken to the Monastery of the Gold Dragon by Brother Ishkal.'

'Ishkal, yes, I remember him,' Dragath hissed. 'It doesn't surprise me that he's taken an interest in some sick human. So you lost your slave — just go and get another one.'

'That won't help me, your Majesty,' Kelkh replied. 'This apprentice was trained to help me in the forge and it would take me too long to retrain another one; too long with a war effort going on.'

'She was trained to help you in the forge?' Dragath frowned. 'You mean she took over the household chores, leaving you free to forge, correct?'

'No, your Majesty,' Kelkh said. 'I mean she knew the lay of the forge and she ... knew how to help me while I was forging.'

'You let a *human* in the forge?' Dragath asked aghast. 'You let her help create weapons that would be used by Drake warriors in the heat of battle?'

'I let her assist a master craftsman in his work,' Kelkh replied, letting his tone turn frosty. 'I take it that there have been no complaints about the quality of my work?'

'No, no complaints, Kelkh,' Dragath said hastily. 'The Emperor is as happy with your work as he has always been. It's speed that is the current issue, and if not having this girl is slowing you down, then you must go and get her.'

'But—'

'No buts, Kelkh. My second order of business is to tell you that you're being moved to the battlefront, and if this girl is instrumental in speeding your craft then she will go with you. If monks must accompany her to keep her well, then that will be arranged too.'

Dragath placed a rolled scroll on the table, sealed with wax and marked with the Emperor's own seal.

'It's an Imperial writ, Kelkh,' Dragath said. 'You will move to the battlefront. We're cutting out the time and risk required to transport your goods to our troops. We want you there so your weapons can go straight to where they 're needed, and you will be on hand to repair any weapons that break.'

Kelkh's skin tarnished as he flushed angrily. 'My weapons don't break, Prince Dragath. To even hint at such a thing impinges on my honour.'

'I am well aware of the quality of your craft, Kelkh,' Dragath replied. 'But unfortunately, not all of the weapons on the battlefield were made by you.'

'So I'm to fix other's mistakes then?' Kelkh balked. 'I must repair inferior weapons when I should be forging my own!'

'Oh, very well,' Dragath sighed irritably. 'You will be left to forge your own craft. There will soon be enough blacksmiths at the battlefront to deal with the demand anyway. But you *will* be there, Kelkh, and you will be there soon. And you will have this girl with you to help speed things along or I will make sure that she never lives long enough for sickness to affect her.'

CHAPTER 19

Aerik, Ebon and Saera stepped wearily past the guards, most of whom ignored them. It was their third trip of the day, hauling two six foot long dragon replicas made of silk and stuffed with sandbags — and, of course, black powder. Aerik's original plan had called for the slaves to hide the black powder in small, unobtrusive decorations that could be scattered around the barracks, but Pan had offered the council an alternative plan that Aerik quickly endorsed.

Every year a celebration was held for Ascension Day, the day where, according to legend, the Drakes were gifted with the great strength and outer appearance of their god, The Great Dragon. Every year they decorated the streets and homes with Dragon lanterns, Dragon piñatas and paper Dragon statues. Pan suggested that they hold their attack until the lead up to the festival and hide the black powder in plain sight, where no Drakes would ever suspect them to be.

It was worth the few weeks wait, she argued, for the chance to use the festival as a cover. The Drakes wouldn't check the Dragons being carried in, because they would never consider it possible that a human would have access or the intelligence to create anything dangerous enough to fit in such a small space. Plus, the only way to check would be to cut the Dragon open, which no self respecting Drake would ever wish to do, unless they were secure enough of their status in the eyes of their god.

Huffing and puffing under the weight of the heavy replicas, Aerik, Ebon and Saera moved through the barracks to the back common room, where most of the Drakes congregated when they were off duty. The room had a long balcony that ran the length of the back wall, and it was there that the Drakes sat and drank, hurled abuse at passing human slaves and committed public executions for the sector. Aerik had even heard rumours that the Drakes held archery competitions from that balcony, using humans as targets — he didn't know if it was true or not, but he wouldn't have been surprised to discover it was.

They placed the stuffed Dragons in two corners of the room and scurried back out under the disdainful gaze of the other Drakes. The last two Dragons were now in place and all that was left was to get out of the barracks and wait until the festival night, when they would light the fuses and destroy the building. They had chosen festival night because the building would be almost deserted — it was the only night of the year when no humans would be on duty at all. The death of human slaves was unacceptable in their planning. Destruction of the barracks was the objective, with all the fear and uncertainty that came with it.

They made it outside without incident and were crossing the wide courtyard in front of the building when they heard one of the Drakes shouting for them. Fighting back the urge to bolt, Aerik, Ebon and Saera turned around and dropped to their knees as the Samurai approached. Without offering any explanation the Drake walked in a slow circle around them, studying them with a critical eye. He finally stopped in front of Saera and grabbed her by the jaw, turning her head this way and that as he examined her face.

'You're a new slave to this province, aren't you?'

'I am, my Lord,' Saera replied, carefully concealing her disgust.

'Yes, I knew I hadn't seen you before,' the Samurai nodded. 'I think I'll have you accompany me this afternoon. I need a new serving girl for the common room.'

Saera stiffened and Aerik wondered if there was some innuendo buried beneath that order that he was unaware of. Regardless, he wouldn't allow Saera to be spirited away by this Drake, but neither could he allow the public outcry that would follow if he killed a Samurai in an open courtyard. He remembered the training regimes that he himself had taught people under his command; always try to deflect the issue or defer it to a later date. If you can get away, you can disappear.

'My Lord,' Aerik said respectfully. 'I wish no disrespect and I know that my companion would be honoured beyond words to serve you in any capacity possible, but we're already under orders from Samurai Captain Sakea. We must finish our duties to him before we accept any others.'

Aerik had dredged the name of the Samurai Captain from the intelligence reports Kebble had given him, and judging from the sour expression on the Drake's face, he had chosen well.

'Then you'd best get moving,' the Drake said, glancing over Ebon's shoulder. 'Captain Sakea is on his way over here right now and he doesn't look happy.'

Aerik kept his face calm, but his stomach was churning horribly. Of all the bad luck. But Aerik knew his own lessons well and he moved automatically to the next rule; put as much distance between yourself and the danger as possible.

'Good master, I beg your permission to be on our way,' he said. 'Samurai Captain Sakea has asked us to find certain goods for him in the market, and he will be wondering why we're still here.'

Aerik left it at that, hoping the Drake would be smart enough to make the connection — if Sakea was upset about the slaves still being here, then he would also be upset at the Samurai for keeping them from their appointed task. But this Drake was either too stupid or too suspicious to cotton on, and the Samurai Captain drew closer and closer. Aerik's mind worked in overdrive, falling back on the last rule of training; when all else fails, run like hell.

The Drake looked over Ebon's shoulder once more, waving respectfully at Captain Sakea to attract his attention, and in that instant, Aerik struck. The Drake was taken completely off guard as Aerik heaved him backwards, but his training and natural skill brought him back to a fighting stance almost instantly. That moment of instability was all they needed, and they were racing across the courtyard towards the crowded streets.

Shouts of anger erupted behind them and Aerik resisted the urge to look over his shoulder, throwing all of his energy into his sprint. He darted to one side, nearly falling over as a young man emerged from a shop, pushing a hand cart in front of him. The young man gaped in surprise, then in fear as three arrows thudded dully against the cart's frame.

'They're firing arrows,' Aerik shouted to warn Ebon and Saera, though if they heard him they showed no sign — they just kept their heads down and ran.

Aerik knew his luck was running short when he heard the

bellowed order that all humans had learned to dread. The order, screamed by the Drakes, was for all slaves to stop and kneel immediately. Ordinarily, it meant that one of them had done something wrong and would be punished; right now it was to remove the obstacles from the street and give the archers a clear line of sight.

Pumping his legs as fast as he could, Aerik made for the first open alleyway. Ebon and Saera were already running for it and would reach it a few seconds ahead of him. The question was, would he make it before he was riddled with arrows?

For a brief moment, he thought he was going to get there. Despite the kneeling slaves and the cloud of arrows that thudded against the cobblestones and leapt up to slap at his legs, he thought he would get there. Then one of the missiles hit him in the shoulder, hard. It was straight and impossibly accurate, and Aerik knew it must have come from an enchanted crossbow. He hit the ground, screaming as wave after wave of pain radiated from the bolt and sent his muscles into spasms. He knew the Drakes were coming and he wondered if they would reach him before the next bolt did.

A booted foot struck the ground in front of his face, and Aerik knew his time was up. He wished he could have held Rebecca one last time, he wished he could have seen her free. A fresh wave of pain radiated from his shoulder as rough hands grabbed him by the tunic and the belt, then hauled him into the air. He saw Ebon's face pressed against his own as he was slung over the big man's shoulder, and only then did he realise that he might not die after all.

Saera stood in front of them, holding a thick wooden goods pallet as a shield against the arrows and crossbow bolts that flew down the street. When she heard Ebon's shout, she left the pallet in the street and sprinted back into the alley, while Aerik prayed that the makeshift barricade would stay upright until she was clear. He watched the pallet rock under the repeated blows and saw dozens of arrow tips poking through the thick wood. He saw it sway dangerously and start to topple, then his sight was cut off by the brick walls of the alleyway.

'Aerik, are you all right?' Ebon asked.

'Everything hurts,' he gasped.

'It's the enchantment on the crossbow bolt,' Ebon replied. 'It's not life threatening, thank gods, but you'll have to deal with it a little longer until we can find somewhere safe to get it out.'

'I'll be fine, just get me away from here,' he said, gritting his teeth against the pain. He almost fainted as Ebon took off and the jolt of the heavy footsteps slammed through his shoulder, but he muffled his cries to a hiss and held on.

He fought against the pain for what felt like an eternity, though he knew it was probably less than an hour. No one knew the alleyways of the city like the slaves, and none of the slaves knew them better than the revolutionaries. The Drakes used the main roads, avoiding the narrow, smelly, grimy alleyways, considering them beneath their honour. They left the alleys for the slaves so they could reduce how much they saw the humans.

It had always been a great advantage that the Drakes showed such disdain for the alleyways. Perhaps one day that would change, but for now it was a slave lifeline and Aerik was happy it was so.

They finally reached a secluded dead end, that from the smell of it was used as a rubbish tip. No windows looked out into the street and there were no inquisitive faces poking around, so Ebon gently lowered Aerik to the ground while Saera kept watch.

'Are you ready?' Ebon asked.

'It can't feel any worse, Ebon,' Aerik replied. 'Do it.'

He gasped in pain as Ebon yanked the bolt out, gritting his teeth to stop himself from screaming. For the next few seconds it felt as though his whole body was on fire, then slowly the pain drained away to a dull throb in his shoulder. With the poison gone and the bolt no longer pumping more into his system, it was only ordinary aches and pains that he had to deal with.

'Where are we?' he asked weakly.

'I'm not entirely sure,' Ebon shrugged. 'Somewhere in the south of the Tingra ghetto, I think.'

'Ah, the old stomping grounds.'

Ebon nodded as he tore strips from his tunic to bind Aerik's wound. Aerik kept still while his friend worked, trying to think through the haze of pain.

'They're going to be searching for us,' he said finally. Ebon just nodded and kept winding the cloth around the wound. 'And they'll get us, too, if we don't find somewhere to hide.'

'They might get us even if we do find somewhere,' Ebon replied. 'Depends whether they want to do a house to house search or not.'

'They will,' Aerik sighed. 'They lost face to us back there, and they're prickly enough about their honour without having it sullied by a human.'

'So what's the plan then?' Saera asked, looking over her shoulder at the pair of them.

Aerik closed his eyes and gritted his teeth, prevented from speaking for a moment as Ebon tightened the bindings and tied them off. When Ebon was finished, he let out the breath he'd been holding and fought off a wave of dizziness.

'We're in the Tingra ghetto, right?' he asked finally.

'If not in, then only a few blocks away,' Ebon replied. 'Unfortunately, the manor's clear on the other side and we'd never make it through the ghetto unnoticed.'

'That's okay,' Aerik said. 'We're in my old neighbourhood. I'm sure I can find someone here who remembers me.'

Ebon heard a groan of annoyance and was pretty certain he heard a few oaths muttered just below audible level as well — no slave who valued their life swore too loudly, just in case it was a Drake patrol come knocking. The door swung open to reveal a tall, broad shouldered man with an aged seamed face and shoulder length brown hair. He looked at Ebon with no recognition and his face darkened with anger at the interruption. Before he could say a word, Aerik stepped out from behind the door and smiled at him.

'Hello, Japheth,' he said. 'You're looking old.'

Japheth's jaw dropped when he saw Aerik, his mouth working noiselessly as he tried desperately to think of something to say.

'Aren't you going to invite us in?' Aerik asked.

'Of course,' Japheth replied, snapping his jaw shut and stepping back from the doorway.

Aerik, Ebon and Saera all hurried inside. Ebon paused to scan the street one last time for Drakes or informants before shutting and locking the door. He turned back to see Aerik and Japheth embracing each other as long lost friends.

'Aerik, by the gods I never thought to see you alive,' Japheth said. 'You disappeared the night Monta and Tisa were killed, and no one ever heard anything of you again. Then they found a Drake dead in your house ...'

'It all seems such a long time ago,' Aerik sighed, thinking back to that day.

'It *was* a long time ago, my friend,' Japheth said. 'I've missed you. Drinking scrum has never been the same without you, and as for these new bards — well, they just wish they were as good as you. What brings you back here now?'

Aerik glanced at Ebon and Saera, weighing his words before he answered. 'I'm in trouble, my friend. The Drakes are searching for me and they'll be starting a house to house search very soon, if they haven't already.'

'The Drakes are searching for you? What did you do?'

'More things than I can count,' he chuckled, half to himself. 'But in this case, we lied to a Samurai and then ran away instead of letting the Drakes take Saera for themselves.'

Japheth looked at Saera, who nodded. He studied her face looking for deception, but seemed satisfied by the simmering anger he saw in her face.

'Those damn lizards,' he said, keeping his voice a whisper from force of habit. 'Let me get you some food first, then we'll talk about the best plan for sneaking you out—'

Japheth was interrupted by a light knock on the wall from the neighbouring house. He froze instantly and all colour drained from his face. Aerik sighed and swore under his breath, but he remembered enough of his old life to get up and pass the warning knock on to the neighbours on the other side of Japheth's home. The knock was a simple alert — it meant that the Drakes were moving down the street, searching homes.

'No cellar,' Ebon said quickly. 'And running gets us nothing.'

'No need for either,' Aerik smiled. 'Japheth's wife is a midwife, which means she picks up a lot of favours from other slaves that need her help. Three years ago, after the last gales of winter, Japheth called in a favour and had one of our friends reinforce the ceiling beams.'

'Good old Timbal,' Japheth said. 'He worked in that wood shop for years before the Drakes took him.'

Aerik reached out and squeezed his old friend's arm in understanding. 'Show us the entry hatch to the roof and we'll make good use of Timbal's work.'

Japheth nodded and led them to the back corner of the main room where a hatch was cleverly concealed in the thatched ceiling. He dragged a chair over and ushered the three of them into the ceiling, then replaced the hatch and chair so the Drakes wouldn't suspect anything.

Aerik, Ebon and Saera lay in silence on thick timber beams that had been added for strength. The thatch that made up the ceiling also concealed the beams, which meant that the Drakes had no chance of knowing they were there — unless they did something stupid, of course.

Their hearts lurched as they heard the heavy thumping on Japheth's door and the low growl of Drake voices. They heard Japheth murmur a subdued reply and then there was silence. The creak of footsteps moved throughout the room, slow and steady as the Drake moved from one end of the house to the other. For one heart stopping moment, the Drake paused underneath the roof hatch and Aerik thought he meant to open it and look in. He gripped the hilt of his blackened knife and carefully slid it from its sheath, but to his relief the footsteps started again and the Drake walked back to the door. There was another low growl and Japheth's humble reply, then the door slammed shut and there was only silence.

For half an hour they waited in silence, each minute dragging longer than the next. When they finally heard the scrape of the chair and the creak of the roof hatch, they were so drained they barely had the strength to drag themselves out. Japheth helped them down and sat them on straw stuffed bags where they collapsed gratefully.

'Now, Aerik,' Japheth said, 'I think you need to tell me what this is all about.'

While Japheth chopped vegetables and prepared a stew for dinner, Aerik told his story — from his harrowing escape from The Stable on the night of Monta's death, to his elevation to the leadership of several resistance cells and his membership in the slave council. He kept the specifics of who and where a secret, not from lack of trust but from fear for his friend's safety.

When he was finished, Japheth ladled out the thick stew and handed a bowl to each of them. He sat opposite his friend and ate in thoughtful silence.

'The leader of the resistance, Aerik,' he said finally. 'What on earth possessed you to do that?'

'A leader, not *the* leader,' Aerik replied. 'And it was the deaths of Monta and Tisa that possessed me to do it, as well as the attempt on my own life.'

'Fair point,' Japheth grunted. 'But what in god's name do you think you can achieve?'

'Freedom, Japheth. The more we push the Drakes, the more trouble we become for them. One day we'll have such a force that they'll have to listen to us, or risk losing everything they've built.'

'Either that or they'll just decide to kill every human in the city and start afresh.'

'They can't do that and you know it. They'd be cutting their own throat.'

'Bad choice of words,' Japheth said.

'You know what I mean,' Aerik replied. 'They would lose so much in trade and production that they'd cripple themselves. They're too dependent on us.'

Japheth shook his head and Aerik left it at that. It had taken a lot for him to save them from the Drakes, and even then he'd done it with a great deal of apprehension. One day he would understand.

'I want you to join me,' Aerik said suddenly. He was pretty sure he knew the answer, but it was worth a shot. 'Help us fight for what should have been ours by right. If we win, then a human will never again have to fear for their life when a Drake walks by. Your life and your destiny would be your own.'

Japheth sighed and Aerik prepared himself for a flat refusal, but the big man surprised him. 'Tell me what you've got planned and I'll tell you what I can do to help. I won't join you, not yet, but I'll give you anything I can.'

Aerik smiled at the unexpected response and even Ebon seemed happy at the prospect, but Saera scowled suspiciously.

'Our aim was to hit the barracks and destroy it on festival night.'

'That's tomorrow night,' Japheth frowned.

'Yes, it is, but don't worry. Our packages are already in place, we just need to get inside and set the fuses. If we can get the three of us inside, it can be done in less than five minutes.'

'Except that the Drakes are looking for us,' Ebon pointed out.

'That's where Japheth comes in,' Aerik smiled. 'I need disguises for the three of us; something that will get us in unnoticed. Then we just walk in the front like all the other slaves and get our job done.'

'Why don't we just go to the Council and ask for more men to help?' Saera asked.

Aerik and Ebon looked at each other, their faces both as dark as the other's. Saera's brow furrowed as she tried to understand their hesitation.

'The council is already a political animal,' Aerik sighed eventually. 'You aren't a part of the meetings Saera. You don't know what it's like. Half the council members have decided that they like being in command of their resistance cells. They're afraid that by joining together, we're going to take what they've created away from them.'

'Those who think like that have banded together behind Kebble,' Ebon added. 'And those who feel that unity means strength have banded behind Aerik.'

'If I go to the council now, they'll see it as a failure on my part,' Aerik said. 'It will give Kebble's faction support and push those who are undecided into his camp.'

'That's a dangerous game to play,' Saera growled. 'You're betting people's lives in an effort to win a popularity contest.'

'I agree,' Aerik sighed. 'Unfortunately, the consequences of not playing the game mean even *more* lives and the chance to lose all that we've accomplished. That's something I refuse to do. Now, Japheth, what suggestions do you have for our disguise?'

Japheth rubbed his chin thoughtfully as he looked them all up and down. 'Well, the Drakes are looking for two men and a woman. I could give you some of my wife's clothes and see Martrietta for a wig.'

'No,' Ebon said, his face reflecting equal parts horror and embarrassment.

'No,' Aerik agreed. 'That's been done before and the Drakes will be looking for it. We'd be better to dress Saera as a man and go in that way.'

Japheth looked Saera up and down again, this time sizing her up for a male wardrobe. 'Possible,' he said finally. 'We could take her hair out of that ponytail and put it in a slave braid, then dress her in some of my clothes. They're a bit big, but the bagginess should blur the shape of your body. We'll still have to tie down your ... ah, upper body. The Drakes would notice them pretty quickly.'

Saera looked at Japheth and raised her eyebrows, while he flushed with embarrassment. 'What exactly is wrong with my upper body?'

'Don't worry, Japheth, we understand what's required,' Aerik said, patting him on the shoulder. 'That's not a problem.'

'I was only teasing,' Saera said, her face braking into a grin. 'No fair spoiling my fun.'

'Fun comes later, when we have the time.' Aerik said. 'Now Japheth, what do you have for us?'

'I could put some chalk in your hair and use a few moulded rags to change your body shape. We can also stuff cotton in your cheeks to blur your face lines. We've done it before.'

'Sounds perfect,' Aerik nodded. 'Remember, we need it done by tomorrow night.'

Japheth looked a little daunted, but he nodded and jumped to his feet. 'Then I'd better go out and get these things organised.'

With that, Japheth put on his cloak and disappeared into the night. The others gathered up the dirty dishes, washed them all and put them away — leaving food scraps out invited the rats. When they finished and dried off their hands, Aerik spread a blanket out on the floor and lay down to get some sleep. He heard Saera sit down next to him and he rolled over tiredly to look at her.

'Can I talk to you?'

'As long as you're quick,' he yawned.

'I will be,' she nodded. 'I want to go and get reinforcements from the Manor. We can gather a group of our own men and send them into the barracks. There'll be fewer guards because of the festival, so we'd have a better chance of slipping our people in.'

'Especially if we create a diversion out the front,' Aerik added. 'You're right, Saera. We would be better off with more men, but you have to understand the balancing act we're playing at the moment. I'm trying to get the council to adopt a more subtle style of planning attacks, while Kebble just wants to fight face to face.'

'That's suicide,' Saera balked.

'I know that and you know that, but Kebble disagrees,' Aerik said. 'He's let his revenge cloud his better judgment. He's become what you would have if you hadn't curbed your anger.'

'You mean if *you* hadn't curbed my anger,' she grinned. 'Aerik, if you succeed in this plan by using stealth and tactics instead of brute force, then the council will see you're right no matter how many people you use. But if you fail, or even if you succeed but lose lives, then the council will see that as proof your ideas don't work.'

Aerik looked at her thoughtfully, mulling over her words. He ran several scenarios through his mind as he thought of whether having more men would help or hinder him, and how he would use them if he decided he did need them.

'People's lives are more important than people's opinions,' Saera said. 'Don't risk the mission or our lives just to impress the council.'

'Saera, impressing the council could mean the lives of many humans, and if it's done right, it could mean the freedom of our people,' Aerik sighed. 'But you're right — my plans are for nothing if this mission fails. Have Ebon do your hair in a male slave braid while I find you some of Japheth's clothes. Disguised like that, you should be able to get to the Manor and organise a team.'

'What do I tell them?'

'Come back to me when your hair's done,' Aerik said. 'I should have worked it out by then. Oh, and I'll need you back here by tomorrow afternoon. I want you with us for the diversion.'

Saera hopped to her feet and nodded. 'I'll be here. I promise.'

Chapter 20

'Annah and Rajin, you two are next.'

Annah jumped to her feet and stepped into the centre of the padded mat on one side of a painted red square. On the other side stood Rajin, a gold scaled Acolyte who was roughly the same level of advancement as Annah was. Dala had chosen them as a pair for their first sparring match and Annah hoped that she was up to the challenge.

Dala sat on a bench watching her students and comparing notes with Ishkal who sat next to her. He had made a point of being around Annah as much as possible since her run in with the human slave, and Annah was comforted by his presence. She turned towards them and bowed low, then turned and bowed to Rajin.

'The same sparring rules apply here,' Dala said. 'Single strike to a red patch on your opponents padding or three strikes on a blue patch gets you one point. First to ten points wins the match.'

Annah and Rajin both kept their eyes on the other, but nodded slowly to show that they understood. Dala waited a few moments longer, then clapped her hands twice to start the match.

Rajin rushed towards Annah and jabbed his fists at her with blinding speed. Annah dropped back, ducking and weaving away from his attacks with such skill that Rajin couldn't land a punch on her, let alone hit one of the coloured patches. His frustration started to tell the longer he fought, and before long his punches became angrier and less calculated. If Annah had wanted to, she could have landed several blows on Rajin and almost ended the game, but her fists remained bunched at her sides.

'She misses many opportunities,' Dala said.

'I think she's afraid to strike,' Ishkal replied. 'She knows the opportunities are there, I guarantee it.'

'Why is she afraid? We've promised her the protection of the Order to keep her safe.'

'Dala, you've grown up a Drake and a monk of the Gold Dragon,' Ishkal sighed. 'You've always been privileged and you've never had to fear for your life from the hand of another. No one would dare threaten you, but Annah has been a slave for as long as she can remember. For her to speak the wrong words in the wrong tone was a death sentence, let alone for her to strike a Drake. It will just take time.'

'Perhaps,' Dala nodded. 'But time grows shorter. The rest of her skills are far above what's expected of an Acolyte, all except her fighting skills.'

'She has the skill,' Ishkal insisted. 'She just needs the will to use it.'

Dala's reply was cut short as the gates to the training hall slid open and a big, iron scaled Drake limped through, trailed by a stammering secretary.

'Please, sir, if you would just wait in the audience hall I could have some news brought to you,' the secretary said desperately. But from the Iron Drake's expression, he wasn't about to wait anywhere. Ishkal took one look at him and his face broke into a mirthful grin.

'Kelkh,' he laughed. 'What on earth are you doing here?'

At the sound of Kelkh's name, Annah stopped dodging around the mat and looked over. Rajin took advantage of her distraction and landed a savage blow to her stomach. Kelkh was running across the room before Ishkal could stop him. He dropped his shoulder and powered into Rajin sending him flying across the mat.

'Hit her again and you'll get worse!'

'Kelkh, wait,' Ishkal shouted, hurrying over. 'Annah and Rajin are sparring. It's part of her training.'

'So is honour in combat,' Kelkh spat. 'She had clearly stopped when that slime hit her.'

'Then they've both learned a valuable lesson, my friend,' Ishkal smiled. 'Annah has learned not to stop in a fight for any reason, and Rajin has learned the consequences of being dishonourable.'

Kelkh's mouth twitched into a smile, but he was unable to keep it up for long. It took a moment for Ishkal to realise how tired his friend looked and how much weight he carried on his shoulders.

'Kelkh, what is wrong?'

'I need to take Annah back with me,' he said heavily. 'I've been ordered to the front lines and I need her to come with me.'

Speaking in a low voice, Kelkh told Ishkal everything that had happened between him and Dragath, from the visit to the forge to the explicit order for him to regain his apprentice. When he was finished, Ishkal was grim with anger.

'He wouldn't dare. He wouldn't dare to harm Annah while she's under the protection of the Golden Order.'

'He would and you know it,' Kelkh said. 'He would see it as a point of honour to have her dead. Please, Ishkal, let her come with me.'

'But he would risk a revolution by disobeying the word of the Gold Drakes,' Ishkal protested.

'Dragath would make sure that the evidence didn't point to him,' Kelkh said. 'And even if it did, the Abbot wouldn't risk civil war within the Empire over the life of a human.'

'He would, especially when she's under our protection,' Ishkal said. 'But I see your point; Annah would still be just as dead. I'll talk to the Abbot and see what I can arrange. Damn Dragath!'

'You'll get no argument from me.'

Ishkal was as good as his word, and while Kelkh and Annah enjoyed a simple dinner together, he spoke to the Abbot. The old Drake wasn't happy about Annah leaving, especially after his vision that may or may not have been linked to her, but Ishkal was persuasive — and like it or not, Kelkh was recognised by Drake law as Annah's legal owner, and that gave him final say in her comings and goings. The Abbot reluctantly agreed, but he charged Kelkh with her safety until such time as she could be returned to the monastery.

Ishkal left the Abbot and joined Annah and Kelkh for dinner, where he broke the news to her that she would be leaving. As he expected, she was torn between her happiness at rejoining Kelkh and returning to the forge, and sadness at leaving Ishkal and her training at the Monastery.

'Annah,' Ishkal said, 'don't think of this as goodbye, think of it more as a holiday. You'll be returning to the forge that you love, and in good time you'll return to us to complete what you've started.'

Annah nodded and blinked back her tears. 'Thank you, master,' she said, keeping her back straight and looking Ishkal in the eyes like he had taught her.

'You're welcome, Annah,' he replied. 'Now run along and pack your bags. And be sure to take your dream stones with you.'

Choking back her emotion, Annah turned and fled towards her room, leaving Ishkal and Kelkh alone to work out the finer details. In a scant few hours, Annah was once again winging away on Mange with all of her possessions, carrying parts of her old life to a new and mysterious place.

The journey took several days, even with Mange's strong wings carrying them at dizzying speeds across the Empire. Kelkh and Annah took the time to rekindle their friendship, though Kelkh, gruff as always, would never have admitted as much. She knew straight away that he had missed her, and that made it easier to postpone her training with Ishkal.

They spoke little through the day, spending their time hunched into their cloaks to ward off the wind. At night they sat around the fire and talked of Annah's time at the monastery, Kelkh listening attentively despite the bottle of scalett that always sat next to him. He glowed to hear about her acceptance as a full Acolyte in the Order and his eyes misted over when she showed him the bracers he had made sitting snugly around her wrists. He muttered something about the dust in the clearing as he wiped his eyes, then changed the topic abruptly. Annah just smiled.

They reached the border on the sixth day and Kelkh started searching for the main army encampment. Dragath had given him its last known location, but war was a fluid thing — if the Drakes had made a break in the Cat-Men's lines, then they would have shifted their encampment forward to keep the supply depots close at hand. Relying on Mange's eyesight, Kelkh slackened the reins and gave the Rock Dragon freedom to seek out the camp.

After three tiring hours of search, Mange flew over a low mountain range and revealed a whole new horizon stretched out before them. Kelkh took one look at the land and hauled on Mange's reigns to pull the great beast down. Mange circled the grassy, weatherworn top of one mountain, dropping lower with each pass as Annah wondered what was going on. By his third revolution, the ground was only a meter below and Mange's speed had dropped to almost nothing.

'Annah, jump down.' Kelkh said grimly.

'Of course, master,' she replied, sliding off Mange's back. 'Is something wrong?'

'Not if I'm fast enough,' he muttered. 'I want you to stay here until I come back for you. Do you understand?'

'Of course, master.'

Kelkh nodded and kicked Mange's flanks, and the Dragon immediately pumped his wings and shot into the air. Annah watched them go, confusion and fear roiling in her stomach. When Kelkh was nothing more than a blob in the distance, she switched her gaze to the two massive armies sprawled across the valley, moving slowly closer to battle.

Kelkh hurtled through the sky, watching the land unfold before him like a map. The mountain range was bunched on either side of the wide valley, which stretched for miles and provided the only feasible route through the area. The two armies were camped at either end of the valley and were currently moving towards a colossal battle in the centre. They hadn't met each other yet, but it wouldn't be long before they did. Drake officers flew above their infantry companies on Keldarkan Dragon mounts, ordering them into formation for the imminent charge while the archers and cavalry support checked their bowstrings and tightened their harnesses.

As he reached the middle of the valley and approached the rear of the Drake formations, Kelkh fought the buffeting wind to stand up in his saddle and get a better view. In the distance, a wide river cut a channel through the mountain walls from the foothills to the valley. Trees and shrubs grew close to the river banks, almost hiding the water's surface from sight as they took advantage of the shelter that the rocky walls provided. Through the gaps in the green ceiling, Kelkh saw what had made his warrior instincts scream in warning; he saw the thick layer of ice that covered the surface of the river.

As he drew lower to the rear formations of the Drake army, he looked out for the closest cluster of Keldarkan dragons which indicated the officers of the rearguard. The officers looked up in surprise to see a large war dragon strapped with forge equipment land in front of them.

'The camp is two leagues to the North, Forger,' the emerald scaled Captain said disdainfully. 'I suggest you get there now and out of the way of my men. The battle will begin shortly.'

'Turn your men around, Captain,' Kelkh replied. 'The Cat-Men are moving to attack your flank. They'll be here in minutes.'

'Fear not, old Forger,' the Captain said patronisingly. 'The mountains are impassable on either side of the valley. There's no need to be afraid, the Cat-Men won't be able to flank us.'

'They will if they follow the river through the mountains,'

Kelkh snapped. 'That channel will drop them right in your lap.'

'The river is too deep and too rapid for anything to travel along it,' the Captain growled. 'My scouts checked it thoroughly several days ago. Now I've been more than patient with you, but it's time to move on!'

'I know what I'm talking about, damn it. I fought in the Cat-Men wars a decade ago,' Kelkh said. 'They have shamans who can—'

A fierce roar cut through the air, issuing a powerful challenge to any who dared accept it. The Captain turned away from Kelkh and squinted to make out the hulking figure of a Lion-Rah who stepped from the centre of the Cat-Men ranks. Even from a distance it was a massive specimen, eight feet tall with muscles that bulged beneath its tawny fur. It stood on two feet like a Drake, but its fingers were short and stubby, ending in razor sharp claws. Its head was that of a grassland Lion, huge with a blunt snout and long fangs, and surrounded by a thick reddish-brown mane.

The Lion-Rah threw his hands to the sky and let loose another colossal roar, calling the blessing of his gods upon his army. Kelkh barely watched the spectacle, ignoring it with the practiced detachment of a veteran soldier, but he saw the fear in the green troops around him. The warriors of the Cat-Men army took up their leader's cry, stomping their feet and smashing their weapons against their shields.

'This is a diversion,' Kelkh snarled. 'When they finally attack, it will be because their flanking troops are about to drive a knife into your side.'

'Sir, we could spare Skink Company,' a Lieutenant said. 'We could send them to the lake around the river mouth and scout the area. If the Cat-Men attack the front line, we can still bring them back in time to support the main column.'

The Captain glared at his subordinate and gathered the reigns of his mount. 'I'm going to check on the Company Commanders one last time. I want this man out of here before I return!'

The Captain flicked his reins and took to the sky to survey his troops. The Lieutenant sat uncomfortably in his saddle, hoping that Kelkh would move along and save himself the embarrassment of being physically removed from the battlefield.

'My name is Kelkh Ironbound,' Kelkh tried one last time, 'former Samurai Captain of—'

'Of the Royal Guard,' the Lieutenant said. 'I have heard stories about you from my father.'

'Then help me, damn it,' Kelkh said. 'We're running out of time! Have you ever fought against the Cat-Men?'

'No sir,' the Lieutenant replied. 'I earned my commission against the humans on the border of Darendall.'

'The humans are nothing like the Cat-Men,' Kelkh growled. 'They don't have any magic. But the Cat-Men have shamans who can freeze the ice on that river, and that would give them a clear path to our rearguard!'

'I can't disobey my orders, sir,' the Lieutenant said. 'Not even for you.'

'You were ordered to get me out of here, nothing more,' Kelkh replied. 'Give me command of one company and I guarantee that I'll leave and head straight for the lake, and you won't have disobeyed any orders; if I'm wrong, you can blame everything on me and still have the troops back in time.'

The Lieutenant stared up at the sky as he tried to decide what to do. Heaving a deep sigh he took a golden seal from his belt and handed it to Kelkh.

'Take Skink Company,' he sighed. 'They're recruits so keep them on a short leash. Look for an orange pennant with an emerald Skink in the centre. Give them this seal and tell them that Samurai Lieutenant Meelik sent you.'

'Thank The Dragon that someone in this regiment has half a brain,' Kelkh growled. 'Don't worry, son, you've probably just saved this battle.'

Kelkh kicked Mange's flank and took off for Skink Company. He saw the pennant without any difficulty, being waved in the breeze by some over eager flag bearer. He honed in on the small group of Keldarkan Dragons tethered beneath the flag and brought Mange to hover over them.

'Who's in charge of this company?' Kelkh roared.

'I am,' a young Ensign replied uncertainly. 'What do you want, Forger?'

'As of now, your company is under my command.' Kelkh flicked the golden seal off his thumb and the young Ensign caught it as it dropped, looking at it uncertainly.

'Lieutenant Meelik sent me,' Kelkh said impatiently. 'The Cat-Men are moving to attack our flank and we need to stop them before it is too late.'

'Lieutenant Meelik sent a Forger to lead my Company?' the Ensign balked.

'You can take it up with him after the battle,' Kelkh snapped, fed up with the delay. 'Until then, get your company moving double time to the lake around the river mouth. *Now.*'

When Kelkh broke through the brush surrounding the lake, he almost believed nothing was wrong. The lake was as still as glass, shimmering like molten gold under the weak early spring sun. If it wasn't for the frozen surface of the river feeding into the lake, Kelkh might have thought he was mistaken about the whole thing.

The Drakes of Skink Company were almost bent double, gasping for breath as they enjoyed their first reprieve since Kelkh had taken command. They'd pushed themselves hard to reach the lake ahead of Kelkh's fears, and now as they stood around the tranquil lake they wondered if it had all been for nothing.

'Don't get too comfortable,' Kelkh bellowed. 'I want archers formed in a single line around the outskirts of the lake, targeting the river mouth. Infantry will form up in front of them but *out of their line of fire*, am I clear? If you need to stand or kneel in the lake, then do it. Sergeants, you're in direct command of your squads. All officers with Keldarkan Battle Dragons will form up on me — you're now our cavalry. Move out!'

Kelkh watched the green troops mill around the lake shore while the frustrated Sergeants tried to enforce order. He heard grumbling from the troops and even from some of the young officers as they muttered about a wild goose chase, but the more experienced sergeants knew what they were doing. They had all fought before and they understood the urgency of Kelkh's commands, as well as the reasoning behind them. The Dragon willing, they would get the troops into position in time and they might all have some chance.

'You there,' Kelkh said, pointing to one of the officers flying behind him. 'I need you to scout out the river. Find those Cat-Men and get me any information you can about them. How far away they are, how many of them there are, anything you can spot that might be useful.'

Kelkh's orders were cut short as a low rumble echoed off the cavern walls. It sounded like the beat of a hundred drums, soft at first but rapidly getting louder. They were out of time; the Cat-Men were upon them.

'Don't bother scouting,' he said to the anxious officer. 'Get all the information you can from your first pass, then fly to the rearguard command centre and find Samurai Lieutenant Meelik. Tell him everything you see, but *only* him. He'll know what to do from there.'

The officer gave Kelkh a nervous salute, then moved his Dragon to a better vantage point of the battlefield. Kelkh ignored him, his eyes locked on the river mouth.

'Archers, ready your arrows,' he shouted. 'The Dragon is watching us today, so make him proud of his descendants.'

Kelkh's words were almost drowned out by the pounding of feet and the screech of claws on ice. The rumble reached a crescendo of power, bursting a moment later as a flood of Cat-Men ran to the end of the iced river and leaped into the lake. They pushed through the waist high water, churning the mud and silt in their wake as they charged for the shore.

'Fire!'

The hum of arrows cut through the air, startling the Cat-Men from their frenzy. They realised that they were surrounded by a Drake army an instant before the arrows struck home, tearing into their scattered ranks. Their pain filled roars were heard even over the thumping footsteps of the rest of their army, warning those on the river of the danger that lay ahead — but Kelkh was not going to give them the chance to regroup.

'Charge!'

With a collective battle cry, the Drake infantry churned through the lake waters, already turning red from the bodies of the dead, and cut through the confused Cat-Men like chaff. The next wave of enemy troops paused by the river mouth to make some kind of attacking formation, just as Kelkh had anticipated. Some of the younger Drake soldiers looked up as the Keldarkan Dragons flew over their heads, forming a loose wedge with Kelkh at their tip.

The river had cut a deep channel through the mountain rock, giving the Cat-Men nowhere to go but forward, right into Kelkh's dragon charge. Kelkh saw the spotted golden pelts of the wickedly fast Cheet-Rah, the powerful orange and black striped Tig-Rah and the tan fur of the Jag-Rah. He saw them cry out in challenge and saw some of the more enterprising soldiers raise their bows. He saw the crack in the Cat-Men formation that would crumble under his sword.

Bellowing the war cry of the Royal Guard, Kelkh pushed Mange into a dive and crashed through the first line of defence. Mange smashed heavily onto the ice, crushing two Cat-Men under his bulk, then reared on his back legs to protect Kelkh from the archers and free his front claws to swipe at anything close by. Kelkh leaned sideways in his saddle and swung his blade at a nearby Cheet-Rah. The swift creature managed to block the blow, but the sheer power knocked it off balance making it easy prey for the next Drake crashing through. Kelkh moved seamlessly to his next target, a huge Tig-Rah that roared in challenge and charged towards him.

The Tig-Rah ducked beneath Mange's claws and ran under the Dragon's belly. It popped up from one side underneath the wing and jabbed its sword at Kelkh, who caught on his crosspiece and pushed it aside. On his backswing, Kelkh drew an angry red line across the Tig-Rah's chest. The Cat-Man roared in pain and tried to duck back under Mange's belly, but Kelkh was too quick, stabbing at its shoulder. It roared again and slashed at Kelkh's leg with its claws, drawing four lines of blood, but Kelkh shunted away the pain and concentrated on staying alive. He kicked Mange's flanks and pushed the Dragon into a crouch, forcing the Tig-Rah to jump out of hiding or risk being crushed into the ice. Kelkh leaned over in his saddle and finished his foe with a single thrust as it emerged.

When he straightened up once again, three new enemies leaped into the air to attack him. Mange lashed out with his front claws nearly taking the head from the shoulders of one of them, and swung his tail to catch the second in its back, sending the limp body flying into the chaos of battle. The third landed awkwardly between Mange's wings. Kelkh punched out with his sword hilt, catching the Cat-Man in the snout and knocking its head backwards. With a deft movement, he pulled a thin metal shaper from his forge belt with his left hand and jammed it into the Cat-Man's throat.

As his latest foe slid to the icy surface of the river, Kelkh found himself in a small island of inaction in the battle. To his left, a Cheet-Rah scaled the back of a young officer's Dragon, running up the spine and stabbing the Drake in the back. To the right, another officer fought on foot, surrounded by dead enemies, his Dragon lying motionless on the ground. They had achieved the chaos that Kelkh had set out for, but now the Cat-Men were regrouping and the cavalry would start to take real losses. He didn't know how long these green soldiers could hold out.

As if answering his silent prayer, a deep battle horn sounded from behind him, the signal that the infantry had pushed through the lake and arrived at the river mouth. Kelkh kicked Mange into the air, hoping the other officers would remember the signal and do the same. The Dragons rose into the air numbering two thirds of their original strength — most of the missing Dragons had lost their riders and continued to raise havoc in the Cat-Men ranks, but they were attacking aimlessly, and for the most part ineffectively. Kelkh did a quick head count, then turned back to the battle to watch over his troops.

The infantry hit the confused Cat-Men like a battering ram, crashing through their first line with devastating ease. They pushed the enemy further back along the riverbed until they met the organised core of troops i n a furious melee. While the Cat-Men were savage and ferocious fighters, the Drakes were far better skilled, but they were young, inexperienced and heavily outnumbered. Cat-Men and Drakes fell side by side turning the icy river surface bright crimson, until the momentum of the Drake spearhead faltered, then stopped completely.

The Drakes fought valiantly, until a group of heavily armed Tig-Rah slammed into their lines and launched a savage counter attack. The Jag-rah followed their comrades into battle, sprinting forward and leaping over the first three ranks of the Drake infantry to tear at the middle ranks. The battle could have been over then and there, but Kelkh was too experienced to allow that to happen.

'Sound the infantry withdraw,' he shouted. 'Fall back to the centre of the lake! Cavalry, we charge on my mark to cover them.'

Kelkh led the cavalry down the narrow channel of the river, crashing into the Tig-Rah phalanx while his men retreated to the river mouth. He didn't risk his Cavalry long this time, just long enough for the infantry to get a head start. As soon as he took to the sky once more, the Cat-Men yowled angrily and charged after the retreating Samurai. The Drakes reached the river mouth seconds ahead of the pursuit and leaped frantically into the water.

The infantry weren't completely clear of the river mouth when the Cat-Men overtook the rearguard, falling on them with a frenzied bloodlust. The Cat-Men army buried the lagging Drakes and poured into the lake after the main column, mushrooming out from the river mouth as more troops piled out behind them. Hovering above them, just out of arrow range, Kelkh waved the golden standard he had commandeered and bellowed orders at the top of his voice.

On either side of the river mouth, Kelkh's second and third infantry groups crashed into the Cat-Men, closing in on either side of them like a bear trap. The first group spun on their heels and charged back into battle to close the box around the river mouth, keeping the Cat-Men contained and unable to bring the full force of their numbers to bear. The battle lines writhed and flowed as the Cat-Men pushed at the Drake lines, but for the most part the Drakes held.

Kelkh saw the breach moments before it happened, the ripple of troops as the Cat-Men hit the beleaguered line and started to push through. He roared and led his cavalry into the heat of the battle to push the Cat-Men back and reseal the breach. It was a bloody affair, with little of the finesse of his earlier attacks. The Samurai Cavalry let their Dragons do most of the work, then took to the sky and left the infantry behind to finish the job. Kelkh watched as the infantry ranks closed behind him and the breach was repaired, but he knew it was going to be the first of many.

When the second breach occurred, Kelkh once again led the cavalry to attack, but the Cat-Men were ready for them this time. As the Dragons descended, the Cat-Men hurled spears at the Drake riders. Kelkh deftly swerved Mange to one side to avoid the missile, but the officer next to him wasn't so skilled; the spear caught him in the chest, launching him out of his saddle and into the air. His foot caught the reigns of his dragon as he fell, yanking them to one side. Responding to the order, the Dragon swerved to the left, cutting in front of Mange who, unable to slow his momentum, slammed into it. The Dragon jerked in surprise at Mange's unexpected impact and swung its tail reflexively. Kelkh turned just in time to absorb the blow as the tail slammed into him, but he couldn't stop it knocking him free of his saddle.

Keeping a solid grip on his sword, Kelkh watched the ground draw closer and felt the breeze whistle past him. He waited until he was almost on top of the battle when he whispered a prayer that the Cat-Men had already used all their spears and unfurled his wings to stop his descent. He felt the yank at his shoulder blades as his wings filled with air and slowed him to a gentle drop, and he knew he had probably strained half of his back muscles. Shunting the pain aside, he folded his wings away and dropped the final two meters to the lake, right into the thick of the battle.

Before he had even stood from his crouch, a Cheet-Rah soldier closed in on him with a short sword in each hand. Kelkh somehow knocked both incoming blades aside and returned with a vicious swing of his own that hit nothing but air. The mud from the bottom of the lake had been stirred up by all the turmoil of battle, and moving through the thick crimson water was tough — but Kelkh knew it gave him an edge. The Cheet-Rah was the fastest warrior alive on land, but in the muddied water, Kelkh's sheer strength helped him push through despite his crippled leg. When the Cat-Man attacked once more, Kelkh caught its swords with his own and heaved backwards, knocking the Cheet-Rah off balance. Not used to the drag of the lake, the Cheet-Rah took a moment to regain its footing, but that instant was all it took for Kelkh to slide his blade through its defences.

The Cheet-Rah had barely slid into the murky river before two more Cat-Men charged to attack. Kelkh swung his blade through combinations that he hadn't used in years, but were etched into his memory by harsh experience. Even with his leg slowing his movements, he fought the two creatures to a standstill, slowly moving them into a position where he could finish them off. One of them slipped in the mud on the lake bottom, giving Kelkh an opening in his defences.

Kelkh thrust his sword forward, grabbing the Cat-Man by the neck with his other hand and yanking it between him and his other opponent. The other Cat-Man found its blade slicing into its dying comrade instead of the Drake Samurai, and yanked out of its hand as the body slid to the bottom of the lake. Left without a weapon, the Cat-Man hurled itself at Kelkh, trying to drag him under the water. Kelkh tried desperately to regain his balance, but his leg couldn't bear the weight and crumpled beneath him, dropping them both into the lake.

The world turned red as he fell beneath the water, filling his senses with the stench of battle. He felt a sting on his chest as the Cat-Man's claws flailed uselessly at him, but it was only a minor wound. Kelkh closed his eyes to the murky water, knowing that he couldn't see the orange and black striped fur of his opponent even if he had wanted to. Acting by touch, he grabbed one of the Cat-Man's wrists and kept his arm pinned, while his other hand found the creature's neck and squeezed. His lungs started to burn with lack of air, and from the change in the Cat-Man's panicked demeanour, it was feeling the same. Kelkh tried to stand as he pushed the Cat-Man further into the bottom of the lake, but the slippery mud and the flailing enemy made it impossible. Letting go of the Cat-Man's wrist, Kelkh put his hand to the ground to steady himself, and by the grace of The Dragon, found something else in the mud mire. It was the hilt of the sword he had dropped when he was tackled.

Kelkh let go of his enemy and scooped up the sword in one hand and a handful of mud in the other. He burst through the lake surface, gasping for breath, and saw his foe gasping and clutching desperately at a wooden spear that floated nearby. Kelkh launched the wad of mud at the Cat-Man's face, hitting it squarely in the snout as he charged forward. The Cat-Man reared back in surprise, leaving its chest and neck exposed. Kelkh finished it quickly.

Still gasping for breath, Kelkh looked around for his next enemy and wondered why he wasn't being overrun. The limp body of a Cheet-Rah flying past him answered that question quickly enough, and he turned to see Mange clearing a circle of foes around him. Kelkh thanked The Dragon over and over for Mange, as he pushed through the water and climbed on his mount's back, kicking him into the sky to lead his troops.

But his absence had been costly. The Cat-Men had regrouped a solid core of warriors and were counter attacking with vicious efficiency, and their greater numbers were telling. Kelkh could see no less than three places in their lines where a breach was imminent, despite the cavalry's best intentions.

'Hold that line,' he yelled. 'Pull together and hold that line, damn you, or it's all lost.'

The Drakes rallied for a moment, but it was too late. The Cat-Men breached the lines, flooding through and tearing at the Drake defences.

'Dragon, guide me into your arms,' Kelkh sighed, kissed his sword blade and kicking Mange into battle for the last time. Mange drove tiredly forward, but reared back in surprise as another battle Dragon cut in front of him. Kelkh recognised the face of Samurai Lieutenant Meelik as it flashed by, but didn't understand until the braying horns cut through the sky. An entire company of Keldarkan Dragons flew past Kelkh after their Lieutenant, charging into the Cat-Men with unbridled fury, while the stomp of the running infantry reinforcements sounded like war drums on the soft earth.

Kelkh let his shoulders sag and guided Mange away from the fight. They were both tired and injured, and neither of them had fought in a pitched battle for many years. They weren't needed and were no more use in any case. The reinforcements had arrived and the battle was won. Flicking Mange's reigns, he guided the Dragon back to the hilltop where Annah waited for him.

'You! Who in The Dragon's name do you think you are?'

Kelkh ignored the irate Captain and slid gingerly off Mange's back, tired and sore, his crippled leg aching mercilessly. Annah dropped lightly onto the ground next to him and tried to make herself invisible.

'By what right do you commandeer my company and countermand my orders?' the Captain ranted. 'I am Samurai Captain Taka and I demand an answer!'

'Captain Taka, your inaction would have cost massive losses to our army,' Kelkh said bluntly. 'You never ordered me not to lead a company, you just told your Lieutenant to get me out of your sight, which he did — and it's lucky for you that he has a brain in his head! If we hadn't repelled the Cat-Men at the lake, the Cheet-Rah would have peppered your formation with arrows while the Tig-Rah smashed your flank. You would be dead before you realised your mistake and the main column would have paid for it.'

'Insolent worm,' Captain Taka hissed. 'I will not be told what strategies to use by a mere merchant! Oh yes, I remember the forge equipment on your mount. You're a blacksmith, not a warrior. What's the matter, Iron scale, didn't you have the stomach to join the Royal Guard? What dishonour you must bring your ancestors.'

Kelkh's jaw tightened and his hands clenched into fists, but he didn't take the bait. 'Watch your tongue, Samurai Captain, before I take it from you.'

'For a merchant to talk that way to a warrior is a death sentence,' Captain Taka hissed. 'Draw your sword, merchant filth, and prepare to meet The Dragon.'

The crowd parted on one side of Captain Taka and a tall, red scaled Drake stepped through. Captain Taka took one look at the new Drake and unconsciously stood straighter.

'Don't you wish to know something about the Drake you're going to kill?' the red scaled Drake asked.

'Sir, what would I need to know about a mere merchant?' Captain Taka asked.

'I wasn't talking to you, Captain Taka,' the Drake smiled. 'I was talking to Samurai General Kelkh Ironbound, former Marshal of the Eastern Armies and once Commander of the Emperor's Royal Guard. Now currently an honoured SongForger, held in high regard by the Emperor and half the aristocracy.'

Captain Taka's face turned sickly green as the blood fled from his emerald scales. He recognised the magnitude of his mistake at once, but his honour and pride prevented him from grovelling to anyone.

'So, you're Samurai Captain Taka?' Kelkh asked. Taka nodded stiffly, wondering what Kelkh had in mind. 'I believe this is yours.'

Kelkh picked up the muddy, blood spattered sword that he'd used in the battle and handed it hilt first to the Captain. Taka took it gingerly, not quite hiding the confusion on his face.

'Your father commissioned this blade from me after you were given your first command,' Kelkh said. 'He asked that I deliver it to you.'

With that, Kelkh walked past the stunned Captain and embraced the Red Scaled Drake as an old comrade. Captain Taka quickly made himself scarce and the other onlookers, seeing that the entertainment was over, followed not long after.

'It's good to see you again, Kelkh,' the red scaled Drake said.

'It is good to see you, Bauer,' Kelkh replied. 'I see they finally made you a General.'

'With your recommendation behind me, there was never any doubt,' Bauer laughed. 'Come, get your things and I'll show you to your new home, then you and I can catch up on old times.'

'That sounds good,' Kelkh nodded. 'The sooner Annah and I are settled, the happier I'll be.'

'Annah?' Bauer asked. He followed Kelkh's gaze and saw Annah huddled inconspicuously under one of Mange's wings.

'My assistant,' Kelkh explained.

'How ... quaint,' Bauer said. 'At least she won't be the only one around camp. Shall we go?'

'One last thing before we leave,' Kelkh replied. 'Do you have any Captaincies available?'

'More than I would wish for,' Bauer grimaced. 'The Cat-Men are vicious opponents.'

'Indeed,' Kelkh nodded. 'There's a Lieutenant Meelik serving under Captain Taka who I think has the right temperament.'

'And comes with a good recommendation,' Bauer grinned. 'I'll see to it immediately. Now, about that tent ...'

CHAPTER 21

Ishkal sighed and rubbed the itchiness from his eyes. The yellowed parchment blurred in front of his face and he dropped it onto the study desk in disgust. Since Annah left the Monastery, he had spent all his waking hours in the Order Library and most of his sleeping hours, too. With Kelkh looking after her on the battlefront, he had taken the opportunity to search through the Order's records to look for an explanation for her magical power, or some reference to it happening before. It was proving to be a harder task than even he had imagined.

He had always known that the Library of the Golden Order was immense — everyone did. The villagers all around the Empire had folk-sayings based on that fact, and every year hundreds of Drakes from all walks of life made the pilgrimage to see the fabled vault of knowledge. But Ishkal knew the library as well as anyone, save perhaps the Abbot, and he had been confident he would find what he sought.

But after nearly two weeks of fruitless searching through dry histories and ponderous tomes, he was beginning to doubt. There was no word, no hint of any human ever having use of the SongForge anywhere; in fact, the books refuted the idea several times. Ishkal wondered why the writers would take such great pains to reiterate something that was apparently an established fact for centuries.

'Well, it won't be solved in the next few hours,' he muttered.

Leaving the parchment on the table, he dimmed the room's flameless lamps with a word, changed out of his day robes and lay down on his blanket. The thin blanket was spread out directly on the stone floor, but he didn't mind. He didn't feel the discomfort as he closed his mind and fell into a deep meditation, leaving his body to drift off to sleep.

From somewhere near the edge of the room, Ishkal heard a noise. It was the shuffle of a clawed foot, stealthy but somehow unthreatening. He opened his eyes slowly and sat up, looking at his surroundings with calm curiosity. The colours of the books were strangely washed out, as though they had been leeched of all their colour. The blood reds and midnight blues of the leather bindings were so dull they were almost grey, as was the polished wood of the shelves and door frames. Standing against the back wall of the study room was a monk, ancient but strong, with eyes that shimmered like molten gold; his scales gleamed gold, too, the colours untouched by whatever had faded everything else.

'Do you know where you are?' the monk asked.

Ishkal stood slowly, taking the time to think about the question. He was in a study room in the library, he thought, but somehow he knew that wasn't the right answer.

'I'm in a dream,' he said finally. 'A vision?'

The monk nodded, the barest hint of a smile touching his toothy face. 'It could be one or it could be the other. Which one it becomes depends on you. Do you know why you're here?'

'To find some record of the power Annah possesses,' Ishkal

answered immediately. 'To find a history of it so I can help her and guide her.'

'Would you truly wish to help her, I wonder?' the monk said. 'What cost would you be willing to pay if you knew the consequences?'

'Annah is more than just my friend,' Ishkal replied. 'She's family and I will do everything in my power to help her.'

'I have heard such words before,' the monk shrugged. 'Bold words from weak beings that have never had to face the dire consequences of their actions, or of their inactions. Let's test your conviction. Take my hand, or go back to sleep and dream sweet dreams and fantasies.'

Ishkal looked at the proffered hand and after a moment's thought, stepped forward to take it. He felt the warm, dry feel of scale against scale, then he felt a tingle in his hand that quickly shot up his arm and neck until it reached his head. Then he felt as though his mind had exploded.

Visions and feelings crashed through his mind, too quickly to take in, yet somehow he knew it all. He saw future after future, each showing its own horror and its own promise, each unbreakably linked to Annah, and through her to himself and Kelkh. And in each future, good or bad, there was war.

The monk slipped his hand from Ishkal's grasp, leaving him to drop voiceless to his knees. Tears ran down his face as he weighed the value of life and death upon the possibilities of future choices.

'And so you see,' the monk said. 'You see what may come to pass. All of these futures are equally possible and all of them based on the choices of other people. There is only so much you can do to influence events, and no way you can choose a path for the future. Only one action you make will ensure beyond doubt that none of this comes to pass. Annah is the keystone. If you kill her, none of this will happen. Kill her and the future will be a whole new realm of possibilities.'

Ishkal raised his tear stained face and stared at the monk angrily. 'No,' he spat.

'So much death, so much fighting,' the old monk said. 'You saw it in every future you witnessed; war no matter what you do. Only Annah holds the power to change that future by her death.'

'And if she dies, there will be no more war?' Ishkal shouted. 'I saw what caused those wars and they had nothing to do with her. She's an innocent girl who doesn't deserve to die!'

'And?'

'And she's my friend,' Ishkal said. 'I cannot, will not, hurt her. I saw futures in there that ended up with a better world than we live in now. Who's to say that there will be better possibilities if she dies? If there's a possibility we can make something good happen, don't we deserve the chance to command our own future? Doesn't *she* deserve the chance at life?'

The monk nodded and smiled as he waved his hand through the air in front of Ishkal's eyes. 'She does indeed.'

Ishkal blinked in surprise as he found himself on his knees. He remembered the monk saying something about a test, then taking the monk's hand. But after that, he remembered nothing at all.

'You have passed the test,' the monk said. 'Now follow me and remember.'

The monk left the room, walking through the halls of the library with ease. Ishkal had to hurry to keep up, trying to memorise the path they followed, every twist and turn as they moved down into the library archives. The monk walked into a little used corridor, dingy yet still lined with dragon carved candelabra. The monk reached for the sixth dragon on the left side and pulled it towards him.

'Do you see?' the monk asked. 'Do you remember?'

'I do but I don't understand,' Ishkal replied.

'Understanding will come later. But you must work for it.'

The colourless scene faded slowly into nothingness, leaving Ishkal and the monk floating in a sea of black. The monk reared his head back and threw out his arms and wings, which twisted and grew longer and thicker. Ishkal watched in amazement as the monk writhed and changed, mesmerised yet somehow unafraid by the transformation. Ishkal heard the words in his mind as his vision clouded over.

'Remember what you have promised.'

The last vision he saw was of a beautiful Golden Dragon, staring at him from the dark with molten gold eyes.

Ishkal sat bolt upright, nearly cracking his skull on a study table before he realised where he was. It wasn't the dingy corridor where the monk had shown him the candelabra; it was his study room, unchanged from how he had left it. Ishkal leapt to his feet and threw his robe around his shoulders, then sprinted out the door.

He ran through the halls of the library as quickly as his memory allowed, following the route the old monk had shown him. He ignored the greetings of friends and the curious looks of fellow monks, desperate to reach his destination before his memory betrayed him. He breathed a sigh of relief as he approached the archive area and made the last few turns into the small, dingy corridor.

It was exactly the way he dreamed it, dark and dusty, with tarnished candelabra running along either side. He walked to the sixth candelabra on the left side and pulled it towards him. Even though he had been expecting it, he was still surprised when he heard the grate of stone and saw the slab at the end of the corridor slide open. Gathering his thoughts and centring his spirit, he prepared himself for whatever might await him and plunged into the secret room.

Books lined every inch of wall space, stacked carefully in enchanted shelves designed to preserve them for all time. The most easily accessible manuscripts were a stack of scrolls in one corner that had been rolled up and placed neatly on top of one another. Ishkal started towards them when a burst of silvery light erupted in front of him and stopped him in his tracks. The light blazed momentarily before fading and shaping into a fuzzy image of a female Gold Monk, tired and frightened but with a core of determination.

'Whoever you are, you must be wary of what you have found here,' she said. 'The Emperor has ordered us to destroy these books and erase any knowledge of the Baradiarche's existence. But there is only so much we will do willingly and destroying knowledge is not part of it.'

The monk drew herself up, looking defiantly into space as though her audience had disapproved. 'We have the right to defy the Red Scales. Our Clan's status above them in the order of things grants us that right and we have used it — but you should be wary nonetheless. This is something they *will* kill for, Gold Scale or not.'

And with that, the apparition faded into nothing, leaving Ishkal more confused than before. Why would the Gold Drakes wilfully destroy knowledge and why would they do it at the order of the Royal family? It didn't make any sense. He carefully closed the door behind him to prevent anyone disturbing him, no matter how unlikely that occurrence seemed, then he sat cross legged on the floor, took a book from the shelf and began to read.

CHAPTER 22

Aerik, Ebon and Saera walked into the courtyard surrounding the barracks, stumbling under the weight of the black powder stuffed dragon on their shoulders. The guards on duty looked at them briefly, checking them over to see if they matched the descriptions handed out after the commotion of the group's last visit. But Japheth had made their disguises well — Aerik looked nearly fifty, Ebon close to the same and Saera looked like a man in his twenties. The Drakes dismissed them with a grunt and then ignored them.

They walked slowly towards the centre of the courtyard where they planned to place the dragon, then they would set their diversion and get out of the sector as quickly as possible. Saera had organised a group of Aerik's best men to slip in through the back of the complex to set off the black powder bombs inside. She had given them the time, the place and the signal, and all Aerik needed to do was light the fuse.

'Are we ready to go?' Aerik asked.

'Thirty seconds longer,' Saera replied.

'Okay, stand up and stretch your back,' Aerik said. 'Make it look like you've strained something — nothing conspicuous, just a trio of weary slaves.'

Aerik put his hands on Saera's shoulder, acting as though he was making sure she was all right while she massaged her lower back and did her best to look pained.

'Now?' he whispered.

'Now.'

Aerik and Saera kept up the pantomime while Ebon casually knelt down to fix a loose bootstrap and pulled three matchsticks from the lining of his pants. The first match snapped when he struck it, but the second flared to life and he quickly touched it to the fuse. He stood up casually and nodded to the others, then all three of them turned and walked towards the edge of the courtyard. They were halfway there when Saera glanced over her shoulder.

'Boss, squad to the left.'

'Coming towards us, or heading for the barracks?' he asked.

'Towards us.'

Aerik felt his stomach tingle with the beginnings of fear and the wound in his shoulder ached as if to remind him of what had happened the last time he had been caught.

'I don't like the coincidence,' he said. 'We run on my mark. They'll have enough to keep them occupied in a few seconds anyway.'

'Boss, we've got a second squad to the right,' Ebon said.

Aerik looked and up and saw the second squad moving to cut them off. They knew, he thought. They were expecting us.

'New plan,' he said. 'No running, they'll have archers hidden around the courtyard. We'll have to stall for time, then we can make our break when the distraction goes off.'

The three of them dropped to their knees and waited, as all

responsible slaves would when they realised a Drake patrol was heading in their direction. They barely moved a muscle when the Drakes surrounded them, though Ebon and Saera heard Aerik muttering numbers under his breath.

Fifteen, fourteen, thirteen ...

One of the Drakes stepped forward, a Samurai Captain based on the elaborate engraving on his boots. He stopped in front of Ebon and grabbed him under the jaw, forcing his head up so he could see it clearly. He studied it briefly then let go and moved on to Saera, rubbing his hands subconsciously on his cloak to remove the taint of human flesh from his fingers.

Twelve, eleven, ten ...

The Samurai Captain repeated the gesture with Saera, grabbing her jaw and forcing her head up so that he could see it. Apparently he didn't like the defiance in her eyes and he backhanded her hard enough to drop her to the ground. Leaving her there, he moved on to Aerik, wiping his hands again on his cloak.

Nine, eight, seven ...

The Captain stopped in front of Aerik, once again forcing his face upwards and studying his features carefully. A slow smile spread over his toothy mouth as he recognised something in Aerik's face, and Aerik felt his hopes of escape fall away. There was only one option left, provided the Drake didn't kill him outright.

Six, five, four ...

'Take them to the cells,' the Captain said. 'I want them alive for the moment, so they can tell us how they planned to destroy the barracks. I want to make sure that nothing like this ever happens again.'

Aerik kept his expression blank, hiding his surprise so the

Drake would have no extra leverage to use against him. He only needed a few more seconds.

Three, two, one.

The distraction they had set in the middle of the courtyard exploded with a terrifying crash, spraying light and streams of fire in every direction. Four of the Drakes were knocked off their feet and the others were shaken enough that they momentarily shifted their focus from the humans.

Ebon and Saera jumped to their feet, yanking daggers from any nearby belt and trying to flee. When they saw that escape was impossible, they prepared to use the weapons on each other rather than leave themselves to Drake torture. Aerik moved just as swiftly, tackling the Samurai Captain and knocking him into two more of his men. For a single moment he was free to run, but he was torn — he knew that to run away was to condemn Ebon and Saera to death, but he didn't know if there was anything he could really do to save them by staying.

In the end, it was his indecision that was his downfall. A Drake fist caught him savagely on the side of the head, dropping him to the cobblestones. From that twisted vantage point, he watched as two crossbow bolts flew from the shadows, slamming into Ebon and Saera with pinpoint accuracy. The bolts caught them both on the shoulder, making Aerik wince in sympathy as his own wound throbbed. Both of them cried out in pain and dropped their daggers, falling to the ground as the black tendrils of the bolt's magic crackled along their bodies and rendered them immobile.

For several minutes the courtyard was silent while the Drakes reorganised themselves and scoured the courtyard for any other surprises. Aerik forced himself groggily to his knees and was for the most part ignored by his captors. The Drakes were in no hurry to deal with him, they would let him stew in his fear for a while. When the courtyard was searched and declared secure, the Captain returned to his captives.

'Very clever, little human,' he said coldly. 'I would never have imagined that you animals could learn how to make black powder, and I wouldn't have believed you could find the resources even if you did.'

Aerik didn't bother to respond; he just stared into the dark and ignored the Captain completely. The Drake chuckled and drove his fist into Aerik's shoulder, where the crossbow wound had reopened and left a crimson stain on his tunic. Aerik grunted in pain, but kept his silence.

'You think you're strong, little human?' the Captain laughed. 'You think you can resist my torture and hide secrets from me? You can't. You *will* tell me everything you know and then you will beg to tell me more.'

Aerik leaned forward and spat clumsily on the Captain's foot. The Drake looked at him coldly, then punched him in the jaw. Aerik fell to the ground, dazed by the blow even though he had expected it. He felt the Captain's claws scrape against his back as he was dragged into a sitting position once again.

'You will tell me everything, *Aerik*,' the Captain snarled. 'You will tell me all about your resistance, you will tell me about your Council, and you will tell me about your plans to overthrow the Drake Empire.'

Aerik felt as though he had been punched in the stomach. He had been betrayed. Someone who knew him and knew what he was had sold him to the Drakes. Names flew through his mind as he thought of a likely suspect, but he felt too sick to think properly. The Captain dragged him to his feet and pushed him towards his soldiers.

'Take him inside,' the Captain said. 'We will deal with him in due course.'

He stepped over the two prone bodies of Ebon and Saera, still writhing in pain on the ground, and looked down at them, trying to decide how much bother they were going to be.

'Take the arrows out of these two,' he said eventually. 'We'll take them with us, but I won't dishonour any of us by carrying them inside. Make them walk.'

Aerik, Ebon and Saera were pushed towards the barracks, shambling like zombies as the Drakes prodded them along. They reached the barracks door without incident, Aerik too heartsick and Ebon and Saera too hurt to offer any resistance. The Drakes reached out to open the doors when, without warning, they burst open with a crashing boom.

The Drakes stared in astonishment as a wave of black clad figures spilled out of the barracks, and the black figures stopped in shock as they saw the Drakes arrayed before them. For a moment there was complete stillness as both sides tried to figure out what had happened.

It was the black figures who recovered first; they panicked and started to run back into the building, before they realised there was something even more terminal waiting for them inside. The hissing of fuses was more than enough to change their minds. Left without any choice, they charged.

Suddenly Aerik found himself in the centre of a whirlwind, where black clad humans and armoured Drakes battled for their lives. The humans fought to escape, while the Drakes fought on sheer instinct, half of them convinced that they fought evil spirits come to life. Shaking off his lethargy, Aerik gave way to his rage and joined the battle, scooping up a fallen dagger from the ground and charging in.

A stocky Drake battled one of the black figures, and as Aerik approached, the Drake found an opening and thrust his sword home. The human crumpled to the ground with a groan, quickly followed by his killer as Aerik buried his dagger in the Drake's neck. He grabbed the Drake's sword and pulled it free, then turned to find a new foe.

Some of the humans had managed to reach the edge of the fighting and were gathering together. They should have been running, but they had too many friends still caught in the battle and they weren't willing to abandon them. Some of them had even recognised Aerik and were waiting for him to tell them what to do; but after the shock and hurt of the betrayal, he had lost himself to his anger and he didn't even notice them.

He charged forward, but strong hands gripped his shoulders and dragged him away from the fight. Aerik struggled and screamed, but the grip held him strong. Looking over his shoulder, he saw Ebon and Saera dragging him away, while Ebon shouted orders at the top of his voice. At Ebon's command, the black clad humans broke ranks and those at the outskirts of the fighting ran for the alleyways. Aerik saw at least five men who were too deep in the battle to run.

'Ebon, we've got to help them!' Aerik shouted. 'We can't leave them.'

'We can't help them,' Ebon replied. 'We'll just be wasting our lives. The barracks will blow at any time, and if we're still here then we'll be incinerated.'

'You coward,' Aerik screamed. 'They're our friends. We have to help them!'

He struggled violently, trying to break free of their grip, but he wasn't strong enough to do more than slow their escape. Ebon's face was an emotionless mask as he swung the hilt of his stolen sword into Aerik's jaw and knocked him unconscious. Heaving him over his shoulder, Ebon nodded to Saera and they fled into the shadows of the alleyways.

They were three blocks away when the sky erupted in an explosion that almost knocked them off their feet. They stumbled on through the shadows, too frightened to stop.

CHAPTER 23

Annah sighed as the rapture of the SongForge drained from her body, leaving her tired and disoriented while the tent swam into view. It was a large tent, in fact cavernous was a better word, pitched at the rear end of the camp, as far away from the battlefront as it could possibly get while still remaining within the patrol lines. Racks of tools and almost finished weapons took up every inch of canvas around the outside of the tent, leaving the centre free for Annah and Kelkh to forg e without clutter.

Annah looked down at the plain blade in her hands, her mind automatically listing the things she needed to finish before the weapon would be complete to Kelkh's and her own stringent standards. She was sure she would have finished everything if her forging hadn't been interrupted ...

Annah's thoughts were shattered as she heard horns blaring in the distance. She realised belatedly that it was the horns that had interrupted her in the first place. One look at Kelkh showed the same irritation in his face, but he showed more understanding of the situation than she did.

'What is it, master?' she asked as the horns blared again.

'I'm not certain,' Kelkh replied. 'But it sounds like the Cat-Men are attacking the front lines again.'

Kelkh looked irritably at the sword he was working on, one side covered in whirls and lines that made it look like a hurricane sky and the other side currently blank. Muttering oaths under his breath he dropped it on his anvil and yanked the thin forge gloves from his hands.

'I'd better go out and have a look,' he said. 'If I don't, Bauer will just come looking for me anyway. Would you like to come with me?'

'No thank you, master,' Annah replied.

Despite her training at the Monastery and Kelkh's protective presence at her side, Annah didn't feel comfortable with the other Drakes around the camp. She was afraid of them, and she saw the looks of hate and disdain that they gave her. She felt much safer being hidden away in the forge tent, left to her duties. Kelkh nodded and pulled his apron over his head, hanging it on a rack.

'I won't be gone long,' he said, wrapping his sword belt around his waist and disappearing out through the tent flap.

Annah watched him stomp from the tent, then picked up her sword and started humming the Forgesong once again. Within moments she was lost to the music, crafting an item of beauty and an implement of war. As so often happened when she was forging, Annah lost all sense of time and her surroundings, feeling only the flow of the Song and the smooth metal under her fingers. It seemed strange to her that when so much of the world passed by her forge deaf ears, she could still hear one gasp so clearly. It conveyed such fear, such anger that it jolted Annah out of her trance and back to reality.

She looked around the room in confusion, taking a few moments before her eyes adjusted and she saw Bauer standing at the tent flap. She immediately placed her sword to one side and dropped to her knees.

'Forgive me, my Lord,' she said. 'I didn't see you enter. Master Kelkh has left for the battlefield to find you and assist in any way he can.'

Bauer stepped silently inside the tent and looked Annah up and down, taking note of her and the weapons that sat in the racks beside her as though he'd never seen them before. Annah had no idea what she was expected to say, so she remained silent.

'How is it that you have the power of the Forgesong?' he asked, his voice deadly calm.

'I don't know, my Lord,' Annah replied honestly. 'It's something I've only learned recently that I can use, and with Master Kelkh's assistance I—'

'Kelkh?' Bauer asked, cutting her off angrily. 'Kelkh knows about this?'

'He trained me, my Lord,' Annah replied, confusion and fear fighting for supremacy in her mind.

'He *trained* you?'

Annah opened her mouth to reply, but the words froze in her throat as Bauer drew his sword with a swish of silk. He offered no explanation, but he didn't need to; he was a Drake and she was a slave, it was his place to decide her fate. As he loomed above her, Annah was frozen in place, mesmerised by the murder in his eyes. She longed to scream or run, but deep down she knew that neither would gain her anything. Who would help her in a camp full of Drakes?

Annah closed her eyes as Bauer drew back his arm, then her heart leapt for joy as she heard stomping footsteps and irritable muttering outside the tent. She heard the tent flaps thrust open and she opened her eyes to see Kelkh storm inside.

'Damned wild goose chase,' Kelkh muttered. 'By the Dragon, Bauer could at least have the courtesy of being at the battlefront where I can find him.'

'Or here, where you can find me,' Bauer said ominously.

Kelkh's head snapped up at the sound of Bauer's voice, his face twisting into shock as he saw Bauer's sword in his hand, its tip resting at Annah's throat.

'What's going on, Bauer?' Kelkh asked.

'How is it that this *human* has the gift of the Forgesong?' Bauer replied.

'She was born with it,' Kelkh said. 'We're not certain why, but we're trying to find out.'

'We?' Bauer asked, his voice like a whip crack. 'It's *we*, is it? Who are *we*?'

'Myself and Ishkal of the Order of the Gold Dragon,' Kelkh replied. 'What business is it of yours?'

'What business?' Bauer snarled. 'You find a human who can use the Forgesong, and not only do you not kill her, but you compound your blasphemy by actually training her! And then you ask me what business it is of mine?'

'You're getting your weapons and you're getting them twice as fast as you used to,' Kelkh shrugged. 'Does it matter that half of them are coming from a human?'

'Of course it matters!' Bauer screamed. 'Wielding the Forgesong is the highest honour The Dragon can bestow upon a Drake — you of all people should know that. And for it to manifest in a *human* is an affront to our god. She must die, and then I will decide what will happen to you.'

Bauer turned back to Annah and brought his blade down in a double handed stroke that should have split her in two, and would have if Kelkh's blade hadn't blocked it. The ring of metal on metal was deafening, then silence reigned in the tent as Bauer stared death at Kelkh.

'I didn't think you could move that fast anymore, old man,' Bauer said.

'Only with the proper incentive,' Kelkh replied.

Bauer drew back his sword with blinding speed and swung three blows at Annah, aiming at her head, her chest and her stomach. Metal rang loudly as Kelkh blocked each strike with precision, then lashed out with his fist and caught Bauer on the snout. Bauer staggered back, staring at Kelkh in anger.

'You'll be declared a non-Drake and hunted for the rest of your days,' Bauer spat. 'All for the life of a human. Is that what you want? Think about what you're doing.'

'You want to kill a girl for being nothing more than what she was born,' Kelkh replied. 'Think of what *you're* doing. If the Forgesong really is a gift from The Dragon, then we should honour this girl as a recipient of such a gift, not try to kill her for it.'

'She's just a human,' Bauer said. Kelkh stepped in front of Annah, pushing her back out of harm's way. Bauer watched, the anger simmering in his eyes. 'So be it.'

He charged forward, his sword slicing at Kelkh from all four diagonals. Kelkh steadied himself on his crippled leg and met the onslaught using brute strength alone to force Bauer back. Bauer launched into another attack, but was stopped prematurely when Kelkh knocked the blade aside and slammed his forearm into

Bauer's face. Bauer hopped backwards out of sword range, blinking tears out of his eyes from the smarting blow.

'You can't beat me, Bauer,' Kelkh said. 'You never could.'

'That was when you were my Captain,' Bauer replied. 'Before you betrayed the Empire for the sake of a human. And before you were a cripple.'

Kelkh flinched noticeably at both jibes, but he held his position in front of Annah. Bauer just watched and waited for his chance, his face showing hurt and betrayal at Kelkh's actions.

'I'm no traitor, Bauer,' Kelkh said, trying one last time. 'And this girl is no blasphemer. She's special, and we should honour her as a gift from The Dragon.'

'Blasphemy,' Bauer repeated, and Kelkh's shoulders slumped in defeat.

'I don't want to kill you, Bauer,' he said softly.

'And I didn't want you to betray us all,' Bauer snarled. 'It just shows you don't always get what you want.'

He darted forward once more, his sword lashing at Kelkh with undisguised fury. Kelkh parried every strike, moving awkwardly as his crippled leg tried to keep up with the rest of his body. Ever so slowly, he pushed Bauer away from Annah and moved him to the middle of the tent.

With amazing deftness, Bauer grabbed an infantry shield from a nearby rack and hurled it at Kelkh's head, but Kelkh was too experienced to fall for such a trick. Slipping to one side, he reached out with a clawed hand and grabbed the shield buckles, pivoting on his good leg as he spun in a complete circle and sent the shield hurtling back at Bauer. The red scaled Drake gasped in surprise before he was knocked to the ground, groaning and spitting out blood.

Kelkh approached him slowly, wary for any sign of deception. What he would have done had he actually reached Bauer, he did not know — he knew that he couldn't kill him, not in cold blood and probably not even in battle, but he also knew that he couldn't let him live while he was part of the Empire. It was the tearing of canvas that gave him pause, and the screech of cats that made him turn away and bellow with rage.

A patrol of Black Leop-Rah had taken advantage of the main offensive to sneak behind the camp and attack the supply lines. Their black fur made it easy for them to blend into the shadows and their strength made them ferocious fighters. They had chosen Kelkh's forge as their first target, tearing through the tent walls to reach their prey.

Kelkh roared in challenge and charged the Cat-Men, hoping to close the gap between them before they could bring their bows to bear. But with his injured leg hampering him, he only made it halfway before the Leop-Rah lined him up and fired.

Kelkh dived to the ground, feeling the burning sting of an arrow as it tore through his clothes and left an angry mark along his back. Rolling to the side, he grabbed an infantry shield from a rack and threw it over his body. He heard the impact of several more arrows, and then the world was lost in a pitch of feral yowls and metal blades.

Somehow Kelkh regained his feet and fended off three Leop-Rah as they sought to finish him. He hacked at one furry arm that swung a sword his way and was rewarded by a horrible yowl as he hit his mark. Using his shield, his sword, his pommel and anything else that presented itself, Kelkh tore through the Leop-Rah facing off against him.

In one moment of inaction, Kelkh saw Bauer fighting three enemies, his body riddled with arrow bolts. Bauer finished one of his attackers, but took a nasty gash to the shoulder while he recovered from the swing. Annah fought against a lone Leop-Rah, her strange halberd in her hands once again and her monk training keeping her safe. Kelkh doubted the Leop-Rah even knew what hit him when he picked on the girl, and he forced down the urge to barrel through the skirmish to her rescue. Catching another blow on his shield, he forgot about his companions and focused once more on keeping himself alive.

It was several minutes after he finished his last opponent before Kelkh realised that the battle was over. Looking left and right around the tent, he saw the slumped, black furred bodies of the Leop-Rah, the shattered weapon racks and tables of the forge, and the arrow ridden body of Bauer. A horrible thought ran through Kelkh's mind and he looked frantically around the tent for Annah, terrified of what he might find.

He found her not far from where Bauer had fallen, half hidden by a toppled table and clutching thin air as though she still held a halberd shaft in her hands. Two Leop-Rah lay sprawled beside her, cut by what could only have been halberd strikes. Kelkh dropped to his knees and wrapped his arms around her, muttering thankful prayers to The Dragon. Annah started at his touch, but sagged in relief when she realised who it was and burst into tears as she buried her head in his shoulder.

Kelkh held her awkwardly, his hands more adept at war and the forge than at comforting a tearful child. He did it well, though he did not know it, and Annah's wracking sobs soon trailed away into quiet snuffles.

'You've saved her life but for how long?'

Kelkh's head snapped up at the sound of Bauer's voice and his sword was readied before he'd even fully turned. He thrust Annah behind him and set his shield to protect her. He saw Bauer almost at once, his arrow ridden body dragged into a half seated sprawl against a toppled table. Kelkh was amazed that he even lived, let alone had the strength to talk.

'I'll find help, Bauer,' Kelkh said. 'Hold on for a little while longer and I'll bring a healer.'

'So caring, Kelkh, for someone you were about to kill just minutes ago,' Bauer laughed, his words ending in a strangled cough. 'Save your pity and your time. I'm dead no matter what you do, but I go to the grave knowing that she won't be far behind me. I have served the Empire to the last.'

Kelkh watched impassively while Bauer breathed his death rattle, anger and disappointment filling his heart; anger that Bauer had forced him to betray the Empire that he had sworn and fought to protect; disappointment that he hadn't been able to convince his one time Lieutenant and wartime comrade that Annah was worthy of life. Was it worth it, he wondered? Looking down at her, crouched behind him, he knew in his heart that it was.

'What did he mean? That I wouldn't be far behind him?' Annah asked softly.

'He meant that his death will leave a great number of questions unanswered,' Kelkh replied. He was a warrior at heart and subtlety had always been beyond him. 'Why was Bauer here without his honour guards? Why was he, a warrior trained by my own hand, surprised by the Leop-Rah in this tent? Why did a human girl arrive at a Drake camp dressed in the robes of a Monk of the Gold

Order? Why did that human girl who had no combat skills survive an attack?'

He looked grimly around the tent, trying to think quickly and wishing that Ishkal were here to help him.

'Even if the Generals here don't put the pieces together, they will still be suspicious of you, Annah,' he said heavily. 'And Drakes won't allow their suspicions to fester. They'll just kill you and be done with it.'

Annah's face paled and she stared at Kelkh, too shocked to ask him what she should do. He read it in her face regardless.

'We must leave, Annah,' he said. 'We must flee, now. It will look like we died here or were taken by the Leop-Rah. They won't search for us or suspect us. We have equipment here and a little food, but we'll have to scavenge before long.'

Kelkh muttered to himself as he grabbed two saddlebags from amidst the wreckage and began stuffing them with all manner of things. Within minutes he had gathered as much as he dared and, with Annah in tow, he left the tent and hurried to the stables.

They left the encampment on foot, walking for half an hour before they mounted Mange and took to the skies, just to make sure no one spotted them flying away. They flew for as far as their waning strength allowed them before they finally collapsed on a mountainside.

When Annah was bedding down under her threadbare blanket, she realised she'd left the turquoise dream stones Ishkal had given her back at the camp. But it wasn't until she drifted off to sleep that she truly missed them, as the grey mist swirled around her and a strangely familiar laugh filled her mind.

'Welcome back, my apprentice. I knew you would return to me ...'

CHAPTER 24

Aerik rubbed his swollen face, gingerly touching the bruises and cuts that were the legacy of a perfect plan gone wrong. He'd been betrayed and lives had been lost because of it. It hurt worse than he'd expected, being betrayed by one of his own people. He wished he could understand why.

A polite cough at the door drew him from his thoughts and he looked up to see Ebon standing at the doorway. Aerik waved him in, thankful for the company.

'How are you feeling?' Ebon asked.

'Sore, but alive,' Aerik replied. 'You've got a lot of strength in your arm.'

Ebon sighed as he looked at the ugly bruise left over from where he had punched his friend. 'Yeah, I'm sorry about that.'

'Don't be,' Aerik said. 'You kept me alive and your quick thinking kept others alive too. I'd lost myself to my anger, something I've told others so often never to do. I would have thrown myself into battle and died for nothing. All things considered, I'm happier to be alive — and I'm sure Lysa and Rebecca would agree.'

'Good, because we need you here and planning,' Ebon nodded. 'We're due at the council in less than an hour, and so far you're the only one of them with guts to speak against Kebble openly.'

'Yes, the council,' Aerik sighed. 'Kebble will have ammunition today. Have you got the final numbers?'

'Twelve of the twenty that left for the mission,' Ebon replied. 'With three more badly injured, though they're stable and expected to live.'

Aerik dropped his head to his hands and tried to stop the tears before they came. Twelve of his men dead, friends and comrades who trusted in him. Wiping his eyes, he tried to put his anger and hurt aside as he prepared to present his suspicions to the council.

'Let's get this over with,' he sighed. 'The sooner the better.'

Ebon nodded and fell into step behind Aerik as they left the manor and headed towards the council meeting hall. Saera joined them outside Aerik's study, looking suspiciously at every shadow as they walked by. She had assigned herself as his personal bodyguard ever since their near escape from the barracks attack. Aerik hadn't objected because he knew it made her feel better.

They reached the council hall a full ten minutes ahead of schedule, but much to their surprise, they found all the councillors already present and waiting. When Aerik stepped inside, the hum of chatter fell silent and all eyes turned his way. The councillors watched him silently, and then, led by Kebble, they rose respectfully to their feet. Kebble stepped away from the table and wrapped Aerik in a hug, surprising them all; no one had ever seen such emotion from the man before.

'I'm sorry for your loss, brother,' he said. 'Your plan was a good one and would have worked if it hadn't been for the cowardly betrayal of one person. The lives that were lost aren't your fault in any way.'

Aerik didn't trust his voice, thick with emotion at the

unexpected words from his council rival. Whatever Kebble's faults, he would never condone the betrayal of his people to the Drakes. His methods were different from Aerik's, but he believed in the cause just as fully. Any suspicions Aerik had that Kebble had betrayed him evaporated immediately. He nodded in thanks and moved towards his chair, but Kebble placed a hand on his shoulder to stop him.

'We've got something for you, something that's yours by right,' Kebble said. 'One of Jink's cells found it, but the council has agreed it should be your decision what to do with it.'

'What is it?' Aerik asked, sensing the anticipation in Kebble's voice.

'We know where the traitor's being kept.'

The council proceedings were finished in less than half an hour. The only order of business was to ensure that the location of the traitor was passed to Aerik, and to offer condolences to his loss. It was sheer chance that the traitor had been found — one of Jink's spies had gained a servant's position in a Captain's manor and she overheard the Drake Captain negotiating a trustee's package with the man. She was too late to stop the trap at the barracks, but she did manage to bring Jink word of the traitor's location.

Aerik almost ran from the room, with Ebon and Saera following at his heels. Despite their still healing wounds, all three of them had a score to settle. They had been betrayed and their friends had paid the price for it. The law was clear about what had to be done. Blood for blood.

In the space of three hours, Aerik, Ebon, Saera, and the five unwounded survivors from the raid on the barracks all left the manor, keeping to the shadows as they followed the streets and alleyways towards the building Jink had marked.

The Captain's manor was more of a homestead with a house guard than a true military building. It had a high wall that surrounded the manor, wide enough for a Samurai to walk his patrol route, with a square stone tower at each corner. The house stood three stories tall, surrounded by meticulously raked stone gardens and carefully shaped shrubs. A small water fountain completed the tranquil setting, and the guards stopped more than once in their patrol route to stare in admiration at the beautiful scene.

Aerik and his men saw none of it; they saw strengths and weaknesses, they saw points of entry and openings for ambush. They watched from the shadows for almost an hour, thinking, memorising and planning. When it was time to move, Aerik's words were quick and to the point. They knew what they had to do and they knew what their objective was.

The Drake walked his patrol route, bored, checking the walls and walkways for any sign of intruders. He wasn't worried about either — in the five years he'd been assigned to this post no one had ever tried to gain entry. He knew he shouldn't be so lax, not with all the rumours of dark spirits rising in the human sectors, but he was safely in Drake owned land. Vigilance was hard to maintain when there was no enemy to guard against.

The Drake continued on his rounds, whistling quietly to himself as he stooped to pass under the brushing leaves of an overhanging tree. He made a note to mention that to the Captain. Having a tree so close to the manor walls was a danger that provided an enemy with easy access to the compound.

The Drake stopped in his tracks and chuckled at the ridiculousness of that idea. Enemies? What enemies? He was patrolling a manor in the middle of the Empire's capital city, where the closest battlefront was hundreds of kilometres away. Laughing again, he swatted at a blob of pollen that landed on his snout. His laugh turned to a gurgle as a loop of wire dropped around his head and tightened as he was hauled off his feet.

The Drake struggled to hook his claws behind the thin wire, but it was pulled too tight around his neck. He watched helplessly as two black clad figures dropped from the tree above and advanced. Frantically he scrabbled for the sword at his belt, but his movements were already clumsy from lack of air. One of the figures drew a sword of their own, and as the spots started to cloud the Drake's vision, the last thing he saw was the silver moonlight highlighting a matte black blade as it was thrust forward.

'The next patrol's not due for twenty minutes,' Ebon whispered, as he wiped his sword blade on the Drake's cloak. 'That gives us fifteen minutes to get inside, get our traitor and get back out; sixteen at a push.'

'That's all we'll need,' Aerik replied. 'Jink told his spy to leave the door to the servant's quarters unbolted, and we have her directions from there to the traitor's room.'

'I just hope it isn't another trap,' Ebon muttered. 'This would be an easy way to finish the job.'

'It isn't,' Aerik said. 'I know Kebble. He was just as outraged at the betrayal as we were.'

Ebon grunted, not convinced. He gave three owl hoots and waited as six more black figures dropped from the tree. 'We'd better go if we're going.'

Aerik nodded and pulled a length of rope off his shoulder. He handed one end to Saera, who had appeared protectively beside him, then threw the coil off the wall into the rock garden below. When the other end was tied securely, six of them slid over the edge, leaving two of their comrades to guard their route back out.

Hugging the walls and shadows, Aerik led them around the compound, watching the manor carefully until he saw a single candle sitting in a grimy window. At his signal they left the shadows under the wall and crossed the garden, moving swiftly through the stretch of moonlight until they found the shadows of the manor. Saera opened the door and crept inside, while the others waited outside for her to declare it safe. It was a tense thirty seconds before her hand reached out and waved them in, and Aerik breathed a sigh of relief.

They followed the directions to the letter, pausing only once to dispatch an unfortunate guard who had woken up to make a trip to the bathroom in the middle of the night. They reached the door to the traitor's room in only a few minutes and entered without hesitation. They knew there would be no guards in the room; no Samurai would allow themselves to be dishonoured by having to guard a single human.

They moved so quietly that the figure kneeling on the floor

didn't even hear them come in. It wasn't until Ebon and Saera rose up on either side of him that he realised they were there. He struggled briefly and drew a breath to cry out, but the swish of silk as a blade was drawn and the cool touch of Ebon's dagger against his throat quietened him immediately. Aerik stepped into the light, removing his face mask so the traitor could see who had come to find him. He heard the traitor gasp in shock and fear, and only then did he look the man in the face.

'Japheth?' he gasped, the air leaving his body in a rush that made him feel physically ill.

'Aerik, thank the gods you're still alive!' Japheth said. 'The Drakes captured me just after you left. They tortured me until I told them everything ...'

But Japheth's words faded to a murmur after one look at Aerik's face. Aerik had seen the state that Drake victims were left in after torture and Japheth had no marks on his body to indicate anything of the sort. He was being held as a trustee slave in the luxurious manor of a Samurai Captain, not the dungeon of a broken slave. Aerik wasn't fooled, even if he was hurt beyond measure.

'In the name of the gods, Japheth, why?' Aerik asked.

'I told you, Aerik, I was captured—'

'Enough!' Aerik growled. 'You've used our friendship to play me for a fool once already, don't try it again. Why did you throw it away? To gain crumbs from the Drake's table?'

'Our friendship?' Japheth spat, abandoning his pretence. 'I was friends with a slave, a good man who knew his place and lived his life. Who are you? Because you're sure as hell not the friend I knew!'

'Apparently, neither are you,' Aerik murmured, but Japheth ignored him.

'You're a dangerous man who kills Drakes and puts every human in the Empire in danger,' Japheth said. 'They destroyed the whole Mirin ghetto because of people like you. If you'd just shut your mouth and stayed in your place, nothing like that would have happened, but no you had to stir the pot!'

'If I had 'shut my mouth and stayed in my place' I'd be dead, just like Monta and Tisa,' Aerik replied. 'Just like so many of our friends who were worked to the bone or broken in spirit before the Drakes decided to kill them for sport. We're a slave race, and we live and die by Drake whim, Japheth. You're happy to turn a blind eye to the death and misery that our people live with every day, but I'm not. I want Rebecca to grow up in a better world than that.'

Japheth dared to lean forward and spit on Aerik's foot. 'You're a dangerous maverick and you'll achieve nothing but the deaths of our family and friends. It's because of people like you and that bastard, Ebon, that Monta and Tisa were killed! If it wasn't for him, they'd both be alive!'

Japheth's defiant stare withered at the sheer rage he saw reflected in Aerik's face. He paled even further when Ebon let go of his arm just long enough to remove his mask and give Japheth a clear look at his face.

'Perhaps they would still be alive without Ebon's arrival,' Aerik said, his voice dead of all emotion. 'Perhaps not. Perhaps Monta would have been killed the day after for not meeting his quota at the ro-khill paddies. Perhaps Tisa would have stepped left instead of right around a Drake cart on the wrong day of the week.'

Japheth cowered as Aerik stepped forward and knelt in front of him, expecting to be struck or stabbed. But Aerik just waited until

Japheth regained his courage and looked at him once more.

'There's just one thing I want to know, Japheth,' Aerik said. 'You knew all of this when we first arrived at your door. You knew what we were and you knew why the Drakes were after us. Why didn't you turn us in then? Wasn't I a big enough catch?'

Japheth's gaze dropped back to the floor, but Aerik saw the telltale flash of guilt in his face before he turned away.

'That's it, isn't it?' Aerik said. 'You thought I was a nobody in the resistance, so you honoured our friendship and hid me from the Drakes. Then you found out I was a leader on the council and you realised how much you could sell me out for. What did they offer you, Japheth? What was the price of my life?'

Japheth looked around the room, searching for any sign of escape or rescue by the Drakes.

'I guess it doesn't matter,' Aerik continued. 'I think I'd prefer not knowing how much a lifetime of friendship was worth.'

'You don't have to do this, you know,' Japheth said, licking his lips desperately.

'Yes I do, Japheth. By your actions you deliberately caused the deaths of twelve of my men, my friends who trusted me to keep them alive. That debt must be repaid. Blood for blood, that's the law. I can't break it, not even for the memory of the friendship we once had. Believe it or not, I am sorry.'

'The Law?' Japheth asked angrily. 'What Law? There's no law other than what the Drakes give us. You're a slave, damn it!'

Aerik looked at his once friend and remembered all the happy times they had shared in the past. He tried to find some flicker of anger in his heart for Japheth's betrayal, for the deaths that his actions had caused, but all he felt was a hollow ache. He rocked back on his heels and drew his dagger, making Japheth's eyes bulge in fright.

'You have no laws,' Japheth repeated, trying one last time. 'You're just a slave.'

'No, Japheth. Not anymore.'

At sixteen minutes to the second, six black figures climbed over the outside wall of the Captain's barracks and ran into the alleys of the city, vanishing into the night.

Aerik paused at the brink of the shadows and looked back at the blazing light of the manor. So much had passed, but there was so much yet to come. Kebble's sympathy would fade and the battle for control of the Council would be on once again. There was still the problem of what to do with slaves who didn't want to fight. And then there was Annah. Always Annah, the enigma that seemed lodged in his thoughts. Her help would be invaluable to his cause; he just needed to find a way to convince her to help him.

Shaking his head, Aerik shoved his thoughts aside and disappeared into the shadows. Trouble would find him soon enough without him looking to find more.

APPENDIX

THE DRAKES

The Drake Empire is a feudal nation with a strict caste system. Warriors are held in the highest regard and almost all nobles of any standing are or were Samurai warriors. All other professions fall into the category of lesser duties and the honour accorded to each is ranked by tradition.

The Drakes believe that they are offspring of their seven Dragon gods. Each Dragon reputedly granted a measure of their power and skill to the armies that fought with them in the Great Battles, creating the seven Clans of the Drake Empire. In time, the story of the Drake's beginning became legend, and now the Drakes often refer to their seven Dragon sires as a single deity known as 'The Dragon'. They use a seven sided stone to represent Him, one crystal but seven facets of their race.

The Drake's not only rank themselves by occupation, but also by clan. The clans are based on the colour of a Drake's scales, which determine the bloodline of the Dragon sire. The clans do not intermix and any Drake born of such breeding is immediately outcast. The clans have a strict rank order based on the power of the original Dragon sire, and all Drakes honour that system on pain of death.

Each Drake clan has an area in which they are allowed to pursue their occupation. They are not allowed to find employment outside of these strict guidelines.

Gold Drakes

The Gold Drakes are born of the most powerful of the seven Dragons. Like all Drakes they inherit the colour of their scales from their sire, as well as their strength and dexterity. As the most powerful clan, the Gold Drakes could have ruled the Empire, had they wished, however they chose the path of knowledge instead. Forming themselves into an order of monks, the Gold Drakes became historians and philosophers, and eventually students of the magical Forgesong.

Strong, fast, intelligent and wise, the Gold Drakes are the perfect warrior poet.

Red (Ruby) Drakes

The Red Drakes were the next strongest clan after the Gold, and they eagerly accepted the mantle of the ruling class when the Gold clan refused. The Red Drakes, or as they later renamed themselves, the Ruby Drakes, comprise all the Princes and Emperors, and most of the nobles throughout the Empire. Red Drakes who are not born to privilege become company managers or high officials.

Fast and highly intelligent, the Red Drakes are known for their cunning nature and explosive tempers.

Iron Drakes

The Iron Drakes immediately took it upon themselves to become the watchers and guardians of the Empire. They represent stability and structure for every person, Drake and non-Drake alike, and are known as the fiercest and best trained fighters in the land. They either work in the elite guard or command structure of the regular armies, or they serve in the Royal guard.

Exceptionally strong, the Iron Drakes are possessed of a slow wisdom that often surprises those who assume they are just stupid.

Sapphire Drakes

The Sapphire Drakes quickly found that they had a knack for writing and organization. They easily cemented their position as court scribes and company bookkeepers, and later moved into areas of diplomacy.

Intelligent and well spoken, the Sapphire Drakes are gifted with a silver tongue that has done much to advance their clan.

Emerald Drakes

Strong, though not as bright as the other clans, the Emerald Drakes are exceptionally good at following their orders to the very letter. They comprise the majority of the regular army and they do their jobs very well.

Copper Drakes

Smaller than the other clans, the Copper Drakes are skilled with their hands and gifted with an eye for criticism. These gifts have done them very well as artists and artisans, as well as merchant traders. A Copper Drake can see the faults of any merchandise in an instant, though those same faults mysteriously disappear when it comes to selling the goods again.

Black Drakes

The Black Drakes are the most unusual of their kind, born with a great love of the land. They are farmers and tillers of the earth, and are often labelled 'Dirt' Drakes in jest by the other clans. They continue to do what other clans think of as 'human work', simply for the love of the earth and the land. They are the best farmers and woodsmen in the entire Empire, and their goods are much sought after by the aristocracy despite their odd ways.

www.ingramcontent.com/pod-product-compliance
Lightning Source LLC
Chambersburg PA
CBHW031110030726

47496CB00002BA/475

* 9 7 8 0 6 4 5 5 9 9 6 6 4 *